THE DAY EARTH HAD ONLY 80 HOURS TO LIVE!

Bill Graham, special investigator, had only 80 hours in which to save Earth from total destruction by the Viton terror—an invisible evil so deadly that man risked madness and death *by merely thinking about it.*

SINISTER BARRIER is a truly fascinating tale, a hair-raising science-fiction adventure novel certain to win the acclaim of every s-f fan. Eric Frank Russell is one of the enduringly great names in modern science-fiction. Among his outstanding novels have been WASP and THE GREAT EXPLOSION.

SINISTER BARRIER

ERIC FRANK RUSSELL

PAPERBACK LIBRARY, Inc.

New York

PAPERBACK LIBRARY EDITION

First Printing: May, 1964
Second Printing: December, 1966

Paperback Library books are published by
Paperback Library, Inc. Its trademark, consisting
of the words "Paperback Library" and associated
distinctive design, is registered in the United
States Patent Office. Printed in the United
States of America, Paperback Library, Inc.
260 Park Avenue South, New York, N.Y. 10010.

Clipping from a New York daily:—

TO BE READ IN A DIM LIGHT, AT NIGHT.

The late Charles Fort, who was a sort of Peter Pan of science and went about picking up whimsies of fact, mostly from the rubbish heaps of astronomy, would have been interested in an incident that occurred Sunday morning on Fifth Avenue between Twenty-ninth and Thirtieth Streets.

Eight starlings in flight suddenly plummeted to the feet of Patrolman Anton Vodrazka, dead. There was no sign of a wound or any other indication of what caused their end. It was at first thought that they might have been poisoned, as were some pigeons at Verdi Square, Seventy-second Street and Broadway, recently.

S.P.C.A. agents said it was most unlikely that eight birds, even if they had been poisoned, would succumb at the same moment in mid-flight. Another report from the same neighborhood a few minutes later didn't help any. A starling, "excited and acting as if pursued by some invisible terror," had flown into a Childs Restaurant on Fifth Avenue, banged into the lights and fallen in the front window.

What killed the eight starlings? What frightened the ninth? Was there some Presence in the sky? . . . We hasten to pass the idea on to the nearest writer of mystery stories.

Chapter 1

"SWIFT death awaits the first cow that leads a revolt against milking," mused Professor Peder Bjornsen. It was a new slant, and a wicked one, born of dreadful facts. He passed long, slender fingers through prematurely white hair. His eyes, strangely protruding, filled with uncanny light, stared out of his office window which gaped on the third level above traffic swirling through Stockholm's busy Hötorget. But those eyes were not looking at the traffic.

"And there's a swat waiting for the first bee that blats about pilfered honey," he added. Stockholm hummed and roared, a city unconscious of its chains. The professor continued to stare in silent, fearful contemplation. Then suddenly his eyes lifted, widened, flared with apprehension. He drew away from the window, slowly, reluctantly; moving as if forcing himself by sheer will-power to retreat from a horror which beckoned, invisibly beckoned.

Raising his hands, he pushed, pushed futilely at thin air. Those distorted optics of his, still preternaturally cold and hard, yet brilliant with something far beyond fear, followed with dreadful fascination a shapeless, colorless point that crept from window to ceiling. Turning with a tremendous effort, he ran, his mouth open and expelling breath soundlessly.

Halfway to the door he emitted a brief gasp, stumbled, fell. His stricken hand clutched the calendar from his desk, dragged it down to the carpet. He sobbed, hugged hands to his heart, lay still. The spark which had motivated him became extinguished. The calendar's top leaf fluttered in a queer, inexplicable breeze from nowhere. The date was May the seventeenth, 2015.

Bjornsen had been five hours dead when the police got to him. Imperturbably, the medical examiner diagnosed heart disease and left it at that. Snooping restlessly around, Police Lieutenant Baeker found on the professor's desk a note bearing a message from the grave.

"A little knowledge is a dangerous thing. It is humanly impossible to discipline my thoughts every minute of the day, to control my involuntary dreams every hour of the night. It is inevitable that soon I shall be found dead, in which case you must—"

"Must what?" asked Baeker. There was no reply. The voice that could have shocked him with its answer was stilled forever. Baeker heard the medical examiner's report, then burned the note. The professor, he decided, like others of his ilk, had grown eccentric in his old age, being burdened by too much abstruse learning. Heart disease it was, actually and officially.

On May the thirtieth, Doctor Guthrie Sheridan walked with the deliberate, jerky step of an automaton along Charing Cross Road, London. His eyes were shining, frozen lumps, and he kept them focussed on the sky while his legs made their mechanical way. He had the eerie appearance of a blind man following a thoroughly familiar route.

Jim Leacock saw him wending his fascinated way, failed to notice anything abnormal. Dashing up, he yelled, "Hey, Sherry!" all set to administer a hearty slap on the back. He stopped, appalled.

Turning upon him pale, strained features framing eyes that gleamed like icicles seen in bluish twilight, Guthrie seized an arm and chattered, "Jim! By heavens, I'm glad to see you!" His breath was fast, his voice urgent. "Jim, I've got to talk to someone—or go crazy. I've just discovered the most incredible fact in the history of mankind. It is almost beyond belief. Yet it explains a thousand things that we've merely guessed at or completely ignored."

"What is it?" demanded Leacock, skeptically. He studied the other's distorted face.

"Jim, let me tell you that man is not and never has been the master of his fate, nor the captain of his soul. Why, the very beasts of the field—!" He broke off, grabbed at his listener. His voice went two tones higher, held a hysterical note. "I've thought it! I've thought it, I tell you!" His legs bent at the knees. "I'm done for!" He slumped to the pavement.

Hastily, the startled Leacock stooped over him, tore open his shirt, slid a hand down on his chest. No beat was discernable. The once wildly beating heart had packed up—for keeps. Sheridan was dead. Heart disease, apparently.

At the same hour of the same day, Doctor Hans Luther did a very similar thing. Carrying his deceptively plump body at top speed across his laboratory, he raced headlong down the stairs, across the hall. He fled with many fearful glances over

8

one shoulder, and the glances came from eyes like polished agate.

Reaching the telephone, he dialed with shaking finger, got the *Dortmund-Zeitung,* shouted for the editor. With his eyes still upon the stairs while the telephone receiver trembled against his ear, he bawled into the mouthpiece, "Vogel, I have for you the most astonishing news since the dawn of time. You must give it space, plenty of space, quickly—before it is too late."

"Let me have the details," suggested Vogel, tolerantly.

"Earth is belted with a warning streamer that says: KEEP OFF THE GRASS!" Luther watched the stairs and sweated.

"Ha-ha!" responded Vogel, without mirth. His heavy face moved in the tiny vision-screen above the telephone, bore the patient expression of one accustomed to the eccentricities of scientists.

"Listen!" yelled Luther. He wiped his forehead with the back of a quivering hand. "You know me. You know that I do not tell lies, I do not joke. I tell you nothing which I cannot prove. So I tell you that now and perhaps for thousands of years past, this troubled world of ours . . . a-ah! . . . *a-a-ah!*"

The receiver swung at the end of its cord, gave forth a reedy shout of "Luther! Luther! What's happened?'

Doctor Hans Luther made no response. Sinking slowly to his knees, he rolled his peculiarly glistening eyes upward, fell on his side. His tongue licked his lips sluggishly, very sluggishly, once, twice. He died in awful silence.

Vogel's face bobbed in the vision-screen. The dangling receiver made agitated noises for ears beyond hearing.

Bill Graham knew nothing about these earlier tragedies, but he knew about Mayo. He was right on the spot when it happened.

He was strolling along West Fourteenth, New York, when for no particular reason he cast a casual glance up the sheer side of the Martin Building, saw a human figure falling past the twelfth floor.

Down came the body, twisting, whirling, spread-eagling, as horribly impotent as a tossed bundle of rags. It smacked the pavement and bounced nine feet. The sound was halfway between a squelch and a crunch. The concrete looked as if it had been slapped by a giant crimson sponge.

Twenty yards ahead of Graham, a fat woman stopped in mid-step, studied the stain and the bundle while her complexion turned oysterlike. Dropping her handbag, she lay down on the sidewalk, closed her eyes, muttered nonsense. A hundred pedestrians turned themselves into a rapidly shrinking circle with the battered body as its center. They pushed and shoved as they guzzled the sight.

The dead had no face. Its sodden clothes were surmounted by a ghastly mask like one made of scrambled blueberries and cream. Graham felt no qualms as he bent over the corpse. He had seen worse in war.

His strong, brown fingers plucked at the pocket of a sticky vest, drew out a blood-spattered pasteboard. Looking at the card, he permitted himself a low whistle of surprise.

"Professor Walter Mayo! Good grief!"

Swallowing hard, he looked once more at the pathetic remnant sprawled at his feet, then forced his way through the swelling, murmuring crowd. The revolving doors of the Martin Building whirled behind him as he sprinted for the pneumatic levitators.

Fumbling the card with unfeeling fingers, Graham strove to assemble his jumbled thoughts while his one-man disk was wafted swiftly up its tube. Mayo, of all people, to pass out like that!

At the sixteenth floor the disk stopped with a rubbery bounce and a sigh of escaping air. Racing along the passage, Graham reached Mayo's laboratory, found its door ajar.

There was nobody in the laboratory. Everything appeared peaceful, orderly, bearing no signs of recent disturbance.

A thirty-foot long table carried a lengthy array of apparatus which he recognised as an assembly for destructive distillation. He felt the retorts. They were cold. Evidently the experiment had not been started.

Counting the flasks, he decided that the setup was arranged to extract the sixteenth product of something which, when he opened the electric roaster, proved to be a quantity of dried leaves. They looked and smelled like some sort of herb.

Papers on an adjacent desk danced in the breeze from a widely opened window. He went to the window, looked out, down, saw the crowd surrounding four blue-coated figures and a crushed form. A death wagon was drawing in to the curb. He frowned.

Leaving the window open, he searched hastily through the papers littering the dead professor's desk, found nothing to satisfy his pointless curiosity. With one last keen glance around, he left the laboratory. His falling disk swept him past two ascending policemen.

A line of phone booths stood in the foyer. Entering one, he spun the dial, saw a girl's clear features glow into the circular visor.

"Give me Mr. Sangster, Hetty."

10

"Yes, Mr. Graham."

The girl's face dissolved, was replaced by that of a heavy-featured man.

"Mayo's dead," Graham informed, bluntly. "He dropped down the front of the Martin about twenty minutes ago. He dived past sixteen floors, landed almost at my feet. He was unrecognisable except for the scars on his hands."

"Suicide?" The other raised bushy brows inquiringly.

"That's how it looks," Graham admitted, "but I don't think it is."

"Why not?"

"Because I knew Mayo exceedingly well. As a government liaison officer between scientists and the U.S. department of special finance, I have dealt with him personally over a period of ten years. You will remember that I have negotiated four loans for the furtherance of his work."

"Yes, yes." Sangster nodded.

"In general, scientists are an unemotional crowd," Graham continued, "and Mayo was about the most phlegmatic of the lot." He gazed earnestly at the little screen. "Believe me, sir, Mayo was not capable of self-destruction—at least, not while in his right mind."

"I believe you," said Sangster, without hesitation. "What do you wish to have done?"

"The police have every reason to treat this as a simple case of suicide and I cannot interfere because I have no status in such cases. I suggest that all necessary strings be pulled to make sure that the police dismiss this matter only after the most thorough investigation. I want them to sift this to the bottom."

"It shall be as you ask," Sangster assured. His rugged features grew large as they were brought nearer to the distant scanner. "The appropriate department will intervene."

"Thank you, sir," Graham responded.

"Not at all. You hold your position only because we have complete faith in your judgment." His eyes lowered to a desk not visible in the screen. A rustling of papers came over the wires. "Mayo's case has a parallel today."

"What?" ejaculated Graham.

"Doctor Irwin Webb has died. We were in contact with him two years ago. We provided him with sujcient funds to complete some research which resulted in our war department acquiring a self-aligning gunsight operating on magnetic principles."

"I recall it well."

"Webb died an hour ago. The police phoned because they

11

found a letter from us in his wallet." Sangster's face became grim. "The circumstances surrounding his death are very strange. The medical examiner maintains that he died of heart disease—yet he expired while shooting at nothing."

"Shooting at nothing?" echoed Graham, incredulously.

"He had an automatic pistol in his hand, and he had fired two bullets into the wall of his office."

"Ah!"

"From the viewpoint of our country's welfare and scientific progress," continued Sangster, speaking with much deliberation, "the deaths of such able men as Mayo and Webb are too important to be treated lightly, especially when mysterious circumstances intervene. Webb's case seems to be the more peculiar of the two. I want you to look into it. I would like you, personally, to examine any documents he may have left behind. Something of significance may be lying around there."

"But I have no official standing with the police," Graham protested.

"The officer in charge of the case will be notified that you have governmental authority to examine all Webb's papers."

"Very well, sir." Sangerster's face faded from the visor as Graham hung up. "Mayo!—and now Webb!"

Webb lay on the carpet midway between the door and the window. Flat on his back, with his dead eyes wide open, the pupils were almost hidden where they turned up and under the top lids. The cold fingers of his right hand still grasped a dull blue automatic loaded with segmentary bullets. The wall toward which the gun pointed bore eight abrasions; a small group of weals where quarter sections of two split missiles had struck home.

"He shot at something along this line," Lieutenant Wohl said to Graham, stretching a thin cord from the center of the weals to a point four or five feet above the body.

"That's what it looks like," agreed Graham.

"But he wasn't shooting at anything," Wohl asserted. "Half a dozen people were passing along the passage outside when they heard his gun suddenly start blasting. They burst in immediately, found him like this, breathing his last. He strove to say something, to tell them something, but the words wouldn't come. Nobody could have got in or out of his office without being seen. We've checked on the six witnesses and they're all above suspicion. Besides, the medical examiner says it's heart disease."

"Maybe it is," Graham evaded, "and maybe it isn't."

A cold eddy wafted through the room as he spoke those

12

words. A subtle tingling slid up his spine, stirred his back hairs and passed away. His inward self became filled with a vague unease, elusive but strong, like that of a rabbit which suspects the presence of a hawk it cannot see.

"All the same, I'm not satisfied," continued Lieutenant Wohl. "I've got a hunch that this Webb suffered from delusions. Since I've never heard of heart disease causing hallucinations, I reckon he's taken something that's caused both."

"You mean that he was a drug addict?" Graham queried.

"I mean just that! I'll gamble that the autopsy will show my hunch is correct."

"Let me know if it does," requested Graham.

Opening the doctor's desk, he commenced to search carefully through the neatly arranged files of correspondence. There was nothing to satisfy his interest, nothing to which he could attach special significance. The letters without exception were orthodox, innocent, almost humdrum. His face registered disappointment as he shoved the files back into place.

Closing the desk, he transferred his attention to the huge safe built into the wall. Wohl produced the keys, saying, "They were in his right-hand pocket. I'd have looked through that safe, but was told to hold off for you."

Graham nodded, inserted a key. The cumbersome door swung slowly on its bearings, exposed the interior. Graham and Wohl gave vent to simultaneous exclamations. Facing them hung a large sheet of paper bearing a hasty scrawl:

Eternal vigilance is the impossible price of liberty. See Bjornsen if I go.

"Who the deuce is Bjornsen?" snapped Graham, plucking the paper from the safe.

"Don't know. Never heard of him." Wohl gazed in frank puzzlement at the sheet, and said, "Give it to me. It carries marks of writing from a sheet above it. Look, the impressions are fairly deep. We'll get a parallel light beam on it and see if we can throw those imprints into relief. With luck, they'll prove easy to read."

Graham handed him the sheet. Taking it to the door, Wohl passed it outside with a quick utterance of instructions.

They spent the next half-hour making careful inventory of the safe's contents; a task that revealed nothing except that Webb had been a painstaking bookkeeper and had kept close watch on the business side of his activities.

Prowling around, Wohl found a small pile of ash in the grate. It was churned to a fine powder beyond all possibility of reclamation—the dust of potent words now far beyond reach.

"Grates are relics of the twentieth century," declared Wohl.

"It looks like he stuck to this one so that he could burn documents in it. Evidently he had something to conceal. What was it? From whom was he hiding it?" The telephone buzzed, and he hastened to answer it, adding, "If this is the station maybe they'll be able to answer those questions for us."

It was the station. The face of a police officer spread across the midget visor while Wohl pressed the amplifier stud so that Graham could listen in.

"We brought out the words on that sheet you gave us," the officer said. "They're pretty incoherent, but maybe they'll mean something to you."

"Read 'em out," Wohl ordered. He listened intently while the distant police officer recited from a typewritten copy.

"Sailors are notoriously susceptible. Must extend the notion and get data showing how seaboard dwellers compare with country folk. Degrees of optical fixation ought to differ. Look into this at first opportunity. Must also persuade Fawcett to get me data on the incidence of goitre in imbeciles, schizophrenics especially. There's wisdom in his madhouse, but it needs digging out."

The reader looked up. "There are two paragraphs, and that's the first."

"Go on! Go on, man!" urged Graham, impatiently. The officer continued while Graham kept eagle eyes upon the visor, and Wohl looked more and more mystified.

"There is a real connection between the most unexpected and ill-assorted things. Oddities have links too surreptitious to have been perceived. Fireballs and howling dogs and second-sighters who are not so simple as we think. Inspiration and emotion and everlasting cussedness. Bells that chime unswung by human hands; ships that vanish in sunlit calm; lemmings that migrate to the valley of the shadow. Agruments, ferocity, ritualistic rigmarole, and pyramids with unseen peaks. It would seem a nightmarish hodge-podge of surrealists at their worst—if I didn't know Bjornsen was right, terribly right! It is a picture that must be shown the world—if it can be shown without massacre!"

"What did I tell you?" asked Wohl. He tapped his forehead significantly. "A narcotic nut!"

"We'll see about that." Bringing his face closer to the telephone's scanner, Graham said to the distant officer, "File that sheet where it'll be safe. Make two more typewritten copies and have them sent to Sangster, care of the U.S. department of special finance at their local office in Bank of Manhattan."

He switched off the amplifier, pronged the receiver. The tiny television screen went blank.

14

"If you don't mind, I'd like to go with you to the station," he told Wohl.

They went out together; Wohl convinced that here was work for the local narcotic squad; Graham pondering the possibility of the two deaths being natural despite their element of mystery. As they crossed the sidewalk both felt a strange, nervous thrill. Something peered into their minds, grinned and slunk away.

Chapter 2

No new information awaited them at the station. Fingerprint men had returned from Mayo's laboratory as well as from Webb's office, had developed and printed their photographs. There were a mass of prints, some clear, some blurred. Most had been brought out with aluminium powder; a few—on fibrous surfaces—with iodine vapor. The great majority were prints left by the scientists themselves. The others were not recorded on police files.

Experts had gone with complete thoroughness through the dead men's rooms and discovered not the slightest thing to arouse their own suspicions or confirm Graham's. They reported with the faint air of men compelled to waste their time and talents on other people's fads.

"There's nothing left but the autopsy," declared Wohl, finally. "If Webb's a drug addict, the case is cleared up. He died while shooting at some crazy product of his own imagination."

"And Mayo jumped into an imaginary bathtub?" queried Graham.

"Huh?" Wohl looked startled.

"I suggest an autopsy on both—if it's possible to hold one on what's left of Mayo." Graham reached for his hat. His dark gray eyes were steady as they looked into Wohl's blue ones. "Phone Sangster and let him know the results." He hurried out with characteristic energy.

A pile of wreckage cluttered the corner of Pine and Nassau. Graham got a glimpse over the head of the surging crowd, saw two crumpled gyrocars which appeared to have met in head-on collision. The crowd thickened rapidly, pushed, stood on tiptoe, murmured with excitement. He could sense their psychopathic tension as he passed. It was like moving through an invisible aura of vibrancy. The mob-noumen.

"Disaster is to crowds what sugar is to flies," he commented to himself.

Entering the huge pile of Bank of Manhattan Building, he took a pneumatic levitator to the twenty-fourth floor. Pushing through a gold-lettered door, he said, "Hello, Hetty!" to the

16

honey-blonde a the switchboard, and passed on to a door marked *Mr. Sangster*. He knocked and went in.

While Sangster listened quietly, he made a full report, concluded, "And that's all there is, sir. It leaves us with nothing except my own doubts concerning Mayo, and the peculiar fact of Webb firing a pistol."

"And it leaves us this person Bjornsen," said Sangster, shrewdly.

"Yes. The police haven't been able to get a line on him. They've hardly had sufficient time yet."

"Do the postal authorities hold any mail for Webb, from this Bjorsen?"

"No. We thought of that. Lieutenant Wohl phoned and asked them. Neither the mail carrier nor the sorters remember letters from anyone named Bjornsen. Of course, this unknown —whoever .he may be—might not have sent letters or, if he did, they may not have carried the sender's name on the envelop. The only mail for Webb comprises two conventional letters from scientist friends of his college days. Most scientists seem to maintain a wide but erratic correspondence with other scientists, especially fellow experimenters working along parallel lines."

"Which this Bjornsen may have been," Sangster suggested.

"Now there's an idea!" Graham pondered it a moment, then reached for the phone. He got his number, absentmindedly pressed the amplifier stud, winced when the receiver promptly bellowed into his ear. Resting the receiver on Sangster's desk, he said into the mouthpiece, "Is that the Smithsonian Institute? May I speak to Mr. Harriman?"

Harriman came on, his dark eyes level in the screen. "Hello, Graham. What can I do for you?"

"Walter Mayo is dead," Graham told him, "and Irwin Webb, too. They passed away this morning within an hour of each other." Harriman's face expressed his sorrow while Graham gave him brief details of the tragedies. Graham asked, "D'you happen to know of any scientist bearing the name of Bjornsen?"

"Yes. He died on the seventeenth."

"Died?" Graham and Sangster shot to their feet, and the former said, grimly, "Was there anything unusual about his end?"

"Not that I know of. He was an old man, well past his allotted span. Why do you ask?"

"Never mind. Do you know anything more concerning him?"

"He was a Swedish scientist specializing in optics," replied Harriman, obviously mystified, "and he passed his prime twelve

17

years ago. Some people thought him in his second childhood. His death gained eulogies in a few Swedish papers, but I have noticed no mention of it in the press over here."

"Anything else?" Graham persisted.

"Not much. He was rather obscure. If I remember aright, he commenced his decline when he made himself a laughing-stock with some paper he read to the 2003 International Scientific Convention, at Bergen. It was a lot of gibberish about visual limitations, with plenty of spooks and djinns thrown in. Hans Luther also brought the vials of wrath on his own head by being the only scientist of any prominence to treat Bjornsen seriously."

"And who is this Hans Luther?"

"A German scientist, and a very clever man. He's dead. He died not long after Bjornsen."

"What, another?" Graham and Sangster shouted together.

"What's the matter?" Curiosity was the keynote of Harriman's tones. "You don't expect scientists to live forever. They die just like other people, don't they?"

"When they die just like other people," replied Graham, dourly, "we feel regrets and nurse no suspicions. Do me a favor, Harriman. Get me a complete list of all the internationally known scientists who have died since the first of May, together with every cogent detail you can rake up."

Harriman blinked with surprise. "I'll phone you as soon as I can," he promised, and rung off. Almost at once he came on again with, "I forgot to tell you that Luther is said to have died in his Dortmund laboratory while gabbling some incoherent nonsense to his local paper. He had a heart attack. His death was attributed to dementia and cardiac exhaution, both brought on by overwork."

He hung on the line, watching for the effect, openly hoping for information. Then he gave it up, repeated, "I'll phone you as soon as I can." He disconnected.

"This thing gets crazier the further we look into it," commented Sangster. He flopped into his chair, tilted it back on its hind legs, frowned his dissatisfaction. "If the deaths of Mayo and Webb weren't natural, they certainly weren't supernatural. Which makes plain, straightforward homicide the only alternative."

"Murder for what?" inquired Graham.

"That's just the hell of it! Where's the motive? There simply isn't any! I can imagine half a dozen countries who might regard the super-swift amputation of America's best brains as a suitable prelude to war, but when Swedish and German scientists get dragged in—with maybe a dozen more nationalities on

18

the list Harriman's compiling—the entire situation becomes complicated to the point where it's absolutely fantastic." Picking up his typewritten copy of Webb's notes, he waved it dismally. "As fantastic as all this stuff." He cocked a speculative eye at the brooding Graham. "Your hunches started us on this hunt after heaven-alone-knows-what. Have you got any ideas to back them up?"

"None," Graham confessed. "Not one. We haven't yet found enough facts to provide basis for a plausible theory. It's up to me to dig up more details."

"From where?"

"I'm going to see this fellow Fawcett whom Webb mentioned in his jottings. He ought to be able to tell me something interesting."

"Do you know Fawcett?" Sangster registered surprise.

"I've never heard of him. But Doctor Curtis, who is Webb's half-sister, may be able to put me in touch. I know Doctor Curtis well."

A slow smile came into Sangster's heavy face. He said, "How well?"

Graham grinned and replied, "Not as well as I'd like."

"Humph! So that's the way it is! Combining business with pleasure, eh?" He made a negligent gesture. "Oh, well, best of luck! If only you can nail down something more substantial than mere suspicions we can get the Federal Bureau of Investigation on the job."

"I'll see what I can do." The telephone shrilled as Graham reached the door. He hesitated, one hand on the door-knob, while the other grabbed the receiver, laid it on the desk, operated the amplifier.

Wohl's features glowed into the screen. He could not see Graham who was standing outside the scanner's angle of vision. He stared straight at Sangster while he spoke.

"Webb must have had the itch."

"The itch?" echoed Sangster, confusedly, "Why?"

"He'd painted his left arm, from shoulder to elbow, with iodine."

"What the devil for?" Sangster threw an appealing look at the listening Graham.

"Nothing. There wasn't anything the matter with his arm. My theory is either he had the itch or he did it to gratify his artistic instincts." Wohl's tough face cracked into a hard grin. "We've not finished the autopsy yet, but I thought I'd better let you know about this. When you've given it up, I can pose you another just as daffy."

"Out with it, man!" snapped Sangster.

"Mayo had the itch, too."

"Do you mean that he'd painted his arm as well?"

"Yes, with iodine," confirmed Wohl, maliciously enjoying himself. "Left arm, shoulder to elbow."

Staring fascinatedly at the screen, Sangster drew in a long, deep breath, said, "Thanks!" He replaced the receiver, gave Graham a despairing look.

"I'm on my way," said Graham.

Doctor Curtis had a strict, professional air of calm efficiency which Graham liked to ignore. She had also a mop of crisp black curls and a curvaceousness which he liked to admire with frankness she found annoying.

"Irwin had been behaving strangely for more than a month," she told him, unnecessarily eager to keep his attention on the subject about which he had come. "He would not confide in me despite my concern for him, which, I'm afraid, he chose to regard as feminine curiosity. Last Thursday, his peculiar attitude strengthened to a point of such ill-concealed apprehension that I began to wonder if he were on the verge of a nervous breakdown. I advised him to take a rest."

"Did anything occur last Thursday which might have caused him to worry unduly?"

"Nothing," she assured with confidence. "Or nothing that might affect him so seriously as to make him unbalanced. Of course, I must admit that he was extremely upset by the news of the death of Doctor Sheridan, but I don't see why that—"

"Excuse me," Graham interrupted. "Who was Sheridan?"

"An old friend of Irwin's. A British scientist. He died last Thursday, of heart disease, I understand."

"And still they come!" Graham murmured.

"I beg your pardon?" Doctor Curtis opened large, black eyes inquiringly.

"Just a comment," he evaded. Leaning forward, his muscular features intent, he asked, "Did Irwin have a friend or acquaintance named Fawcett?"

Her eyes widened more. "Oh, yes. He is Doctor Fawcett, the resident specialist at the State Asylum. Surely he cannot be involved in Irwin's death?"

"Not at all." He noted the obvious puzzlement which now overlay her normally tranquil pose. He was tempted to take advantage of it and put several more questions he wished to ask, but some queer subconscious quirk, some subtle hint of warning, made him desist. Feeling himself a fool to obey his inward impulses, he went on, "My department has a special interest in your brother's work, and his unfortunate end has left us with several features to clear up."

Apparently satisfied, she gave him her cool hand. "Do let me help you."

He held it until she had to drag it away. "You help by boosting my morale," he chided.

Leaving her, he ran down the steps leading from the twentieth floor surgery, reached the skyway which ran past mighty building-piles at a level three hundred feet above the ground.

A police gyrocar whined along the skyway, stopped before the surgery just in time to meet him as he got to the bottom of the steps. Lieutenant Wohl thrust his head out of its side window.

Wohl said, "Sangster told me you'd be here. I've come to pick you up."

Clambering into the sleek machine, Graham asked, "Has something broken loose? You look like a hound-dog on the scent."

"One of the boys discovered that Webb's and Mayo's last phone calls were both made to some big brain named Professor Dakin." He pressed the accelerator stud, the two-wheeled speedster plunged forward, its encased gyroscope emitting a faint hum. "This Dakin lives on William Street, right near your own hideout. Know him?"

"Like my own hands. You ought to know him, too."

"Me? Why?" Wohl whirled the wheel, took a skyway bend with a cop's official recklessness. The gyrocar kept rigidly upright while its occupants rolled sidewise in their seats. Graham clung to the hand-rail. Four other drivers on the skyway got the momentary meemies as they bulleted past, glaring after them.

Pulling in some breath, Graham said, "When did the police abandon the moulage method of making casts?"

"Five years back." Wohl aired his knowledge. "We now photograph impressions with stereoscopic cameras. Impressions on fibrous surfaces are recorded in relief with the aid of the parallel light beam."

"I know all that. But why is that method now used?"

"Because it's handier and absolutely accurate."

"Take it on from there," suggested Graham.

"It's been used ever since they found a way to measure stereoscopic depth by means of . . . heck!"—he risked a swift and apologetic glance at his passenger, and concluded—"the Dakin steroscopic vernier."

"Correct. This fellow is the Dakin who invented it. My de-

21

partment financed his preliminary work. Frequently we get results for our money."

Wohl refrained from further comment while he concentrated on handling his machine. William Street slid rapidly toward them, its skyscrapers resembling oncoming giants.

With a sharp turn which produced a yelp of tormented rubber from the rear wheel, the gyrocar spun off the skyway and onto a descending corkscrew. It whirled down the spirals with giddying effect.

They hit ground level still at top pace, and Wohl straightened out, saying, "Those whirligigs sure give me a kick!"

Graham swallowed a suitable remark, his attention caught by the long, low, streamlined, aluminium-bronze shape of an advancing gyrocar. It flashed toward them along William Street, passed with an audible swish of ripped air, shot up the ramp to the corkscrew from which they'd just emerged. As it flashed by, Graham's sharp eyes registered the pale, haggard face staring fixedly through the machine's plastiglass windshield.

"There he goes!" exclaimed Graham, urgently. "Quick, Wohl —that was Dakin!"

Frantically spinning his wheel, and turning the gyrocar in its own length, Wohl fed current to the powerful dynamo. The machine leaped forward, hogged a narrow gap between two descending cars and charged madly up the ramp.

"He'll be about six turns above us and near the top," Graham hazarded.

Grunting assent, Wohl muscled his controls which the police speedster spiralled rapidly upward. The fifth twist brought them behind an ancient, four-wheeled automobile holding the center of the shute and laboriously struggling along at a mere thirty.

They gave an impromptu demonstration of the greater mechanical advantage of two wheels with power on both. Cursing violently, Wohl swerved, fed juice, shot around the antiquated obstruction at fifty, leaving its driver jittering in his seat.

Like a monster silver bullet, their vehicle burst from the corkscrew onto the skyway, scattered a flock of private machines, dropped them behind. The speedometer said ninety.

Half a mile ahead, their aluminum-bronze quarry hummed full tilt along the elevated artery and maintained its lead.

Moving his emergency power lever, Wohl grumbled, "This is going to make junk of the batteries."

The gyrocar surged until its speedometer needle trembled over the hundred mark. The gyroscope's casing broadcast the angry sound of a million imprisoned bees. A hundred and ten.

The tubular steel supports of the skyway railing zipped past like a solid fence, with no intervals apparent between them. One-twenty.

"The Grand Intersection humpback!" Graham shouted, warningly.

"If he hits it at this crazy pace he'll jump more than a hundred feet," growled Wohl. He narrowed his eyes as he squinted anxiously forward. "His 'scope will give him a square landing, but it won't save his tires. One of them will burst for sure. He's driving like a blithering maniac!"

"That's what makes it so obvious that something is damnably wrong." Centrifugal force held Graham's breath for him as they cut around another decrepit four-wheeler whose driver managed to gesticulate within the split-second available.

"Every jalopy ought to be banned from the skyways," Wohl snarled. He stared ahead. The shining shape of their quarry was whirling headlong around the shallow bend leading to Grand Intersection. "We've gained a bare hundred yards. He's driving all out, and he's got a special sports model at that. You'd think someone was chasing him."

"*We* are," remarked Graham dryly. His eyes sought the rear-view mirror while his mind considered the likelihood of Dakin being pursued by someone other than themselves. What was Dakin running from, anyway? What did Mayo take a death-dive to escape? What did Webb shoot at as his dying act of defiance? What wiped out Bjornsen and made Luther expire with a gabble on his lips?

He gave up the fruitless speculation, noted that the road behind was clear of other chasers, raised his eyes as something threw a dark shadow over the gyrocar's transparent roof. It was a police helicopter hanging from spinning vanes, its landing wheels a yard above the hurtling car.

The two machines raced level for a few seconds. Wohl jabbed an authoritative finger at the police star across his vehicle's bonnet, then waved urgently toward the crazy car ahead.

Making a swift gesture of comprehension, the helicopter's pilot gained height and speed. Hopping great roofs, his machine roared through the air in desperate attempt to cut the skyway bend and beat Dakin to the intersection.

Without slackening pace in the slightest, Wohl hit the bend at full one twenty. Tires shrieked piercingly as they felt the sidewise drag. Graham leaned heavily on the nearside door; Wohl's bulk pressed crushingly on him.

While centrifugal force held them in that attitude, and the tortured gyroscope strove to keep the machine upright, the tires gave up the battle and the car executed a sickening double-eight. It swooped crabwise across the concrete, missed a dawdling phaeton by a hairbreadth, flashed between two other gyrocars, wiped the fender off a dancing four-wheeler and slammed into the side. Miraculously, the rails held.

Wohl gaped like a goldfish while he dragged in some air. He nodded toward the hump where the skyway curved over another elevated route which swept past it at right angles.

"Holy smoke!" he gasped. "Look at that.

From their vantage point four hundred yards away the crest of the hump appeared to bisect the midget windows of a more distant pile of masonry. Dakin's machine was precisely in the center of the crest with the police helicopter hovering impotently over it.

The fleeing car did not sink in perspective below the crest as it should have done in normal circumstances. It seemed to float slowly into the air until it reached the tops of the bisected windows and exposed a line of panes between its wheels and the crest. There, for one long second, it poised below the helicopter, apparently suspended in defiance of the law of gravity. Then, with still the same uncanny slowness, it sank from sight.

"Mad!" breathed Graham. He dabbed perspiration from his forehead. "Utterly and completely mad!"

He rolled his window downward until a deep dent in its plastiglass prevented it from descending farther. Both men listened intently, apprehensively. From over the crest came a short, sharp sound of rending metal, a few seconds of silence, then a muffled crash.

Without a word they struggled out of their battered gyrocar, sprinted along the skyway, over the long, smooth hump. They found a dozen machines, mostly modern gyrocars, drawn up beside a thirty-foot gap in the rails. White-faced drivers were grasping twisted railposts while they bent over and peered into the chasm beneath.

Shouldering through, Graham and Wohl looked down. Far below, on the side of the street opposite the lower and transverse skyway, a mass of shapeless metal made a tragic heap on the sidewalk. The face of the building that reared itself ten floors from the spot bore deep marks scored by the wreckage on its way down. The ruts of the road to oblivion.

A rubbernecking driver jabbered to nobody in particular, "Terrible! Terrible! He must have been clean out of his mind! He came over like a shell from a monster gun, smacked the side-rails, went right through and into that building. I heard him land down there." He licked dry lips. "Like a bug in a can. What a wallop! Terrible!"

The speaker's emotions were voiced for the rest. Graham could sense their awe, their horror. He could sense the excitement, the sadistic thirst, the corporate soul-stirring of the inevitable mob now gathering three hundred feet below. Mob hysteria is contagious, he thought, as he felt it rising like an invisible and hellish incense. One could get drunk on it. Men who were cold sober individually could be drunk collectively; drunk on mass-emotions. Emotions—the unseen intoxicant!

Another feeling drove away these morbid thoughts as fascinatedly he continued to stare downward: a feeling of guilty fear, like that of a man holding dangerous and punishable opinions in some far country where men are hanged for harboring the wrong thoughts. The sensation was so strong and emphatic that he made a mighty effort to discipline his mind. Dragging his gaze from the scene beneath, he nudged Wohl into attention.

"There's nothing we can do. You've reached the end of Dakin's trail and that's that! Let's get going."

Reluctantly, Wohl backed away from the gap. Noticing the defeated helicopter landing on the skyway, he hastened toward it.

"Wohl, homicide squad," he said, briefly. "Call Center Station on your short-wave, will you, and ask them to have my machine towed in for repairs. Tell them I'll phone a report through shortly."

Returning to the still gaping group of drivers, he questioned them, found one who was bound for William Street. This fellow had an ancient four-wheeler capable of a noisy fifty. Wohl accepted a lift with becoming condescension, climbed in crinkling his nose in disgust.

"Some move with the times, some jump ahead of the moment, and some just stay put." He picked disdainfully at the worn leatherette on which he was sitting. "This hell-buster has stayed put since Tut built the pyramids."

"Tut didn't," Graham contradicted.

"Tut's brother, then. Or his uncle. Or his sub-contractor. Who cares?" His head jerked backward as the driver let in a jumpy clutch and the car creaked forward. He uttered a potent name, looked aggrieved, said to Graham, "I'm letting you tote me around because, being just another wage-slave, I've got to do as I'm told. But I've still no notion of what you're seeking, if anything. Does your department know something special that isn't for publication?"

"We know nothing more than you do. It all started with

me having some vague suspicions, and my superiors backing them up." He gazed speculatively at the cracked and yellowish windshield. "I first smelled the skunk. For my pains, I've now got to dig out the stinker—or sing small."

"Well, I've got to hand it to you for getting hunches and having the nerve to play them." He bounced around on his seat, said complainingly, "Look, homicide on the job, in a jalopy! That's where it gets us. Everybody dies, and even we're in a corpse-wagon." He bounced again, hard. "I can see by the way things are shaping that I'll finish up playing with feathers and treacle. But I'm with you as long as I stay sane."

"Thanks," Graham responded, smiling. He studied his companion. "By the way, what's your other name?"

"Art."

"Thanks, Art," he corrected.

Chapter 3

THEIR careful search of Dakin's place revealed nothing worthy of note; no last, dramatic message, no hidden jottings, no feature that could be considered in any way abnormal. As a route to the solution of their indefinable puzzle, it was somewhat of a dead-end.

Discovering the late scientist's original and crude model of his vernier, Wohl amused himself by projecting its standard stereoscopic cube upon a small screen. Twiddling the micrometer focusing screw that controlled the cube's perspective, he made the geometrical skeleton flat enough to appear almost two-dimensional, then deep enough to resemble an apparently endless tunnel.

"Cute!" he murmured.

Graham came out of a back room holding a small, nearly empty vial of iodine in his fingers.

"I looked for this on another hunch. It was in his medicine chest along with enough patent cure-alls to stock a drugstore. Dakin always was something of a hypochondriac." He put the vial on the table, surveyed it morosely. "So that means exactly nothing." His dissatisfied glance went round the room. "We're only losing time in this place. I want to see Doctor Fawcett, at the State Asylum. Can you run me there?"

"I'll phone first." Using Dakin's instrument, he talked to his station, cut off, said to Graham, "There will be no autopsy on Dakin. They can't dissect pulp!" He put away the vernier, pocketed the vial, opened the door. "Come on. Let's have a look at your asylum—some day it may be home, sweet home!"

Darkness was a shroud over the Hudson. A sullen moon scowled down through ragged clouds. Incongruously, a distant neon repeatedly flashed its message in blood-red letters fifty feet high: BEER HERE. Observing it, Wohl subconsciously licked his lips. Fidgeting on the sidewalk, they waited for the gyrocar which Wohl had ordered over the phone.

The machine hummed down the street, its long floodlight blazing. Wohl met it, said to the uniformed driver, "I'll take her myself. We're going to Albany."

Climbing into the seat, he waited until Graham had plumped beside him, eased the machine forward.

Graham said to him, warningly, "We're in a hurry—but not that much."

"What d'you mean?"

"Please, I'd like to get there in one lump. I don't function so well in several parts."

"Nobody functions so well when you get after them. Are you a stockholder in the local graveyard?" Wohl's beefy face quirked. "There's one comfort about hanging around with you."

"What's that?"

"I'll die with my boots on."

Graham smiled, said nothing. The car picked up speed. Twenty minutes later he was hugging the rail as they cornered. Still he said nothing. They pelted northward, reached Albany in hours—good going even for Wohl.

"This is well outside my official stamping-ground," Wohl commented, as they pulled up outside their destination. "So far as I'm concerned, I'm off duty. You've merely brought a friend along."

The new State Asylum sprawled its severe, ultra-modern architecture over a square mile of former parkland. It was very evident that Doctor Fawcett was the leading light in its administration.

He was a skinny little runt, all dome and duck's feet, his top-heavy features triangular as they sloped in toward a pointed goatee beard, his damn-you eyes snapping behind rimless pince-nez.

His small form even smaller behind a desk that looked the size of a field, he sat stiffly upright, wagged Graham's copy of Webb's jottings. When he spoke it was with the assertive air of one whose every wish is a command, whose every opinion is the essence of pure reason.

"A most interesting revelation of my poor friend Webb's mental condition. Very sad, very sad!" Unhooking his pince-nez, he used them to tap the paper and emphasize his pontifications. "I suspected him of having an obsession, but must confess that I did not realize he'd become so completely unbalanced."

"What made you suspicious?" Graham asked.

"I am a chess enthusiast. So was Webb. Our friendship rested solely upon our mutual fondness for the game. We had little else in common. Webb was entirely a physicist whose work had not the slightest relation to mental diseases; nevertheless, he showed a sudden and avid interest in the subject. At his own request, I permitted him to visit this asylum and observe some of our patients."

"Ah!" Graham leaned forward. "Did he give any reason for his sudden interest?"

"He did not offer one, nor did I ask for one," replied Doctor Fawcett, dryly. "The patients who interested him most were those with consistent delusions coupled to a persecution complex. He concentrated particularly upon the schizophrenics."

"And what may those be?" put in Wohl, innocently.

Doctor Fawcett raised his brows. "Persons suffering from schizophrenia, of course."

"I'm still no wiser," Wohl persisted.

With an expression of ineffable patience, Doctor Fawcett said, "They are schizoid egocentrics."

Making a gesture of defeat, Wohl growled, "A nut's a nut whether in fancy dress or otherwise."

Fawcett eyed him with distaste. "I perceive you are a creature of dogmatic preconceptions."

"I'm a cop," Wohl informed, blinking. "And I know when I'm being given the runaround."

"You must pardon our ignorance, doctor," Graham chipped in smoothly. "Could you explain in less technical terms?"

"Schizophrenics," answered Fawcett, speaking as one speaks to a child, "are persons suffering from an especial type of mental disease which, a century ago, was known as dementia praecox. They have a split personality the dominant one of which lives in a world of fantasy that seems infinitely more real than the world of reality. While many forms of dementia are characterized by hallucinations which vary both in strength and detail, the fantastic world of the schizophrenic is vivid and unvarying. To put it in as elementary a manner as possible, he always has the same nightmare."

"I see," commented Graham, doubtfully.

Putting on his glasses with meticulous care, Fawcett stood up. "I will let you see one of the inmates in whom Webb is interested."

Showing them through the door, he conducted them along a series of passages to the asylum's east wing. Here, he reached a group of cells, stopped outside one, gestured.

They peered cautiously through a small, barred opening, saw a naked man. He was standing by his bed, his thin legs braced apart, his unnaturally distended abdomen thrust out. The sufferer's ghastly eyes were fixed upon his own stomach with unwavering and hellish concentration.

Fawcett whispered rapidly, "It is a peculiarity of schizophrenia that the victim often strikes a pose, sometimes obscene, which he can maintain without stirring for a period of time impossible to the normal human being. They have phases when they become living statues, often repulsively. This particular case is a typical poseur. His stricken mind has convinced itself that he has a live dog inside his abdomen, and he spends hours watching for a sign of movement."

"Good heavens!" exclaimed Graham, shocked.

"A characteristic delusion, I assure you," said Fawcett, professionally unmoved. He looked through the bars as if academically considering a pinned moth. "It was Webb's irrational comments about this case that made me think him a little eccentric."

"What was Webb's reaction?" Graham glanced again into the cell, turned his eyes thankfully away. The thought in his mind was the same as that in Wohl's—but for the grace of fate, there go I!

"He was fascinated by this patient, and he said to me, 'Fawcett, that poor devil has been prodded around by unseen medical students. He is mutilated trash tossed aside by supervivisectionists.' " Fawcett stroked his beard, registered tolerant amusement. "Melodramatic but completely illogical."

A shudder ran through Graham's muscular frame. Despite iron nerves, he felt sick. Wohl's face, too, was pale, and both sensed the same inward relief when Fawcett led the way back to the office.

"I asked Webb what the deuce he meant," Doctor Fawcett continued, quite unperturbed, "but he only laughed a little unpleasantly and quoted that adage about when ignorance is bliss it is folly to be wise. A week later he phoned me in a state of considerable excitement and asked if I could get him data concerning the incidence of goitre in imbeciles."

"Did you get it?"

"Yes." Fawcett dived down behind his huge desk, slid open a drawer, came up with a paper. "I had it here ready for him. Since he's dead, the information comes too late." He flipped the paper across to Graham.

"Why," Graham exclaimed, looking it over, "this states that there is not one case of goitre among the two thousand inmates of this asylum. Reports from other asylums give it as unknown or exceedingly rare."

"Which doesn't mean anything. It's evidence only of the negative fact that imbeciles are not very susceptible to a disease which isn't common." He glanced at Wohl, his tones slightly acid. "When a disease isn't common, it's because not many people are susceptible to it. Probably the same data

30

applies to any two thousand bus drivers, or paint salesmen—or cops."

"When I catch goitre, I'll tell you," promised Wohl, surlily.

"What causes goitre?" Graham put in.

Fawcett said, promptly, "A deficiency of iodine."

Iodine! Graham and Wohl exchanged startled glances before the former asked, "Has a superfluity of iodine anything to do with imbecility?"

His goatee wagging, Fawcett laughed openly. "If it did, there would be a great proportion of idiots among seafaring folk who eat foods rich in iodine."

A message burned into Graham's mind, red-hot. Wohl's face betrayed the fact that he'd got it also. A message from the illogical dead.

Sailors are notoriously susceptible.

Susceptible to what? To illusions and to maritime superstitions based upon illusions?—the sea serpent, the sirens, the Flying Dutchman, mermaids, and the bleached, bloated, soul-clutching things whose clammy faces bob and wail in the moonlit wake?

Must extend the notion, and get data showing how seaboard dwellers compare with country folk.

Displaying a forced casualness, Graham retrieved Webb's notes from the desk. "Thanks, doctor. You've been a great help."

"Don't hesitate to get in touch with me if I can be of further assistance," Fawcett advised. "If you do eventually arrive at the root cause of poor Webb's condition, I'd appreciate the details." His short laugh was more chilling than apologetic. "Every competent analysis of a delusion is a valuable contribution to knowledge of the whole."

They returned to New York as fast as they had left, their cogitating silence being broken only once when Wohl remarked, "The entire affair suggests an epidemic of temporary insanity among scientists whose brains have been overworked."

Graham grunted, offered no comment.

"Genius is akin to. madness," persisted Wohl, determined to bolster his theory. "Besides, knowledge can't go on increasing forever without some of the best minds giving way when they strain to encompass the lot."

"No scientist tries to learn the lot. Knowledge already is far too much for any one mind, and that is why every scientist is a specialist in his own field though he may be an ignoramus about things totally outside the scope of his own work."

It was Wohl's turn to grunt. Concentrating on his driving

with no better results at the sharpest corners, he voiced not another word until he arrived at Graham's address. Then he dropped his passenger with a brief, "See you in the morning, Bill," and hummed away.

The morning was bright, symbolic of a new day that brought early developments. Graham was standing before his mirror, his electric shaver whirring busily, when the telephone shrilled. The youth in the visor eyed him and said, "Mr. Graham?"

"Yes, I'm Graham."

"This is the Smithsonian," responded the other. "Mr. Harriman had a message for you late last night but was not able to get in touch with you."

"I was in Albany. What's the message?"

"Mr. Harriman said to tell you he has been to all the news agencies, and finds they've reported the deaths of eighteen scientists within the last five weeks. Seven of them were foreigners, and eleven American. The number is about six times the average, as the news agencies rarely report more than per month."

"Eighteen!" ejaculated Graham. He studied the face picked up by the faraway scanner. "Have you got their names?"

"Yes." The youth dictated them while Graham copied them down. He gave their respective nationalities. "Anything more, sir?"

"Please convey my thanks to Mr. Harriman and ask him to phone me at the office when convenient."

"Very well, Mr. Graham." The youth disconnected, left him pondering deeply.

"Eighteen!"

On the other side of the room the telenews receiver's gong chimed softly. Crossing to it, he raised the lid, exposed the press-replica screen which, in his apparatus, was licensed for the *New York Sun's* transmissions.

The *Sun's* early morning edition began to roll at sedate reading-pace across the screen while he watched it with part of his mind elsewhere. Presently, his eyes sharpened and his concentration returned as another headline appeared.

SCIENTIST'S DEATH DIVE

Professor Samuel C. Dakin fifty-two years old William Street physicist, took the Grand Intersection humpback in his sports gyrocar last evening, and plunged to death at more than a hundred miles an hour.

The report continued to half-column length, included a photograph of the wreck, several references to "this departed

32

genius," and stated that the police were looking into the cause of the tragedy. It concluded with a comment to the effect that this was the third successive death of a New York scientist since the previous morning, "those of Professor Walter Mayo and Doctor Irwin Webb having been detailed in our yesterday evening edition."

From the automatic-record locker beneath the screen, Graham extracted his photographic copy of the *Sun's* evening issue. Mayo's and Webb's cases were in juxtaposition; the former headed: MAYO FALLS FROM MARTIN; and the latter: ANOTHER SCIENTIST DIES. Both reports were superficial, revealing nothing more except that "the police are investigating."

Wohl turned up just then. He charged into the apartment, his eyes agleam. He waved the *Sun* aside with a short, "I've seen it."

"What's all the excitement about?"

"My hunch." He sat down, breathed heavily. "You're not the only one who gets hunches." He puffed, grinned apologetically, puffed again. "They've held those autopsies. Mayo and Webb were full of dope."

"They were drugged?" asked Graham, incredulously.

"It was mescal," Wohl went on. "A special and very highly refined form of mescal. Their stomachs contained strong traces of it." A pause while he got his breath. "And their kidneys were rich in methylene blue."

"Methylene blue!" Graham's mind struggled in vain to make something rational of this information.

"The boys followed up these facts pretty fast. They found mescal, methylene blue, and iodine in Mayo's, Webb's and Dakin's laboratories. We'd have found them ourselves if we'd known what to look for."

Graham nodded agreement. "It's fair to assume that an autopsy on Dakin would have produced the same result."

"I would think so," Wohl approved. "The boys also discovered that the junk in the furnace of Mayo's distillation set-up was Indian hemp. God knows how he'd smuggled it in, but that's what it was. It looks as if he must have been about to experiment with drugs other than mescal."

"If he was," declared Graham, positively, "it was solely by way of scientific experiment. Mayo was never a drug addict."

"So it seems," said Wohl, dryly.

Graham tossed him the list provided by Harriman. "Take a look at that. According to the Smithsonian, those eighteen have rolled up during the last five weeks. The law of averages suggests that three or maybe four of those deaths were normal

33

and inevitable." He seated himself on a corner of the table, swung one leg to and fro. "That, in turn, suggests that the others were not normal. It also means that we're involved in something a darned sight bigger than first it seemed."

Scanning the list, Wohl commented, "Not only big, but crazy. All drug cases have their crazy aspects. This one's so daffy that it's stuck on my mind since last night." He made a face. "I've kept on picturing that guy we saw in the cell—pregnant with dog."

"Let's forget him for a while."

"I wish I could!"

"What we've got to date," Graham continued, thoughtfully, "poses several questions the answers to which ought to lead us somewhere." He stabbed an indicative forefinger at the list which Wohl was still holding. "We don't know on what basis those news agencies determine their average of three. Is it over the last twelve months, or the last five years, or the last twenty? If it's a long-term average, and this month's deaths beat it by six times, what were last month's casualties and last year's? In other words, what are the total deaths since the start?—and what started them?"

"The first suicide began them," Wohl declared, "The rest were imitative." He handed back the list. "Take a look over police files sometime. You'll find time after time when murder and suicide were temporarily contagious. One spectacular and well-publicized crime often induces several others of similar type."

"I've said from the beginning and I still maintain that these weren't suicides. I knew Mayo and Dakin very well indeed. I knew Webb by repute. They just weren't the psychological types likely to indulge in self-destruction, even if full of drugs."

"That's the point," Wohl emphasized, stubbornly. "You knew them sober. You didn't know them snowed-up. A guy hopped to the eyeballs isn't the same individual—he's someone else. He's capable of anything, including shooting at thin air or jumping off a roof."

"I'll give you that much." Graham looked bothered as he folded the list and put in in his pocket. "This mescal feature is a puzzler."

"Not to my mind, it isn't. The drug traffic is spread by personal recommendation. I reckon that some scientist, driven half-nuts by overwork, has found a new-fangled stimulator more dangerous than he knows. He's used it, suggested it to others, and some of them have tried it. Maybe it worked for a while, but, like arsenic, it's accumulative. It piled up inside

34

them until eventually they went gaga one by one." He spread broad hands. "And here we are!"

"I wish it were as simple as that—but something inside me says that it isn't."

"Something inside you," scoffed Wohl. "Another dog!"

Preoccupied, Graham watched the morning *Sun* still crawling across his screen. He opened his mouth to voice a suitable retort, closed it without speaking. The blurred words on the screen suddenly sharpened, became clear. He stood up as Wohl followed his gaze.

NOTED EXPERT'S END

Stephen Reed, sixty, of Far Rockaway, created a scene outside the Central Library on Fifth Avenue this morning and then threw himself under an express load-carrier. He was killed immediately. Reed was one of the world's leading authorities in optical surgery.

Graham switched off the receiver, closed down the screen, reached for his hat. "Nineteen!" he said, softly.

"Oh, holy smoke!" Wohl got up, followed him to the door. "Here we go again!"

Chapter 4

As usual, most of the half a hundred witnesses of the last of Stephen Reed had vanished beyond trace. Someone hurriedly had called a cop, the police officer had phoned his station, and a reporter waiting there had passed the news to the *Sun*.

It took two hours to find three onlookers. The first was a pear-shaped man with sweaty jowels.

He said to Graham, "I was passing this guy and not taking much notice. I got enough to worry me, see? He let out an awful yell, did a sort of dance and ran into the traffic."

"And then?"

"I could feel what was coming and looked away."

The next proved to be a bulky blonde. She was edgy. She held a small handkerchief in her hand and nervously nibbled at one corner of it while she talked.

"He gave me a turn. He came along like someone watching for a ghost. I thought he'd seen one. He shouted, waved his arms about, and rushed madly into the road."

"Did you hear *what* he shouted?" Graham asked.

She gnawed the handkerchief again. Her pale blue eyes were scared.

"He upset me so much that I didn't catch it. He bawled loudly and hoarsely, at the top of his voice. Something about, 'No! No! For pity's sake, no!' and a bit of other crazy stuff."

"You didn't see anything that might have caused him to act like that?"

"No—that was the worst of it!" She had another chew, shifted her eyes around as if straining to see the unseeable.

"She'll be consulting clairvoyants before this week is through," commented Wohl, as she departed.

The third witness, a suave, well-groomed man with a cultured voice, said, "I noticed Mr. Reed walking toward me with a most peculiar look in his eyes. They were bright and glassy, as if he'd primed them with belladonna."

"Done what?" put in Wohl, curiously.

"Primed them with belladonna, like we do on the stage."

"Oh." Wohl subsided.

"He was looking alertly all over the place, up and down and around. He had an air of apprehension. I felt that he was seeking something he did not want to find."

"Go on," urged Graham.

"As he came near me his face went white. He seemed stricken with sudden and acute fear. He made desperate gestures, like a man trying to ward off a fatal blow, screamed incoherently and raced into the road." The witness shrugged fatalistically. "A twenty-ton load-carrier hit him. Undoubtedly, he died instantaneously."

"You didn't hear what he said?"

"I'm afraid I didn't."

"There was nothing to indicate the reason for his fear?"

"Not a thing," assured the other, authoritatively. "The incident moved me so much that I sought immediately for a cause. I could not find one. It appeared to me that he must have been overcome by some feature not apparent—a tumour on the brain, for example."

"We are very much obliged to you." Graham watched the suave man go. He brooded silently while Wohl picked up the phone and called the morgue.

What was that subtle, unidentified essence in the human make-up which occasionally caused Malaysians to run amok, foaming at the mouth, kriss in hand, intent on wholesale and unreasoning slaughter? What other essence, similar but not the same, persuaded the entire nation of Japanese to view ceremonial suicide with cold-blooded equanimity? What made fanatical Hindus gladly cast themselves to death before the lumbering juggernaut? Was this present outbreak due to the insidious hold of some new virus, breeding and spreading in places more civilised, perhaps stimulated horrifically by mescal, iodine and methylene blue?

He gave up the speculation as Wohl pronged the phone. Wohl turned to him with the martyred air of one burdened for past sins.

"They won't be carving Reed for a while, but they've found he fits the general pattern in one respect: he'd painted himself with iodine."

"Left arm?"

"No. Evidently he believed in variety, or perhaps he was plain ornery. He did his left leg, hip to knee."

"Then we can add him to our list," decided Graham. "We can say he's another case without being able to define said case."

"Yes, I guess so."

"You know, Art, this drug-addict theory of yours may

apply to the mescal, but what about the other items being used in association with it? Methylene blue and iodine aren't drugs in the sense that you mean. They're innocuous, they're not habit-forming. They don't make folk go haywire."

"Neither does water, but plenty of people take it with whisky."

Graham made an impatient gesture. "That's beside the point. As I see it, we've two logical steps still to take. The first is to give this Reed's place the once-over. The second is to seek expert advice on what mescal, methylene blue and iodine can do to people when used like all these bodies have been using it."

"Reed's dump is way out," Wohl remarked. "I'll get the car."

The home of the late Stephen Reed was a bachelor's villa run by a middle-aged and motherly housekeeper. Outside of domestic arrangements, she knew nothing and, when told the tragic news, promptly became incapable of telling anything she might have known.

While she retired to her room, they raked expertly through Reed's study. They found a formidable mass of papers through which they searched with frenzied haste.

"The chief will be the next to have a heart attack," Wohl prophecied, grabbing himself another handful of letters.

"Why?"

"The local boys ought to be in on this. The way you make me go rampaging around other people's bailiwicks would give him an apopletic stroke. You may not know it, but you've got me headed straight for demotion."

Graham grunted derisively, continued with his search. It was some time before he came up with a letter in his hand.

"Listen to this." He read it aloud. "Dear Steve, I'm sorry to learn that Mayo is giving you some of his stuff. I know you're deeply interested, of course, but must tell you frankly that to play with it is a waste of valuable time. My advice is that you throw it in the ashcan and forget it. It will be safer there, as I know only too well." He glanced up. "It bears Webb's address, and it's signed, 'Irwin.'"

"What's the date on it?"

"May twenty-second."

"Not so old."

"A double-link," Graham observed. "Mayo to Webb and Reed. It's being passed from one to another. I expected that."

"So did I." Wohl turned over papers, scanning them rapidly.

"Personal recommendation, like I told you. Though it looks like Webb tried to discourage Reed for some reason."

"The reason was that to fool around with it meant death —and Webb knew it even then! On May twenty-second he knew that his days were numbered as surely as I know that I'm standing here in my pants. He wasn't able to do much about it, but he tried to steer Reed away from the grave."

Looking up from his rummaging, Wohl complained, "You say the damnedest things. You'll be suggesting that the finger is put on us next."

"I'm not so sure that it won't—once we start really to get someplace."

The same cold shiver insinuated itself into his back muscles, and he flexed his shoulder-blades in an effort to shake it off. He had a keen sense of psychic frustration, as if his brain were permitted to probe in all directions except one. Whenever it tended that way a warning bell sounded within him and his questing mind obediently withdrew.

Cramming a handful of insignificant papers back into its file, he growled, "Not a thing. All about eyeballs and optic nerves. He slept with 'em and ate 'em."

"Same here," agreed Wohl. "What's conjunctivitis?"

"Eye-trouble."

"I thought it was something to do with railroad switching." He thumbed through the last of his sheets, returned them to their place. "He's got no laboratory or surgery here. He operated at the Eye and Ear Hospital, in Brooklyn. We ought to try there, eh?"

"I'll call the office first. Time I reported." Using Reed's phone, Graham had a long talk with Sangster, finished, said to Wohl, "We're wanted there sooner than immediately. They've been waiting for us since first thing this morning. Sangster's acting like somebody's swallowed an atom-bomb."

"*We?*" emphasized Wohl raising his eyebrows.

"Both of us," Graham confirmed. "Something mighty important is in the wind." Rubbing his chin, he surveyed the room in open disappointment. "This place is as fruitful as a vacuum. Whether or not we're wanted urgently, we'd better try that hospital on our way—it's our last chance to get an item out of Reed."

"Let's go."

Doctor Pritchard, a tall, slender and youthful individual, got them after the hospital's secretary had passed them from hand to hand. Welcoming them, he gave them chairs, took off his white coat.

"I suppose you wish to question me about poor Reed?"

"You know he's dead?" Graham shot at him.

Pritchard nodded soberly. "The police informed us. They phoned soon after it happened."

"Whether it was suicide is a moot point," Graham told him. "Maybe he bumped himself deliberately, maybe he didn't, though I don't think he did, myself. Nevertheless, the evidence shows that he was far from normal at the time. Can you explain his condition?"

"I can't."

"Have you noticed him behaving queerly of late?"

"I don't think so. I was his assistant, and I'm sure that I'd have noticed any exceptional peculiarity of his." He thought a moment. "Up to three days ago he was more than usually preoccupied. That is nothing extraordinary in a person of his character and profession."

"Why up to three days ago?" Graham persisted.

"I've not seen him since then. He'd taken short leave of absence, to complete some work."

"He gave you no indication of the nature of that work?"

"No. He was never communicative about his outside interests."

"Did you know Professor Mayo or Doctor Webb?"

"I've heard of them. I don't know them."

"Did Reed ever mention either of them to you? Or has he spoken of being involved with them in any way?"

"No," said Pritchard, positively.

Graham gave Wohl a look of defeat. "A dead end!" He returned his attention to Pritchard. "Reed was an eminent opthalmic surgeon, I understand. Would that cause him to take an especial interest in drugs?"

"Within certain limits it might."

"Have you anyone here who is an authority on drugs in general?"

Pritchard pondered again. "I reckon Deacon is our best for that—d'you want him?"

"Please."

He rang a bell. To the attendant who responded, he said, "Ask Doctor Deacon if he's free to come here for a minute."

Deacon arrived looking irritated. He was rubber-gloved and had a beam-light strapped over his iron-gray hair.

"This is a devil of a time to—" he began. He saw Graham and Wohl, added, "I beg your pardon."

"Sorry to disturb you, doctor," Graham soothed. "I'll save your time by being brief. Can you tell me what happens to a

40

person who paints himself with iodine and doses himself with mescal and methylene blue?"

"He ends up in an asylum," asserted Deacon, without hesitation.

Wohl uttered a painted, "Youps!" and stared down at his stomach.

"You mean that literally?" pressed Graham. "It would expedite insanity?"

"Nothing of the sort! I mean no more than that he'd be insane to do anything so pointless."

"That isn't what I want, doctor. I'm asking for the physical effects, without regard for the motive."

"Well," said Deacon, more amiably. "I don't pretend to advise you as authoritatively as could certain other specialists, but I'd say the mescal would drive the subject higher than a kite if he absorbed a sufficient dosage. The methylene blue would cleanse the kidneys and discolor the urine. As for the iodine, it would function as a germicide, stain the skin and, being a halogen, would permeate the whole system in very short time."

"Do you think the three in association might create another and more positive effect—say by one assisting the reaction of another, like a catalyst?"

"You've got me there," Deacon confessed. "Multiple interactions are still the subject of research and will continue to be for many years to come."

Graham stood up, thanked him and Pritchard, then said to Wohl, "Looks as if Reed was a very late comer in this deadly game. He never had time to say much, do much. Whatever is behind this can hit quick and hit hard."

"It's harder to hit a moving object," observed Wohl, with grim humor. He followed Graham out. "Back to Sangster now?"

"Yes. We'd better get there fast. He'll be jumpy if we don't reach him soon."

Sangster had with him a tall, middle-aged and dapper individual of military appearance. Frowning pointedly at the clock as the two arrived, he introduced the newcomer as Colonel Leamington.

"The entire investigation has been taken out of this department's hands," Sangster announced, without beating about the bush. Reaching across his desk, he handed Graham a paper.

The sheet rustled in his fingers as Graham read, "Your application for immediate transfer to the United States Intelligence Service has been approved, and said transfer is effected as from this date. You will take your commission and accept orders from Colonel John H. Leamington who, until further notice, you will regard as your departmental superior."

Gulping as he noted the famous signature at the bottom of the letter, he looked inquiringly at Sangster. "But, sir, I have made no such application."

"You may tear the letter up, if you wish," Sangster remarked.

Colonel Leamington intervened with, "The position, Mr. Graham, is that we wish you to continue your investigation with better facilities than are accorded you in your present position."

"Thank you," he answered, somewhat dazed.

"One of our news-agency men reported the questions made by Harriman on your behalf. It drew our attention to a matter that otherwise might have escaped us for some time." He stroked his neatly clipped mustache, his face serious, very serious. "Eleven of these departed scientists were Americans. They were men of incalculable value to their country. Great as it may be, their loss is as nothing when compared with the menace of further losses. The Government cannot ignore their sudden and mysterious demise."

"I see."

"Then you accept this commission?" pressed Colonel Leamington.

"Yes, yes, of course!" He studied the letter with concealed pride which was not lessened by Wohl's open envy. To be one of the Government's most tried and trusted band, one of Uncle Sam's most privileged operators!

Taking his ring from Leamington, he put it on the right hand, third finger. It fitted perfectly, and he knew that it must have been prepared in anticipation of his acceptance. He also knew that upon its super-hard iridium inner surface were delicate inscriptions too small to be seen with the naked eye; microscopic data giving his name, height, weight, Bertillon measurements and fingerprints formulae, as well as his Service number and a faithful though infinitely small copy of his own signature.

This modest ornament was his only badge, his only warrant of authority, its meaning concealed from all but those equipped to read—but it was the open sesame to officialdom everywhere.

As these thoughts passed through his mind there came a faint and eerie sense of overhanging peril; the warning note again, vague, indefinite, but thoroughly disturbing. He looked once more at his ring, knew that it could be regarded from another and ghastlier angle: it might prove the sole means of identifying him in horrible, mangling death—as many others had been so identified.

What was it that Webb had talked about? "Mutilated trash cast aside by super-vivisectionists."

Pushing the memory aside, he said, "One thing, colonel: I would like to have the continued co-operation of Lieutenant Wohl. He's in this as deeply as me—and we need each other."

He evaded Wohl's look of gratification, listened while Leamington replied.

"Har-humph! Somewhat irregular, but I think it can be arranged. I have little doubt that the chief of police can be persuaded to grant Lieutenant Wohl a roving commission until such time as he's seen this job through."

"Thank you, sir," Graham and Wohl chorused.

Sangster's phone yelped for attention, he answered it, passed it to Graham, saying, "Harriman."

"Hello, Harriman," called Graham. "Yes, I got your list. Thanks a lot!" He paused as the second phone on Sangster's desk clamored deafeningly, and Sangster reached to take it. "There's a deuce of a row here. The other phone bawling. What what that you said?" He paused, listened, then, "Sorry, Harriman, I can't tell you anything just yet. Yes, six times the average is something that calls for an explanation, and that's what I'm out to get—if it can be got!"

He ceased speaking while Sangster put down the other phone and whispered, "Doctor Curtis, for you."

"Listen, Harriman," he continued hurriedly, "all these scientists are people of different nationalities, ages and types. The conclusion is that nothing is being aimed at any one country—unless someone is clever enough and ruthless enough to bump some of his own in order to avert suspicion. I doubt that."

Harriman said, "There's nothing political about this, any more than there is about a new disease."

"Exactly! Different as they may be, these scientists *must* have shared one thing in common—the thing that directly or indirectly brought about their deaths. I want to find that common denominator. Rake me up every detail you can discover about the persons on your list and any earlier cases you may see fit to add. Phone them to"—he looked inquiringly at Leamington, was given a number, and finished—"to Colonel Leamington at Boro 8-19638."

Ringing off, he took up the other phone, spoke rapidly. The others studied his changing expression as he talked.

Finishing, he told them, "Doctor Curtis has received a

long-distance call from Professor Edward Beach. He said that he had just read the accounts of Webb's and Mayo's deaths. He expressed much sorrow, but Doctor Curtis thought him unusually curious about the details of the tragedies."

"Well?" prompted Leamington.

"This Beach is an old friend of Webb's, according to Doctor Curtis. I know him, too. He's the man who designed the stereoscopic owl-eye camera which the police use in conjunction with Dakin's vernier. He is employed by the National Camera Company, at their Silver City plant, in Idaho. Beach is precisely the sort of scientist likely to have valuable information concerning Mayo, Webb and Dakin." He paused a moment, to lend impressiveness to what he was about to say, then added, "Especially since he made a point of asking Doctor Curtis whether she knew if Webb, like Mayo and Dakin, had been working on Bjornsen's formula prior to his end."

"Bjornsen!" ejaculated Sangster.

"You can see the implication," Graham went on. "Beach is linked to these others exactly as *they* were linked to each other—by correspondence based on mutual interests. He's got a place in this death-chain, but death hasn't reached him yet! He's a prospective victim still in condition to talk. I've got to see him and make him talk before he becomes body number twenty." He consulted his watch. "With luck, I can catch the 10:30 strat-plane for Boise."

Wohl said, "Do I come, or are you on your own?"

"I'll take this by myself. While I'm on my way, phone Battery Park Stratosphere Station, Art, and book me a seat on the 10:30."

Reaching for the phone, Wohl asked, "And after that, I do what? Give me something to follow—I hate wasting time."

"You can make a cross-check on the data Harriman's getting. See if you can make contact with the police authorities in all the places where these scientists died, ask them for full and complete details of the deaths. Get them to check thoroughly on every item no matter how minute or seemingly unimportant. Bully, cajole or do whatever else you can to persuade them to obtain exhumation orders and conduct autopsies." He looked at Leamington. "Is all this okay with you, Colonel?"

"I'm satisfied to let you run this your own way," Leamington approved. "I'm taking it for granted that the man who starts something is best fitted to finish it."

"We're worrying about quite a lot of people who started something that none of them finished," Graham pointed out.

"This thing—whatever it is—has a remarkable aptitude for finishing the starters before they get anywhere." He grinned ruefully. "I'm not immortal, either—but I'll do my best."

Snatching his hat, he was gone, bound for Battery Park, the 10:30 strat-plane and the worst disaster in the history of the New World.

Chapter 5

THE New York-Boise-Seattle stratosphere express dived down from the atmosphere's upper reaches, cut its oxygen from its pressurized cabin, levelled with a thunderous burst of rockets, swept beneath the undersides of fleecy clouds.

With the little town of Oakley nestling on its banks, Goose Creek rolled under the fleet vessel's bow. Far to port and well to stern gleamed the northern fringes of Utah's Great Salt Lake. About a hundred and fifty miles to go—a mere ten minutes' run!

A cigarette that Graham had lit over Oakley was still only half consumed when the strat-plane banked away from the valley of the Snake and curved toward Boise. The turn brought Silver City on the port side where it was easily perceivable in the dry, dustless atmosphere of the locality. Its white and cream-colored buildings glowed in the sunlight. Bobbin-shaped chemical reservoirs of the National Camera plant, slung on huge towers, stood out clearly on the city skyline.

Thrusting his feet at the footrests to resist body-surge caused by the ship's rapid deceleration, Graham took two more drags at his cigarette, cast another glance at the far vista of Silver City. For a moment, it was still there, sharp and clear in detail upon the horizon; the next moment it had gone in a mighty cloud of heaving vapor.

Crushing his cigarette between unnerved fingers, he rose partway in his seat, his eyes staring incredulously at the far-away spectacle. The cloud bloomed hugely, swelled with the primal vigor of an oncoming dust-storm, its bloated crests curling angrily as they gained altitude. Small black specks soared above this upper edge, hung momentarily in mid-air, dropped back into the swirling chaos.

"God in heaven!" breathed Graham. His eyes strained unbelievingly. He knew that for the strange specks to be visible from such a distance they must be big, very big—as large as buildings. In those tense seconds it was as if he were endowed with a front seat at the dropping of a bigger and better atom-bomb—with people in the back seats watching seismographs a thousand miles away.

The strat-plane's tail swung round, concealed the distant drama. Unaware that anything abnormal was taking place, its pilot brought the vessel down in a long, dexterous curve that dropped Silver City behind intervening spurs of the Rockies. Making a perfect landing, the great machine rushed over the concrete, its rockets blasting spasmodically. With a final swerve, it stopped alongside a tower-topped building that bore in large white letters the word: BOISE.

Graham was first out. Descending the portable steps in a manner that startled its handlers, he hit the concrete, made to run around the ship's tail, but stopped, appalled.

About a hundred civilians and officials were scattered over the stratosphere station's areaway, but none advanced to greet the arrival. They stood stock still at various points around the space, their faces turned to the south, their eyes narrowed as they strove to bring a long range into focus.

In that direction, sixty miles away, yet thrusting high above minor sprawls of the Rockies, was the cloud. It was not mushroom-shaped as other ominous clouds had been. It was twisted and dark and still growing. It had become an awful pillar that reached to the very floors of heaven and sought to thrust through like a gaseous fungus rooted in hell; a great, ghastly erection of swirling, flowing, sullen clouds poised like a visible column of earthly woe and lamentations.

The noise! The noise of that far phenomenon was infinitely terrible even though muted by distance; a sound of tortured, disrupted air; a sound as if something insane and gargantuan were running amok through the cosmos, ripping, tearing, rending everything on which it could lay its mammoth hands. Titan on a bender!

All faces were pale, uncomprehending, while that far column poked its sable finger into the belly of the void, and from the void came an eldritch yammering like stentorian laughter booming through the caverns of beyond. Then, abruptly, the cloud collapsed.

Its gaseous crown continued to soar while its semi-solid base fell back. It dropped from sight with all the shocking suddenness of a condemned felon plunging through a trap. The thing was gone, but its swollen soul still rose and drifted westward, while its hellish rumbles and muffled roars persisted for several seconds before they faded and died away.

The hypnotized hundred stirred, slowly, uncertainly, as in a dream. Five officials moved stupidly toward the idling strat-plane, their minds confused by the vision in the south. To one

47

side of the concrete area, a private flyer resumed his walk toward his sports machine. Graham beat him to it.

"Quick! Take me to Silver City—government business!"

"Eh?" The flyer regarded him with preoccupied air.

"Silver City," repeated Graham, urgently. His powerful fingers gripped the other's shoulder, shook it to emphasize his words. "Get me to Silver City as swiftly as you can."

"Why should I?"

"Dammit!" Graham roared, looking dangerous, "d'you want to argue at a time like this? You can take me—or have your machine confiscated. Which is it to be?"

The note of authority in his voice had its effect. The flier came to life, said hastily, "Yes, sure! I'll take you." He did not ask who Graham was, nor demand his purpose. Clambering hurriedly into his highly streamlined, two-seater, ten-jet job, he waited for his passenger to get in, then blew fire from the tail. The sports model raced along the concrete, lifted, screamed at a sharp angle into the blue.

Their destination lay beneath an obscuring pall of dust that was settling sluggishly as they progressed. It was just as they roared immediately overhead that a vagrant blast of wind cleared away the desiccated murk and bared the site of what had been Silver City.

Looking down, the pilot yelled something which became lost in the bellow of the stern tubes, fought to regain the controls that momentarily had slipped from his grasp. With cherry-red venturis vomiting fire and long streams of vapor, the ship zoomed close to the ground, brought into near view a scene that made Graham's stomach contract sickeningly.

Silver City was gone; the area it once had occupied was now an enormous scar on the face of Idaho, a five-miles-wide wound dotted with wreckage through which crept, crawled and limped a pathetically small number of survivors.

Jittery with shock, the pilot made an impromptu landing. Choosing a smooth stretch of sand on the north fringe of the scar, he brought his machine down, touched, lifted, touched, tilted, dug the starboard wingtip into soft soil. The machine reeled in a semicircle, tore off its wing, fell on its starboard side with the port wing sticking grotesquely into the air. The pair scrambled out unhurt. They stood side by side and studied the scene in complete silence.

Only one hour ago this had been a neat, clean and busy city of some thirty-five thousand souls. Now it was a field torn from the domain of hell, a crater-pitted terrain relieved only by low mounds of shattered bricks, tangles of distorted girders. Pale cobras of smoke still waved and undulated to the tune of distant groans. Here and there, a stone parted raspingly from its neighbor, a girder contracted in iron agony.

There were other things; things from which eyes avert and minds recoil; things photographed, but not for publication. Gaudy gobs and crimson clots inextricably mixed with tatters of wool and shreds of cotton. A jello shape in shredded denims. A parboiled head still exuding steam. A hand stuck to a girder, fingers extended, reaching for what it never got—and giving God the high-sign.

"Worse than the Krakatoa explosion," declared Graham, his voice soft, low. "Even worse than the Mònt Pelée disaster."

"What a blast! What a blast!" recited the pilot, gesturing in nervous excitement. "This is atomic. Nothing less than an atom-bomb could have done it. You know what that means?"

"You tell me."

"It means that every inch of this ground is deadly. We're being sprayed every second we stand here."

"That's too bad." Graham nodded at the wrecked plane. "Maybe you'd better take the air, eh?" He made his voice more tolerant. "We don't know that it's atomic—and by the time we find out it'll be too late, anyway."

A figure emerged laboriously from behind a pyramid of twisted girders in the middle distance. It limped around craters, side-stepped shapeless but infinitely terrible obstructions, made a lopsided, lurching run toward the waiting pair.

It was a human being, a man whose rags flapped around his raw legs as he progressed. He came up to them showing dirt and blood camouflaging an ashen face that framed a pair of glowing, half-mad optics.

"All gone," announced the newcomer, waving a trembling hand toward the place whence he had come. "All gone." He chuckled crazily. "All but me and the little flock who are worthy in the sight of the Lord." Squatting at their feet, he rolled his red-rimmed eyes upward, mumbled in tones too faint to be understood. Blood seeped through rags dangling on his left hip. "Listen!" he ordered, suddenly. He cupped a quivering hand to his ear. "Gabriel sounded his horn and even the song of the birds was stilled." He giggled again. "No birds. They came down in a dead rain. Out of the sky they fell, all dead." He rocked to and fro on his heels, mumbled again.

The pilot went to his plane, returned with a pocket-flask. Taking the flask, the sitting man gulped potent brandy as if it were water. He gasped, gulped some more. Emptying it, he handed it back, resumed his rocking. Slowly the light of sanity returned to his eyes.

Struggling to his feet, he teetered while he gazed at the

49

others and said, in tone a little more normal, "I had a wife and a couple of kids. I had a real good wife and two damn fine kids. Where are they now?" His eyes blazed anew as they shifted from one to the other, desperately seeking the answer that none could give.

"Don't lose hope," soothed Graham. "Don't lose hope until you know for certain."

"Tell us what happened," suggested the pilot.

"I was fixing a patent no-draft cowl on a chimney in Borah Avenue, and I was just reaching for a piece of wire when the entire universe seemed to go bust. Something grabbed me, threw me all over the sky, then dropped me. When I got up, there wasn't any Silver City any more." He put his hands over his eyes, held them there a moment. "No streets, no houses. No home, no wife and kids. And dead birds falling all around me."

"Have you any idea of what caused it?" Graham inquired.

"Yes," declared the man, his voice pure venom. "It was the National Camera Company, fooling around with something they'd no right to touch. Looking for another ten percent, and damn the consequences. May everybody connected with it be blasted body and soul, now and for evermore!"

"You mean that the explosion was located in their plant?" put in Graham, stemming the tirade.

"Sure!" The speaker's orbs mirrored his hate. "Their tanks blew up. They had a battery of cylinders holding a million gallons of silver nitrate solution, and every gallon of it went up at once, and sent everything straight to Hades. Why do they let 'em keep stuff like that in the middle of a city? Where's their right—and who says so? Somebody ought to be swung for that! Somebody ought to be hoisted higher than the city went!" He spat fiercely, rubbed his swollen lips. Death was in the set of his jaw. "Wiped out peaceful homes, and happy families, and—"

"But silver nitrate in solution won't disrupt like that."

"Won't it, mister?" retorted the victim, his tones sheer sarcasm. He gestured all-embracingly. "Look!"

His listeners looked. They found nothing to say.

Cars began to pour along the road from Boise, the vanguard of a veritable cavalcade that was to continue for a week. A plane swooped overhead, another and another. An auto-gyro bumped to earth half a mile away. Two helicopter ambulances floated inward, prepared to follow suit.

Temporarily disregarding causes, and reckless of consequences, a thousand pairs of feet trod through the graveyard of the West, a thousand pairs of hands pulled cautiously at wreckage, plucked maimed but living creatures from the soil. In his haste to rescue the living, no man thought of tormented atoms spitting invisibly, of hard radiations piercing his own body time and time again.

Ambulances, wheeled and winged, official or rush-converted, raced in, departed only to come again and again. Stretcher-bearers stamped a broad, firm path that later was to become the exact route of Mercy Street. Flying journalists hovered in hastily hired helicopters a few hundred feet above, their tele-visors recording the horror below, broadcasting agony and pathos in extravagant adjectives not one-tenth so moving as the photographic reality depicted on the screens of a hundred million telenews receivers.

Graham and his pilot slaved with the rest, slaved long after dusk had fallen and night had spread its able shroud over the dead that yet remained. A gibbous moon crawled up, spewed its beams over the sights below. The hand on the girder maintained its gesture.

A gore-smeared gyrocar, with silent driver, carried Graham back to Boise. Finding a hotel, he washed, shaved, put a call through to Colonel Leamington.

The news of the disaster had shaken the world, said Leamington. Already the president had received messages of sympathy from fifteen foreign governments as well as from countless individuals.

"We're taking every necessary action to determine as soon and as definitely as possible whether this is another Hiroshima, Black Tom, or Texas City," he continued. "That is to say, whether its cause is attributable to assault, sabotage or accident."

"It's no Hiroshima," Graham told him. "It wasn't an atomic explosion—or not in any sense we understand. It was an ordinary, commonplace bang, a molecular disruption, but on a gigantic scale."

"How d'you know that?"

"They've rushed in Geiger counters from all directions. I questioned a bunch of operators just before I left. They say radiation is not abnormal as far as they've searched. The area seems safe. If anything is radiating, it's something not detectable by the means being employed."

"Humph!" growled Leamington. "I guess we'll get that report here shortly." He was silent for a few seconds, then said, "If it so happens that you come across anything suggesting a connection between this awful disaster and your investigation, you must drop everything forthwith and get in touch with me.

In such circumstances, the whole affair would be far too great for one man to handle."

"There is no evidence of such a connection," Graham pointed out.

"Nothing—until you uncover something!" Leamington riposted. "In view of what has gone before, I feel mighty suspicious. Unless he is one of the few survivors, Beach is now the twentieth on the list exactly as you feared. He is a mouth closed before you could reach him precisely as all the others were closed. I don't like it!"

"Maybe, sir, but—"

"Graham, I repeat most emphatically that if you stumbled on any sort of a link between this holocaust and the work on which you're engaged, you must give up at once and report to me without delay."

"Very well, sir."

"In that event, the best brains in the country must be conscripted to meet the issue." Colonel Leamington's voice trailed off, then came back strongly. "What do you think of the situation yourself?"

Graham hesitated before replying. He knew that he was as far from the truth as he'd been at the start, but he could not force aside the strange, uncanny feeling that had obsessed him since the death of Mayo. It seemed ridiculous to attach importance to sensations which, though strong and persistent, were elusively vague. Was that feeling akin to the hunch which had put him on the track of something yet to be found? Were those psychic warnings somehow related to his investigatory insight? Was it intuition, or empty superstition, or merely jumpy nerves?

Coming to a decision, he spoke slowly and deliberately. "Chief, I've still not the slightest idea of what is behind all this, but I've a notion that there are times when it's dangerous to talk about it." A thought became born in his mind, and he added, "I believe there are times when it's dangerous even to *think* about it."

"Absurd!" scoffed Leamington. "True telepaths don't exist, hypnotism is very much overrated, and there are no known mechanical means of tapping anyone's secret thoughts. Besides, how the devil can any investigation be conducted without thought?"

"That's the hell of it," responded Graham, dryly. "It cannot. Therefore I must take the risk."

"Are you serious, Graham?"

"Never more so! I believe, or rather I feel that there are times when I can stew this affair in my mind, freely and with profit. Just as positively, I feel that there are inexplicable moments when so to think would be sticking out my neck with a vengeance. Why I feel that way is something I can't explain. Maybe I'm nuts—but the deeper I get into this case the more I respect my own nuttiness."

"Why?"

"Because," said Graham, "I'm still perpendicular—while the others are horizontal!"

He put down his receiver, a queer light in his eyes. Somehow, he knew that he was right in his estimate of danger. He must take a risk, an awful risk, against odds infinitely terrible because completely unknown. *Eternal vigilance is the impossible price of liberty*. If he, like Webb, must succumb in vain effort to pay that price, well, so be it!

Police Chief Corbett eventually found one in the top ward of the overflowing Center Hospital. According to him, this fellow was the only employee of the National Camera Company among three thousand survivors rescued from what was left of Silver City.

The patient was bandaged from head to feet, his eyes being covered, only his mouth exposed. A strong odor of tannic acid exuded from him, bore mute witness to his extensive burns. Graham sat at one side of the bed, Corbett at the other.

A weary nurse said, "Five minutes—no more! He's very weak but stands a chance if you'll give him one."

Putting his lips close to a bandage-covered ear, Graham asked, "what exploded?"

"The tanks," came a faint whisper.

"Silver nitrate?" inquired Graham, doing his best to convey incredulity in his tones.

"Yes."

"Can you explain it?"

"No." A dry, swollen and discolored tongue licked along cotton fringes over the burned lips.

"What was your job?" Graham put quietly.

"Lab worker."

"Research?"

"Yes."

Graham wasted a meaning glance on the listening Corbett, then said to the man on the bed, "On what work were you engaged at the time of the disaster?"

There was no reply. The mouth closed under its wrappings, the breathing became inaudible. Alarmed, Corbett signalled a nurse.

Hurrying up, the girl fussed over the patient. "He's all right.

53

You've got two more minutes." She dashed away, her face pale, lined with long duty.

Graham put his question again, got no answer. With a frown, he signed to Corbett to take over.

"This is Police Chief Corbett, of Boise," declared that official, severely. "Your questioner is a member of the United States Intelligence Service. More than thirty thousand people died in yesterday's blast, and the few remaining are in no better shape than you. The discovery of the cause of this tragedy is more important than your loyalty to your employers. I advise you to speak."

The mouth remained stubbornly closed.

"If you refuse to speak," Corbett continued, "means may be found to—"

Waving him into silence, Graham brought his own lips near the recumbent form, and murmured, "Doctor Beach authorises you to tell all you know."

"Beach!" exclaimed the man on the bed. "Why he warned me to say nothing!"

"He warned you?" Graham was thoroughly startled. "He warned you when? Has he seen you *here?*"

"An hour before you came," admitted the other, in a low voice.

With a mighty effort, Graham suppressed a desire to shout, "Then he's alive!" but kept his wits and said, coolly, confidently. "Much may happen in an hour. You can speak without fear."

The other stirred feebly. "We found the new emulsion the day before yesterday," he told them, reluctantly. "Under Beach's supervision, we'd been looking for it for nearly three months. It was an intensive, three-shift, night-and-day job pushed through as if it were costing someone a thousand bucks a second. Beach never let up. It would have taken an individual worker ten years to develop the stuff, but there were sixty of us on the job with all the company's resources at our disposal. Wyman eventually found it Wednesday morning, but we didn't know for certain that he'd actually got it until we tested it a few minutes before the explosion."

"What kind of an emulsion was it, and how did you test it?" Graham encouraged.

"It was a photographic emulsion susceptible to frequencies far into the infra-red, farther than any commercial plates have been able to reach. It touched the ultra-radio band. According to Beach, such an emulsion ought to record things like suns—I don't know why; none of us knew why. We made routine ex-

54

posures with Wyman's compound and, sure enough, we developed negatives recording things like little suns."

"Go on! Go on!" Graham urged.

"We looked them over curiously and talked about them a lot. These suns were small spheres of invisible radiation, three or four of them, floating above the roof of Number Four Extraction Shed. Somehow—I can't explain how or why—the sight of them made us greatly excited in a sort of horrible, heart-leaping way. Beach was home at the time the test proved positive, so Wyman phoned him, and was in the middle of telling him about it when—*wham!*"

"But Beach definitely knew of the existence of these phenomena before you succeeded in photographing them?"

"Of course! I don't know where he got the information, but he had it all right—from somewhere."

"He never gave you any clue to the nature of these objects?"

"No. He told us only what they ought to look like on a negative. Nothing more. He was tight-mouthed on the subject."

"Thanks!" said Graham. "I guess you've helped me plenty."

Leaving his chair, he paced slowly out of the ward, followed by the deeply puzzled Corbett. Continuing along the curved drive leading to the road, they stopped by the police chief's gyrocar.

In response to some weird impulse, some strange but urgent notion he could not identify or explain, Graham drove his thoughts away from the recent examination and compelled them to concentrate elsewhere. It was difficult to govern his own mind in such dictatorial fashion, and for several seconds he sweated in mental agony while he forced his stubborn thoughts into an innocuous path. He drew a woman from his memory, let his mind enjoy her picture, the curl of her crisp, black hair, the curve of her hips, the tranquil smile which occasionally lit her heart-shaped face. Doctor Curtis, of course. Being male, he had no trouble in considering her unprofessionally. She'd no right to expert status, anyway; not with a form like that!

His memory was still conjuring her calm, serene eyes for him to look into when Corbett got into his car and rumbled, heavily, "Pity that guy couldn't tell us what those sun-things might be."

"Yes," agreed Graham, hardly hearing. He closed the car's door upon the burly chief. "I'll call at your office soon after dinner." He walked hastily away, the vision still firmly held in the grasp of his own peculiarly vivid imagination.

Lowering his plastiglass window, Corbett called after him, "Those little suns need investigating, I reckon. They've got

55

plenty to do with all this—I'll gamble my life on that!" Receiving no comment, the chief cast a disgusted look at Graham's broad back, and proceeded to gamble his life by prodding the starter-switch with a broad forefinger.

The gyrocar whined like an eager dog, slid easily forward, built up speed. Its velocity increased until the machine was screaming along and splitting wind in a way that flapped the sunblinds along the street. Bulleting through a narrow gap in cross traffic, it beat the automatic signals at the intersection, sent shocked pedestrians scuttling in all directions. Madly, it plunged past another block, made a slight curve when crossing the second intersection, plunged headlong into the concrete wall of a corner building. The car crushed itself down to half its normal length, and a two-ton concrete block cracked right through. The sound of the impact was a minor explosion that reverberated time and time again through surrounding streets.

The noise battered imperatively on the ear-drums of the self-hypnotised Graham. He fought fearfully, desperately, half-insanely to hold a feminine face before his mental vision, to reject, keep out, beat off the knowledge that yet another had paid the terrible penalty for being curious about little suns.

While crowds—unconsciously protected by their own ignorance—milled and gaped around the distant wreck, Graham, made vulnerable by his own suspicions, threatened by the unseen, battled with himself as he walked steadily away—battled to view a mirage to the complete exclusion of everything else. He paced onward, grimly onward, fighting to camouflage his own betraying mind; and as he fought, he won.

Chapter 6

THE path was a crazy snake, mottled in the moonlight, twisting and turning as it crawled upward, ever upward. The few hours that had gone since Corbett became paste now seemed a year. Graham pushed the memory away, ducked into the shadow of a natural obelisk that poised at one side of the track. A bilious moon let its sickly beams fall over sullen rocks and brooding pines, illuminating the rough landscape in pale ghastliness.

The hidden man's feverish eyes searched the pools of shadow that lined and pitted the route he had just traversed; his ears strained to catch sounds different from the sibilant rustling of branches, scrape of boughs, burble of distant waters—sounds he could attribute only to things that invariably were silent. Involuntarily, for no other purpose than to soothe his too-alert soul, he was looking for the unseeable, listening for the unhearable, waiting for that which lets no man wait when his time is due.

For a full five minutes he stood thus, his nerves strained, his muscles taut, his mind and body prepared to meet whatever menace might explode from the silence and the dark. But there was nothing, nothing—only harsh rocks that thrust ragged outlines toward equally ragged clouds, only sentinel pines standing guard around the camp of night.

Several times had he stopped and stood thus, examining the trail behind, and each time the path remained empty, undisturbed.

Those stalkers in the ebon hours, slinking in his steps, skulking furtively through the gloom, were creatures of his overwrought mind. He had enough self-possession to know that they were fantastic products of his tired and regimented imagination, yet he could not forbear to seek occasional vantage posts and compel his sleep-hungry eyes to seek confirmation of the nightmares haunting his brain.

He stared until he had convinced himself of his own misapprehension, emerged from the black bar of shadow cast by the obelisk, continued up the trail. Stumbling over broad cracks, slipping in deep ruts, tripping over loose stones part-hidden in the inadequate light, he hastened along.

The path curved tortuously around the mountain, ended in a tiny, elevated valley surrounded by towering walls on all sides but one. A building squatted at the farther end of the valley, hugging low to the ground, architectually cowering. It was no ramshackle erection, but a sturdy conglomeration of concrete and local rock, low-slung, drab, ominous in its complete seclusion.

At the valley's mouth stood an ancient, decrepit fingerpost, its faded board bearing in awkward scrawl the words: MILLIGAN'S STRIKE. He looked at the board, eyes narrowed, peering closely, then glanced back along the trail. Nothing stirred.

Jet shadows cast by surrounding cliffs swallowed his own shadow as he stole through the valley, reached the silent building, surveyed its cold, impassive windows. No light blazed welcome from those glassy squares, no noise of human movement came from within those grim walls. There was no sound save that of a loosened stone rolling somewhere back along the trail. That tiny, distant clatter set him back against the wall, one hand in his pocket. He watched the moonlit mouth for fifteen minutes.

Giving it up, he rapped heavily upon the armorplate door, tried its handle, found it locked. He knocked again, using a large pebble to increase the noise. There was no response. Turning his back to the door, his bloodshot eyes staring through the gloom toward the distant, moonlit finger-post, he swung a heavy, steel-shod boot at the armorplate, hammering it like a gong until the entire building echoed and re-echoed its urgent clamor.

Horror clawed at his heart while he battered frantically for entry. Perhaps others had gone in before him: others who had not knocked or opened, yet had passed silently and insidiously inside; others at whom it was futile to shoot, from whom it was useless to run.

Fighting off his panic, he gave the door a final, tremendous blow. If there was no response within one minute, he was going to bust a metal guard off a window, using a good, heavy rock for the purpose. At all costs he must get in, even if it were necessary to wreck the place. Putting his ear against the armorplate, he listened intently, heard a faint humming that grew into a low whine.

Frank relief brightened his features as the whine ceased. A short, metallic rattle followed; slow, deliberate feet approached the door. A chain clanged, a battery of bolts creaked aside, the lock snapped back, the door opened a bare six inches.

From the blackness a deep, rich voice demanded, "Well?"

Graham introduced himself in six swift words, then asked, "Are you Professor Beach?"

The door opened wide, and the man hidden in the interior gloom said quickly, "Come in, Graham. We've met before. I could not identify you in this infernal darkness."

Entering, Graham heard the door slam and lock behind him. A hand grasped his arm, steered him across a completely obscured floor, stopped him at the other side. Metal grated and clanged before his face, the floor sank under his feet. An elevator, of all things, in such a place as this!

Light floated upward, the floor ceased its descent. Graham saw the other's face in revealing rays. The scientist was still the same tall, thin-featured, dark-haired personage that he used to be. The burden of time rested lightly upon this man, for Graham could note little difference in the face he had not seen for several years. But there was one difference, a startling one —*the eyes*.

Beach's thin, curved, hawklike nose jutted between a pair of cold, hard optics unearthly in their brilliance. There was a hint of mesmerism in their deliberate, calculating and penetrating stare, something overpowering in their weird glow.

"Why the darkness upstairs?" queried Graham, still fascinated by those uncanny orbs.

"Light attracts nocturnal creatures," replied Beach, evasively. "They can be a nuisance." He studied his visitor. "How did you come to look for me here?"

"The editor of the local sheet in Boise knew that you'd been spending a lot of time in this place. He said he was sending a reporter here in the morning, to see whether you were alive or dead. I beat him to it."

Beach sighed. "I suppose a horde of snoopers is inevitable after what has happened. Oh, well——" He ushered Graham into a small, book-lined room, gave him a chair. Carefully shutting the door, he took a seat opposite. His long, slender fingers built a church and steeple while his odd eyes bored steadily into the other. "I am indeed sorry that we should meet again in such terrible circumstances. I presume that your visit is connected with the Silver City disaster?"

"It is."

"But since the department of special finance is not involved, it cannot have an interest in the matter?" Beach's dark, finely curved brows lifted questioningly.

"No," agreed Graham. Taking off his ring, he handed it

59

across. "Probably you've heard about those even if you haven't seen one. Its inner surface bears a microscopic inscription which is my warrant as a member of the United States Intelligence Service. You may check it under a microscope, if you wish."

"Ah, the Intelligence!" The eyebrows sank into a thoughtful frown. Beach rolled the ring to and fro between his fingers, gave it back without bothering to inspect it. "I'll take your word that it is what it purports to be." His frown deepened. "If you want to know why the silver nitrate exploded, I cannot tell you. In the next few weeks I shall be asked for an explanation by policemen, factory inspectors, industrial chemists, press reporters, time and time again. They'll all be wasting breath. I am totally unable to offer an explanation."

"You lie!" declared Graham, flatly.

With a resigned sigh, the scientist came to his feet, walked slowly to the door through which they had entered. Finding a hooked rod, he used it to drag a large screen down from its slot in the ceiling. Satisfied that the screen completely covered the door, he returned to his seat.

"Why do I lie?"

Back hairs were erect on Graham's neck as he answered, "Because you, and you alone, know that the stuff was mysteriously disrupted by some weird phenomena that you were trying to photograph. Because someone working under your command finally took a forbidden picture—and Silver City died in the counterblast!"

He swallowed hard, feeling certain that in speaking thus he had signed his own death warrant, and amazed to find that he still lived. Studying Beach for the effect of his words, he noted only the spasmodic tightening of the folded hands, an almost indiscernible flicker in the burning eyes.

"Whatever wiped out that town," continued Graham, "were the same thing or things that have eliminated an unknown number of the world's best scientists. It is my investigation of the deaths of some of those scientists—American ones—that has led me to you!"

Producing his wallet, he extracted a telegram, passed it to Beach. The latter murmured its words as he read them.

GRAHAM CARE OF BOISE POLICE: SOLE COMMON DENOMINATOR DASH ALL WERE FRIENDS OF BJORNSEN OR FRIENDS OF HIS FRIENDS STOP HARRIMAN.

"That refers to last month's quota of dead." Graham stabbed an accusing finger at the scientist. "*You* were a friend of Bjornsen's!"

"True," admitted Beach. "True." He looked down at his hands, ruminated awhile. "I was a very old friend of Bjornsen's. I am one of the few such who still remain." He raised his gaze, looking his opponent straight in the face. "I will also confess that I have much information which I intend to keep entirely to myself. What are you going to do about it?"

The other's bold defiance might have beaten individuals less persistent than Graham, but the investigator was not to be so easily defeated. Leaning forward, arms akimbo on broad knees, his muscular face intent, the Intelligence man did his best to convey the impression that he knew far more than the other suspected, more than he was ready to state at that moment.

Earnestly, he said, "Irwin Webb left a concealed message that we deciphered, a message telling much of what he had discovered. He declared that it was a picture which must be shown the world—if it can be shown without massacre."

"Massacre!" Beach's voice was harsh. "Is not the fate of Silver City enough? One man finds the picture, looks at it, *thinks* about it—and in a lightning flash thirty thousand pay the penalty with their earthly bodies and perhaps with their very souls. Why, even now your own thoughts are your most dangerous enemy. Knowing what little you may know, thinking about what you know, pondering it, turning it around in your mind, you invite destruction at any given moment, you tag yourself as a child of perdition, you are doomed by the involuntary activity of your own mind." His gaze slid toward the door. "If that fluorescent screen over the door happens to glow, neither I nor the strength of the civilized world can save you from instant death."

"I am aware of the fact," responded Graham, evenly. "My risk is no greater than your own, and cannot be increased by knowing the things you know. I cannot die *more* by knowing more!" He refrained from looking round at the screen, kept his whole attention upon the brilliant eyes opposite. If anything illuminated that screen, he would see it in those eyes. "Since there has been massacre despite the fact that the truth is not generally known, matters could hardly be worse if the truth were known."

"An assumption," scoffed Beach, "based on the erroneous premise that whatever is bad cannot be worse." He kept his gaze on that screen. "Nothing was worse than the bow and arrow—until gunpowder came. Nothing worse than that—until poison gas appeared. Then bombing planes. Then supersonic missiles. Then atom-bombs. Today, mutated germs and viruses. Tomorrow, something else." His laugh was short, sardonic. "Through pain and tears we learn that there's always room for further improvement."

"I'm willing to argue that with you when I'm in possession of all the facts," Graham retorted.

"The facts are beyond belief!"

"Do you believe them?"

"A fair question," Beach conceded, readily. "With me, belief does not enter into the matter. Faith has no relation to what one learns empirically. No, Graham, I don't believe them— I *know* them!" Moodily, he massaged his chin. "The incontrovertible evidence already accumulated leaves no room for doubt in understanding minds."

"Then what are the facts?" demanded Graham, his expression urging the other to speak. "What blotted out Silver City? What cut short the experiments of a clique of scientists, ending their lives in manner calculated to arouse no suspicion? What murdered Police Chief Corbett this afternoon?"

"Corbett? Has he gone too?" With his blazing eyes directed over his listener's shoulder toward the screened door, Beach pondered lengthily. There was silence in the room except where a tiny clock numbered the moments toward the grave. One mind worked hurriedly, while the other waited with phlegmatic grimness. Finally, Beach got up, switched off the lights.

"We can observe that screen more easily in darkness," he commented. "Sit here next to me, keep your eyes on it, and if it glows, force your thoughts elsewhere—or heaven itself won't help you!"

Shifting his chair next to the scientist's, Graham gazed through the gloom. He knew that at last the case was about to break, and his conscience kept nagging him unmercifully.

"You ought to have obeyed orders!" silently screamed the still, small voice within him. "You ought to have made contact with Leamington as you were instructed! If Beach becomes a corpse, and you with him, the world will learn nothing except that you have failed—failed as have all the rest—because you refused to do your duty!"

"Graham," commenced Beach, his voice rasping through the darkness, cutting short the investigator's mental reproaches, "the world has been given a scientific discovery as great, as important, as far-reaching in its implications as the telescope and the microscope."

"What is it?"

"A means of extending the visible portion of the spectrum far into the infra-red."

"Ah!"

"Bjornsen discovered it," Beach went on. "Like many other great discoveries, he stumbled across it while seeking something else, had the sense to realize what he'd found, developed it to usability. Like the telescope, the microscope, it has revealed a new and hitherto unsuspected world."

"A revealing angle on the ever-present unkown?" Graham suggested.

"Precisely! When Galileo peered incredulously through his telescope he found data that had stood before millions of uncomprehending eyes for countless centuries; new, revolutionary data which overthrew the officially endorsed but thoroughly famous Copernican system of astronomy."

"It was a wonderful find," agreed Graham.

"The microscope provides a far better analogy, for it disclosed a fact that had been right under the world's nose since the dawn of time, yet never had been suspected—the fact that we share our world, our whole existence, with a veritable multitude of living creatures hidden beyond the limits of our natural sight, hidden in the infinitely small. Think of it," urged Beach, his voice rising in tone, "living, active animals swarming around us, above us, below us, within us, fighting, breeding and dying even within our own blood-streams, yet remaining completely concealed, unguessed-at, until the microscope lent power to our inadequate eyes."

"That, too, was a great discovery," Graham approved. Despite his interest, his nerves were still jumpy, for he started at the unexpected touch of the other's hand in the gloom.

"Just as all these things evaded us for century after century, some by hiding in the enormously great, some in the exceedingly small, so have others eluded us by skulking in the absolutely colorless." Beach's voice was still vibrant and a little hoarse. "The scale of electro-magnetic vibrations extends over sixty octaves, of which the human eye can see but one. Beyond that sinister barrier of our limitations, outside that poor, ineffective range of vision, bossing every man jack of us from the cradle to the grave, invisibly preying on us as ruthlessly as any parasite, are our malicious, all-powerful lords and masters—the creatures who really own the Earth!"

"What the devil are they? Don't play around the subject. Tell me, for Pete's sake!" A cold sweat lay over Graham's forehead as his eyes remained fixed in the direction of the warning screen. No glow, no dreadful halo penetrated encompassing darkness, a fact he noted with much relief.

"To eyes equipped to see them with the new vision, they look like floating spheres of pale-blue luminescence," declared

Beach. "Because they resembled globes of living light, Bjornsen bestowed upon them the name of Vitons. Not only are they alive—they are intelligent! They are the Lords of Terra; we, the sheep of their fields. They are cruel and callous sultans of the unseen; we, their mumbling, sweating, half-witted slaves, so indescribably stupid that only now have we become aware of our fetters."

"*You* can see them?"

"I can! Sometimes I wish to God that I had never learned to see!" The scientist's breathing was loud in the confines of the small room. "All who duplicated Bjornsen's final experiment became endowed with the ability to penetrate that barrier of sight. Those who saw the Vitons got excited about it, thought about the discovery and walked in the shadow of death. From within limited distance, the Vitons can read human minds as easily as we could read an open book. Naturally, they take swift action to forestall the broadcasting of news which eventually might lead to our challenging their ages-old predominance. They maintain their mastery as coldbloodedly as we maintain ours over the animal world—by shooting the opposition. Those of Bjornsen's copyists who failed to hide the knowledge within their mind, or, possibly, were betrayed by dreams while helpless in their slumbers, have had their minds and mouths closed forever." He paused, added, "As ours may yet be closed." Another pause, timed by the steady ticking of the little clock. "There, Graham, is your living purgatory—to know all is to be damned. An exceptionally powerful mind may seek refuge by controlling its daytime thoughts, all the time, every minute, every second, but who can control his dreams? Aye, in slumber lies the deadliest peril. Don't get into that bed—it might be loaded!"

"I suspected something of the sort."

"You did?" Surprise was evident in Beach's tones.

"Ever since I commenced my investigation I've had queer, uncanny moments when I've felt that it was tremendously important to shift my thoughts elsewhere. More than once I've obeyed a crazy but powerful impulse to think of other things, feeling, believing, almost knowing that is was safer to do so."

"It is the only thing that has spared you," Beach asserted. "But for that, you'd have been buried at the start."

"Then is my mental control greater than that of more accomplished men such as Bjornsen, Luther, Mayo and Webb?"

"No, not at all. You were able to exercise control more easily because what you were controlling was merely a vague hunch. Unlike the others, you did not have to suppress a full and horrible knowledge." Ominously, he added, "The real test will lie in how long you last after this!"

"Anyway, thank heavens for my hunches!" murmured Graham, gratefully.

Beach said, "I suspect that you do not have hunches. If those feelings of yours though vague and unreasoning, were powerful enough to command obedience in defiance of your rational instinct, it is evident that you have extrasensory perception developed to an unusual degree."

"I'd never thought of that," Graham admitted. "I've been too busy to take time off to analyse myself."

"The faculty, though not common, is far from unique." Getting up from his chair, Beach switched on the lights, pulled a drawer from a large filing cabinet. Raking through a mass of press clippings that filled the drawer, he extracted a bunch, looked them over.

"I have data concerning many such cases going back for one hundred fifty years. Michele Lefevre, of St. Ave, near Vannes, in France, repeatedly tested by French scientists. Her extra-sensory perception was estimated as having sixty per cent of the efficiency of her normal sight. Juan Eguerola, of Seville, seventy-five per cent. Willi Osipenko, of Poznan, ninety per cent." He pulled a clipping out of the bunch. "Heres a honey. It's taken from British *Tit Bits* dated March 19, 1938. Ilga Kirps, a Latvian shepherdess, of Riga. She was a young girl of no more than average intelligence, yet a scientific curiosity. A committee of leading European scientists subjected her to a very thorough examination, then stated that she undoubtedly possessed the power of extra-sensory perception developed to such an amazing degree that it was superior to her natural eyesight."

"Stronger than mine," commented Graham as the scientist put the clippings back, turned off the light, resumed his seat.

"The power varies. Ilga Kirps was a Viton hybrid. Extrasensory perception is a Viton trait."

"What!" His fingers gnawing at the arms of his chairs, Graham sat upright.

"It is a Viton faculty," repeated Beach, calmly. "Ilga Kirps was the fairly successful result of a Viton experiment. Your own case was less fruitful, perhaps because your operation was prenatal."

"Prenatal? By God, d'you mean—?"

"I've outgrown the age of saying what I don't mean," Beach assured. "When I say prenatal, I mean just that! Further, I say that had we never been cursed with these luminosities, we should not also be cursed today with most of our complications in childbirth. When someone suffers, it's not the unfortunate accident it's believed to be! Why, Graham, I now accept the possibility of a phenomenon which all my life I've rejected as patently absurd, namely, that of virgin births. I accept that there may have been times when helpless, unsuspecting subjects have been artifically inseminated. The Vitons are continually meddling, experimenting, practising their super-surgery on their cosmic cattle!"

"But why, why?"

"To see whether it is possible to endow human beings with Viton abilities." There was silence for a moment, then Beach added, dryly, "Why do men teach seals to juggle with balls, teach parrots to curse, monkeys to smoke cigarettes and ride bicycles? Why do they try to breed talking dogs, train elephants to perform absurd tricks?"

"I see the parallel," Graham acknowledged, morbidly.

"I have here a thousand or more clippings telling about people mysteriously endowed with inhuman powers, suffering from abnormal or supernormal defects, giving birth to atrocious monstrosities which promptly have been strangled or hidden forever from human sight. Others who have endured inexplicable experiences, unnatural fates. Remember the case of Daniel Dunglass Home, the man who floated from a first-floor window before the astounded eyes of several prominent and trustworthy witnesses? His was a thoroughly authentic case of a person possessing the power of levitation—the Viton method of locomotion! You should read a book called *Hey-Day of A Wizard*. It tells all about Home. He had other weird powers as well. But he was no wizard. He was a Viton-esque-humanoid!"

"Good heavens!"

"Then there was the case of Kaspar Hauser, the man from nowhere," Beach went imperturbably on. "Nothing comes out of a vacuum, and Hauser had an origin like anything else. Probably his was in a Viton laboratory. That, too, may have been the eerie destination of Benjamin Bathurst, British ambassador extraordinary to Vienna, who, on November 25, 1809, walked around the heads of a couple of horses—and vanished forever."

"I don't quite see the connection," Graham protested. "Why the devil should these super-creatures make people disappear?"

Beach's grin was cold and hard in the darkness. "Why do medical students make stray cats disappear? From what wondering, puzzled pond vanishes the frogs that later are to be dissected? Who snitches a pauper's body from the morgue when the viscera runs out a mile farther down the street?"

"Ugh!" said Graham, with frank distaste.

"Disappearances are commonplace. For example, what happened to the crew of the *Marie Celeste?* Or the crew of the *Rosalie?* Where they suitable frogs snatched from a convenient pond? What happened to the *Waratah?* Did that man who, at the last moment, refused to sail on the *Waratah* have extra-sensory perception, or was he instinctively warned off because he was an unsuitable frog? What makes one man suitable, another not? Does the former live in continual peril; the latter enjoy lifelong safety? Is it possible that some peculiar, unidentifiable difference in our mutual make-ups means that I am marked for death while you remain untouchable?"

"That's something only time will show."

"Time!" spat Beach, contemptuously. "We've carried the devil on our backs perhaps a million years and only now are aware that he's there. Homo sapiens—the man with a load of mischief!" He murmured some underbreath comment to himself, then went on, "Only this morning I was studying a case to which no solution had been found in ten years. The details are given in the London *Evening Standard* of May, 16, 1938 and the British Daily Telegraph of several dates thereafter. The 5,456-ton vessel *Anglo-Australian* vanished at short notice, without trace. She was a modern, seaworthy boat plowing through smooth, tranquil waters when she and her crew of thirty-eight abruptly became as if they had never been. She disappeared in mid-Atlantic, within fifty miles of other ships, shortly after sending a radio message stating that all was well. Where has she gone? Where are most of the thousands of people who have been listed and sought for years by the bureau of missing persons?"

"You tell me." Graham's eyes raked the darkness for the screen, failed to find it. Somewhere in the black it was standing, a silent sentry, waiting, guarding them, yet unable to do more than give them split-second warning of invaders that they alone must resist.

"I don't know," confessed Beach. "Nobody knows. All we can say is that they've been seized by agencies only now within our ken, powers unfamiliar but in no way supernatural. They have been taken for purposes at which we can but guess. They have gone as they have been going since the beginning of history and as they'll keep on going in the future. A few have come back, warped in ways we've not been able to understand. Those, we have crucified, or burned at the stake, or shot with silver bullets and buried in garlic, or incarcerated in asylums. Still more have been taken and will continue to be taken."

"Maybe," said Graham, skeptically. "Maybe."

"Only a month ago the New York-Rio strat-plane passed behind a cloud over Port of Spain, Trinidad, and didn't reappear. A thousand eyes saw it one moment, not the next. Nothing has been heard of it since. Nine months ago the Soviet's Moscow-Vladivostok new streamliner vanished in similar way. That's not been heard of, either. There has been a long series of such cases going back for decades, right to the earliest days of aeronautics."

"I can recall some of them."

"What happened to Amelia Earhart and Fred Noonan; to Lieutenant Oskar Omdal, Brice Goldsborough and Mrs. F. W. Grayson; to Captain Terence Tully and Lieutenant James Medcalf; to Nungesser and Coli? Some, perhaps, crashed, but I have little doubt that others did not. They were snatched away, exactly as human beings have been snatched for century after century, singly, in groups, in shiploads."

"The world must be told," swore Graham. "It must be warned."

"Who can tell, can warn—and live?" asked Beach, caustically. "How many would-be tellers lie tongue-tied in their graves? How many thousands more can be silenced as effectively? To talk is to think, and to think is to be betrayed, and to be betrayed is to die. Even we, in this lonely hide-out, may eventually be found by some roaming invisible, overheard, and made to pay the penalty of knowing too much; the price of inability to camouflage our knowledge. The Vitons are ruthless, utterly ruthless, and it is ghastly evidence of the fact that they blew Silver City to hell the moment they found that we'd discovered a means of photographing them."

"Nevertheless, the world must be warned," Graham insisted, stubbornly. "Ignorance may be bliss—but knowledge is a weapon. Humanity must know its oppressors to strike off their chains."

"Fine-sounding words," scoffed Professor Beach. "I admire your persistent spirit, Graham, but spirit is not enough. You don't yet know enough to appreciate the impossibility of what you suggest."

"That's why I've come to you," Graham riposted. "To learn enough! If I leave here ill-informed, the blame for my shortcoming will be yours. Give me all you've got—I cannot ask for more."

"And after that?"

"I'll take the responsibility and the risk. What else can I do?"

Silence in the ebon gloom while the two sat by the wall facing the screen, one nervously impatient, the other brooding grimly. Silence pregnant with swift, conjecturing thoughts and timed my slow, deliberate ticks. It was as if the fate of the world was being weighed in the balance of one man's mind.

Suddenly, Beach said, "Come!' Turning up the lights, he opened a door near the still inactive screen, switched more lights that revealed the neat, orderly length of a compact and well-equipped laboratory.

Darkening the room they were leaving. Beach closed the connecting door, indicated a bell on the laboratory wall, and told the other, "If that screen in the next room glows, a photosensitive cell will operate and cause this bell to ring. If it does ring, you'd better muddle your thoughts swiftly and completely—or prepare for the worst."

"I understand."

"Sit there," ordered Beach. He washed his fingers with a spot of ether, picked up a bottle. "This reaction of Bjornsen's is synergistic. D'you know what that means?"

"It's a purely associative effect."

"Correct! You've your own way of expressing it, but it's as good a definition as I've heard. It's a reaction produced by drugs functioning co-operatively which none can produce separately. You can see what that means—to test the effects of multiples in all possible combinations means a number of experiments running into astronomical figures. Synergy will keep research busy for years. They mightn't have stumbled on this one for fifty years to come. If Peder Bjornsen hadn't had the brains to recognize a stroke of luck when he saw it, we'd all—" He let his voice trail off while he tilted the bottle over a measuring vial, counting the drops with utmost care.

"What makes now?" Graham asked, watching him.

"I'm going to treat you according to Bjornsen's formula. It will blind you for a few minutes, but don't let that scare you—it will only be your rods and cones readjusting themselves. While your sight becomes modified, I'll tell you every detail I've been able to gather."

"Is this treatment permanent in effect, or temporary?"

"It seems permanent, but I wouldn't be dogmatic about that. Nobody's had it long enough to be sure." Putting down the bottle, he came to Graham with the vial in one hand and a small pad of cotton wool in the other. "Here goes," he said, "and listen carefully to what I tell you—my opportunity to repeat it may never come!"

Unconsciously, he was prophetic there!

Chapter 7

THERE were pale streamers struggling across the lowering moon, a deep, almost solid blackness in the valley. The building squatting in sullen loneliness at one end was completely hidden in the murk of night, and also hidden was the figure that edged through its armorplate door and flitted through the gloom toward the sighing pines.

For a moment, the figure became a man-shaped silhouette in the moonlight by the crumbling finger-post, then it faded into the less-revealing background of trees. A pebble rattled on the trail, a twig snapped farther on, then there was only the whispering of multimillion leaves, the moan of night breezes among the boughs.

At the other end of the trail a mountain ash spread concealing arms over a narrow, racy cylinder of highly polished metal. Something dodged around the trunk of the ash, merged with the cylinder. Came the soft click of a well-oiled lock, a low but powerful hum. A startled nightbird squawked its alarm as the cylinder projected itself from the black pool beneath the tree, flashed along the highway, bounded over the farther crest.

The same cylinder stood in the Boise Strat-Station at dawn. On one side, weak stars still twinkled against a backdrop of gradually lightening gray; on the other, the sky mirrored the pink of oncoming day. Morning mists were a gauzy veil on the Rockies.

Yawning, Graham said to Police Lieutenant Kellerher, "There are very special reasons why Beach and myself are leaving at different times and by different routes. It is absolutely imperative that one of us reaches Washington. I hold you personally responsible for picking up Beach in one hour's time, and seeing him safely on the *Olympian.*"

"He'll be on it, don't you worry!" Kellerher assured.

"Good! I'll leave it to you." With another wide yawn, Graham ignored the lieutenant's fascinated stare at his eyes, climbed into the rear seat of a racy looking army jetplane that was ready to rush him eastward.

The pilot bent forward in his seat, gave his machine the

gun. Short plumes of fire and long streams of vapor shot backward from the vessel's tail and from other tubes flushed into the trailing edges of its mirror-polished wings. With a rising howl that soon lost its lead and fell behind them, they dived into the morning sky, their vapor trail stretching and thining, the lagging noise of their jets bouncing off the mountain peaks.

Whizzing high over jagged points of the Rockies which speared the red dawn, the pilot levelled off. Graham gaped repeatedly as he suppressed more yawns, stared through the plastiglass with eyes whose utter bleariness failed to conceal their underlying luster.

The jets shivered steadily half a mile ahead of their sound. Graham's chin sank slowly onto his chest, his eyelids drooped, fluttered futilely, then closed. Overcome by the rhythmic vibration of the jets, and the swing and sway of the plane, he began to snore.

A bump and a swift rush of wheels along the runway awoke him. Washington! Nudging him gently, the pilot grinned, gestured to his clock. They had made excellent time.

Four figures hurried toward the machine as he got out. He recognised two of them: Colonel Leamington and Lieutenant Wohl. The others were burly individuals who carried themselves with an authoritative air.

"Got your wire, Graham," announced Leamington, his sharp eyes afire with anticipation. He pulled the message from his pocket, read it aloud. " 'Case bust wide open. Solution important to peace of world and worthy of presidential attention. Meet me army special due Washington port two forty.' " He worried his mustache. "Your information must be of terrific consequence?"

"It is!" Graham's gaze turned to the sky, his cold, shining orbs focused on seeming nothingness. "Unless I take the greatest care, I won't live to tell it! You'll have to hear me in some underground place, a well-protected site such as the basement of a government building. I'd like you to have a Blattnerphone running, so that you'll have a record of what I've said if it so happens that—despite my care and good fortune—my story is stopped partway through the telling."

"Stopped?" Leamington eyed him with a puzzled frown.

"I said stopped. Mouths can be and have been stopped, any time, any place, without warning. Mine's liable to be slapped shut quicker than any, knowing what I know. I want someplace safer if only insofar as it's less conspicuous."

"Well, I guess that can be arranged," agreed Leamington.

Ignoring the curious expressions with which the others were listening to his remarks, Graham went on, "I also want you

71

to have somebody take Doctor Beach off the *Olympian* when it reaches Pittsburgh tonight. He can be flown here, and he'll confirm my statements—or complete them."

"Complete them?"

"Yes, if they don't get completed by me."

"You talk very strangely, Graham," opined Leamington, conducting the other toward a waiting gyrocar.

"No more strangely than men have died." Getting into the machine, the rest following, he added, "You'll get the whole story, in plain, understandable terms, pretty soon—and maybe you'll be sorry you ever listened to it!"

Talk he did; to an audience of thirty seated on rows of hard, uncomfortable chairs in a cellar two hundred feet below street-level. A fluorescent screen, obtained at short notice from a government laboratory, covered the only door, its super-sensitive coating inert, lifeless, but prepared to emit a warning glow with the passage of invisible intruders. Overhead, a stony barrier between the secret session and the snooping skies, towered the mighty bulk of the War Department Building.

It was a mixed audience, uneasily attentive, expectant and slightly skeptical. There sat Colonel Leamington, with Wohl and the two Federal operatives who had met Graham on his arrival. Left of them fidgeted Senators Carmody and Dean, confidants of the country's chief executive. Willets C. Keithley, supreme head of the United States Intelligence Service, was a broad-shouldered, phlegmatic figure on the right, his personal secretary by his side.

Behind these were a number of scientists, government officials, and advisory psychologists to a total of two dozen. That shrewd face topped with a white mane showed the presence of Professor Jurgens, world's leading expert on mass-psychology or, as his friends preferred to describe it, 'mob reaction.' The thinner, darker features staring over his shoulder belonged to Kennedy Veitch, leading ray expert. The six sitting on his left represented the thousand brains still striving to produce the wavicle-bomb, long-sought-for successor of the atom-bomb. The rest were men equally able, each in his own sphere, some unknown, some internationally famous.

The attention of all became fixed exclusively upon the speaker whose glittering eyes, hoarse voice and expressive gestures drove into their receptive minds the full and dreadful import of his subject. In one corner, magnetised wire ran smoothly through the Blattnerphone, recording the revelation with mechanical accuracy.

"Gentlemen," commenced Graham, "some time back

72

the Swedish scientist Peder Bjornsen stumbled on a new line of research which he followed, bringing it to a successful end about six months ago when he found that he was able to extend the range of human vision. He accomplished this feat with the aid of iodine, methylene blue and mescal, and although the manner in which these components react relatively to each other is not fully understood, there is no doubt of their efficiency. A person treated with them in the manner prescribed by Bjornsen can perceive a range of electro-magnetic frequencies much wider than that permitted to natural sight."

"How much wider?" inquired a doubting voice.

"The extension is in one direction only," Graham answered. "It is far into the infra-red. According to Bjornsen, the limit lies in the ultra-radio band."

"What, seeing heat?" pursued the other.

"Seeing heat—and beyond it!" Graham assured.

He raised his voice above the resulting murmur of astonishment as grimly he carried on. "Exactly how this effect is achieved is something for you scientists to puzzle over. What I am concerned with here, what concerns this country, what concerns the entire world is an astounding fact that this discovery literally has dragged into the light." He paused, then gave it to them straight from the shoulder. "Gentlemen, another and higher form of life is master of this world!"

Surprisingly, there was no burst of voices raised in angry protest, no skeptical jeers, not even a buzz of conversation. Something had hold of them, some communal sense of truth, or perhaps a mutual recognition of the speaker's complete sincerity. So they sat there as if glued to their seats, showing him row upon row of shocked, speculative and apprehensive eyes, their faces betraying the fact that his statement exceeded their most fantastic expectations.

"I assure you that this is factual and beyond all disproof," declared Graham. "I have seen these creatures myself. I have seen them, pale but queerly glowing balls of blueness, floating through the sky. A pair of them skimmed swiftly, silently, high above me as I slunk along the lonely trail from Beach's isolated laboratory in the mountains between Silver City and Boise. One of them bobbed in the air above Boise Strat-Station shortly before my plane took off to bring me here. There were dozens over Washington when I arrived. There are scores over the city at this very moment, some probably swaying above this building. They favor haunts of humanity; for terrible reasons they cluster thickest where our numbers are greatest."

"What are they?" put in Senator Carmody, his plump features flushed.

"Nobody knows. There has not been sufficient time to study them. Bjornsen himself thought them alien invaders of fairly recent origin, but admitted that this was sheer guesswork as he had no data on which to base an opinion. The late Professor Mayo agreed that they're of extra-Terrestrial origin, but opined that they had conquered and occupied this planet many thousands of years ago. On the contrary, Doctor Beach thinks they are native to Earth, just as microbes are native. Beach says that the late Hans Luther went further, and on the strength of evidence about our physical shortcomings, suggested that these things are true Terrestrials, while we are the descendants of animals which they've imported from other worlds in cosmic cattle-boats."

"Cattle!—cattle!—cattle!" The word shuttled around the audience. They mouthed it as if it were foul.

"How much is known about these creatures?" someone put.

"Very little, I'm afraid. They've not the slightest resemblance to human beings, and, from our point of view, they are so utterly and completely alien that I cannot see how it will ever be possible for us to find a common basis that will permit some sort of understanding. They look like luminescent spheres, about three feet in diameter, their surfaces alive, glowing, blue, but totally devoid of observable features. They don't register on an ordinary infra-red film, though Beach has now recorded them with the aid of a new emulsion. They aren't detectable by radar, evidently because they absorb radar pulses instead of reflecting them. Beach asserts that they tend to swarm in the vicinity of radar antenna, like thirsty children around a fountain. He thinks they inspired us to develop radar—and thus provide them with another incomprehensible pleasure at the price of our own sweat."

His listeners' features bore a strange mixture of awe and horror as he continued, saying, "It is known that these weird spheres employ extra-sensory perception as a substitute for sight, and that they have this faculty developed to an amazing degree. That is why they have always been able to comprehend us while we've not been able to see them, for sixth-sense mental awareness is independent of electro-magnetic frequencies. They also utilise telepathy in lieu of vocal chords and hearing organs—or perhaps it's

74

merely another aspect of this same extra-sensory perception. At any rate, they can read and understand human thoughts at short range, but not at long range. Beach gave them the name of Vitons, since obviously they are not flesh, and are composed of energy. They are neither animal, mineral nor vegetable—they are energy."

"Absurd!' ejaculated a scientist, finding at last something within the scope of his training. "Energy cannot hold so compact and balanced a form!"

"What about fireballs?"

"Fireballs?" It caught the critic on one foot. He gazed uncertainly around, subsided. "I've got to admit you have me there. Science has not yet been able to evolve a satisfactory explanation of those phenomena."

Graham said, seriously, "Yet science agrees that fireballs are compact and temporarily balanced forms of energy which cannot be duplicated in any laboratory. They may be dying Vitons. They may be these very creatures, as mortal as us, whatever their life-span, falling in death, dispelling their energy in suddenly visible frequencies." Taking out his wallet, he extracted a couple of clippings. *World-Telegram*, April 17: case of a fireball that bounced through an open window into a house, scorched a rug where it burst. Same day, another hopped erratically two hundred yards down a street and popped into nothingness with a blast of heat. *Chicago Daily News*, April 22: case of a fireball that floated slowly across a meadow, entered a house, tried to rise up a chimney, then exploded, wrecking the chimney."

Replacing the clippings, he smoothed his hair tiredly. "I borrowed those from Beach. He has a huge collection of clippings dating back one hundred fifty years. Nearly two thousand of them deal with fireballs and similar phenomena. When you look through them, knowing what at long last is known, they look different. They're no longer a mere collection of off-trail data. They're a singular collection of cogent, highly significant facts which makes you wonder why we've never suspected what has now been discovered. The terrible picture has been there all along—but we weren't able to get it into proper focus."

"What makes you say that these things, these Vitons, are our masters?" queried Keithley, speaking for the first time.

"Bjornsen deduced it from observation, and his followers came inevitably to the same conclusion. A thinking cow could soon discern the mastery of whoever leads its kind to the slaughterhouse! The Vitons behave as if they own the Earth—which they do! They own you and me and the president and every king or criminal who has been born."

"Like hell they do!" swore a voice at the back.

Nobody looked round. Carmody frowned his displeasure at the interruption, the rest concentrated their attention on Graham.

"Little has been discovered," Graham told them, "but that little means plenty. Beach has satisfied himself that not only are the Vitons composed of energy, but also that they live on energy, feed on it—*our* energy! So far as they're concerned, we exist as energy-producers which kindly nature has provided to satisfy whatever they use for bellies. Thus, they breed us, or incite us to beed. They herd us, drive us, milk us, fattening on the currents generated by our emotions in precisely the same way that we fatten on juice involuntarily surrendered by cattle to whom we have given fodder containing stimulants for lactation. Show me the highly emotional man whose life has been healthy and long, and you show me the Vitons' prize cow, the medal-winner!"

"The devils!" snapped a voice.

"If you ponder this to the full, gentlemen," Graham persisted, "you will realize its awful implications. The nervous energy produced by the act of thinking, also as the reaction to glandular emotions, has long been known to be electrical or quasi-electrical in nature, and it is this output which nourishes our shadowy superiors. They can and do boost the harvest anytime they want, by stimulating rivalries, jealousies, hatreds and thus rousing emotions. Christians against Moslems, whites agains blacks, Communists versus Catholics, all are grist to the Viton mill, all are unwitting feeders of other, unimaginable guts. As we cultivate our food, so do the Vitons cultivate theirs. As we plow our fields, sow and reap, so do they plow and sow and reap. We are fleshly soil, furrowed with Viton-dictated circumstances, sown with controversial ideas, manured with foul rumors, lies and wilful misrepresentations, sprinkled with suspicion and jealousy, all that we may raise fine, fat crops of emotional energy to be reaped with knives of trouble. Every time someone screams for war, a Viton is using his vocal chords to order a Viton banquet!"

A man sitting near Veitch stood up and said, "Maybe you know what some of us are doing. We're trying to make atom-splitting behind the times. We're trying to find a way to bring about the complete dissipation of sub-atomic particles into primal energy. We're trying to make a wavicle-bomb. If we ever get it, boy, it'll be some bomb! Even a little one will rock the world." He licked his lips, looked around. "Are you suggesting that we're Viton-inspired?"

"You haven't made such a bomb?"

"Not yet."

"There's your answer," said Graham, dryly. "Maybe you'll never make one. Or if you do, you may never use it. But if you do make one—and drop one—!"

There came a heavy knock on the door, its sudden sound making several start in their seats. A uniformed man entered, whispered briefly to Keithley, then took his departure. Keithley arose, his face pale, his tones vibrant. He looked at Graham, then at the audience, and spoke slowly, earnestly.

"Gentlemen, I regret to inform you that I have just been told that the *Olympian* has been involved in a collision twenty miles west of Pittsburgh." He swallowed hard. His strain was obvious. "Many people have ben injured, and one killed. The casualty is Doctor Beach!"

Amid a babble of comment from his horrified listeners, he sat down. For a full minute the audience shifted about, muttered, stared at each other, at the screen, at the feverish eyes of Graham.

"Another informed mind has been tossed into oblivion," Graham commented, bitterly. "The hundredth or the thousandth, for all we know!" He spread dramatic arms. "We eat, but we do not roam haphazardly around seeking wild potatoes. We grow them, and in growing them we improve them according to our notions of what potatoes ought to be. Similarly, our emotional tubers are not enough to fill higher and mightier bellies; they must be grown, stimulated, bred according to the ideas of those who do the surreptitious cultivating."

"That," he shouted, bunching a strong fist and shaking it at his wide-eyed hearers, "is the sole reason why human beings, otherwise rational enough, ingenious enough to amaze themselves with their own cleverness, cannot conduct world affairs in a way that does justice to their intelligence. That is the reason why, in this present day and age, we can build glories greater than history has ever held, yet live among the miserable monuments to our own destructive powers, and cannot build peace, security, tranquility. That is the reason why we advance in science, and all the emotion-producing arts, and all the exciting graces, but not in sociology, which has been hamstrung from the beginning."

Expressly, he rolled wide an imaginary sheet of paper, and said, "If I were showing you a microphotograph of the

77

edge of an ordinary saw, its peaks and valleys would be a perfect graph representing the waves of emotion which have upset this world with damnable regularity. Emotion—the crop! Hysteria—the fruit! Rumors of war, preparations for war, accusations of preparations for war, actual wars, ferocious and bloody; religious revivals, religious riots; financial crises; labor troubles; color rivalries; ideological demonstrations; specious propaganda; murders, massacres, so-called natural disasters, or slaughter in any emotion-arousing form; revolutions and more wars."

His voice was loud, determined as he went on. "Despite the fact that the enormous majority of ordinary men of all colors and every creed instinctively yearn for peace and security above all else, this world of otherwise sane, sensible people cannot satisfy that yearning. *They are not allowed to satisfy it!* Peace, real peace, is a time of famine to those higher than us in the scale of life. There must be emotion, nervous energy, great, worldwide crops of it, brought into being, somehow, anyhow."

"It is atrocious!" swore Carmody.

"When you see this world riddled with suspicion, rotten with conflicting ideas, staggering beneath the burden of preparation for war, you can be certain the harvest time is drawing near—a harvest for others. Not for you, not for you —you are only the poor, bleeding suckers whose lot it is to be pushed around. *The harvest is for others!*"

He bent forward, his jaw jutting aggressively his eyes burned into theirs. "Gentlemen, I am here to give you Bjornsen's formula that you may test it for yourselves. Maybe there are one or two among you who think I've been no more than making noises. God knows, I really wish that I'm deluded! So, soon, will you!" His grin was hard and completely humorless. "I ask, I demand that the truth be given the world before it becomes too late. Humanity will never know peace, never build a heaven upon earth while its collective soul bears this hideous burden, its collective mind is corrupted from birth. Truth must be a weapon, else these creatures would never have gone to such drastic lengths to prevent it from becoming known. They fear the truth, therefore the world must learn the truth. The world *must* be told!"

Sitting down, he covered his face with his hands. There were things he could not tell them, things he did not want to tell them. Before morning some of them would have gained the ability to test the facts, they would gaze into the dreadful skies—and some of them would die. They would die scream-

78

ing the guilty knowledge that filled their minds, the fear that stuffed their leaping hearts. They would fight futilely, run uselessly, babble the dying protests of the damned, and expire helplessly.

Dimly, he heard Colonel Leamington addressing the audience, telling the scientists to go their separate ways with care and circumspection, to take with them mimeographed copies of the precious formula, to test it as soon as possible and inform him of the results immediately they were obtained. Above all, they were to exercise mental self-control, keeping well apart so that at worst their minds could betray them only as individuals and not as a group. Leamington, too, appreciated the danger. At least, he was taking no chances.

The governmental experts went out one by one, each accepting his slip of paper from Leamington. All looked at the seated Graham, but none spoke. Their faces were grim, and ominous thoughts already were burgeoning in their minds.

When the last of them had gone, Leamington said, "We've prepared sleeping quarters farther below this level, Graham. We must take good care of you until the facts have been checked, because Beach's death means that you're now the only one with first-hand information."

"I doubt it."

"Eh?" Leamington's jaw dropped in surprise.

"I don't think so," asserted Graham, wearily. "Heaven alone knows how many scientists have had private information about Bjornsen's discovery. Undoubtedly, some dismissed it on sight, as manifestly ridiculous—or so they thought. They never bothered to test it for themselves, and their omission saved their lives. But there may be others who have confirmed Bjornsen's claims and have been fortunate enough to have escaped detection up to the moment. They will be terrified, haunted men, driven half-mad by their own knowledge, afraid to risk ridicule, or precipitate their own end, or even cause a major holocaust by shouting from the housetops. They'll be down, way down somewhere out of sight, skulking silently around, like sewer-rats. You'd have hell's own job finding them!"

"You think that general dissemination of the news will cause trouble?"

"Trouble is putting it mildly," Graham declared. "The word for what will happen isn't in the dictionary. The news will be broadcast only if the Vitons fail in their positive attempts to prevent it. If they deem it necessary, they'll have no compunctions about wiping out half the human race to preserve the blissful ignorance of the other half."

79

"Supposing that they can do it," Leamington qualified.

"They've organized two world wars and have kept us emoting in suspense for the last twenty years over the possibility of a third and even bigger one." Graham rubbed powerful hands together, felt dampness oozing between the pores. "What they could do before they can do again."

"You're not suggesting that they're so all-powerful that it's futile to struggle against them, are you?"

"Most definitely not! But I don't under-estimate the enemy. That's a mistake we've made too many times in the past!" He noted Leamington's wince without commenting upon it. "Their numbers and strength still remain a matter of speculation. Pretty soon they'll be swarming all over the place, looking for ringleaders of mutinies, dealing with them quickly, thoroughly—and finally. If they discover me, and remove me, you'll have to seek some other survivor. Bjornsen told his friends, and there's no telling just how far the news has spread through purely personal channels. Dakin, for instance, got it from Webb, who got it from Beach who got it from Bjornsen. Reed got it from Mayo and back to Bjornsen by another route. Dakin and Reed got at third-hand, or fourth-hand or maybe tenth-hand, but it killed them just the same. There may be a few others who, more by luck than anything else, have managed to keep alive."

"It is to be hoped so," said Leamington, with a touch of gloom.

"Once the news does get out, those of us who know it now will all be safe. The motive for removing us will then have ceased to exist." There was pleased anticipation in his tones, the glee of one who looks forward to ridding himself of an intolerable burden.

"If the results gained by these scientists bear out your statements," interjected Senator Carmody, "I, personally, shall see to it that the president is informed without delay. You can depend upon all the action of which the government is capable."

"Thanks!" Nodding gratefully, Graham arose, went out with Leamington and Wohl. They conducted him to his temporary refuge many levels deeper beneath the War Department Building.

"Say, Bill," spoke Wohl, "I collected a mess of reports from Europe that I've not had a chance to tell you about. There have been autopsies on Sheridan, Bjornsen and Luther, and the results were exactly the same as in the cases of Mayo and Webb."

"It all ties up," remarked Colonel Leamington. He patted

Graham on the shoulder, performing the action with an amusing touch of paternal pride. "Your story is one that is going to strain the credulity of the world, but I believe you implicitly."

They left him to the much-needed sleep he knew he would not get. It was impossible to slumber with the crisis so near to hand. Mayo had gone, and he had seen him go. He had seen Dakin flee from a fate that was fast, determined, implacable, and he had anticipated and heard Corbett's similar end. Tonight—Beach! Tomorrow—why?

In the cold, damp hours of early morning, the news burst wide over a startled planet, broke with breath-taking suddenness and with a violence that transcended everything. The whole world howled in horror.

Chapter 8

IT was three o'clock in the morning of June the ninth, 2015, and the seldom-mentioned but superbly efficient United States Department of Propaganda was working overtime. Its two huge floors in Home Affairs Building were dark, deserted, but half a mile away, hidden in a two-acre basement comprising a dozen great cellars, slaved the department's complete staff augmented by eighty willing helpers.

One floor above them, held by an immense thickness of concrete and steel, rested the mammoth weights of several old-fashioned presses, clean, bright, oiled, kept for years in constant readiness against the time when there might be a nation-wide breakdown in the television news-reproduction system. One thousand feet higher soared the beautifully slender pile that was the home of the semi-official *Washington Post*.

Into the hands of the bustling four hundred, jacketless, perspiring, were being drawn the threads of communication over an entire world. Television, radio and cable systems, stratplane couriers, even the field-signalling sections of the fighting forces were theirs to command.

For all the intense activity, there was no sign of it at ground-level. The Post Building stood apparently lifeless, its mounting rows of windows reflecting a multitude of sallow moons. Unconscious of the frantically active battalion far below him, a patrolling police officer stamped his lonely way along the sidewalk, his eyes on a distant illuminated clock, his mind occupied with nothing more damning than the cup of coffee at the end of the beat. A cat ran daintily across his path, vanished into the shadows.

But down, down, down, far underneath the brooding monoliths, buried amid a million unsuspecting sleepers, the four hundred toiled in preparation for the awful dawn. Morse keys and high-speed autotypers rattled brief, staccato messages or longer, more ominous ones. Teletypers chatted furiously through chapters of information. Telephones shrilled and emitted metallic words while, in one corner, a powerful

82

multi-channel shortwave transmitter forced impulses through its sky-high antenna and out to faraway ears.

News flowed in, was dissected, correlated, filed. Bleeker has completed the test, reports that he is watching two spheres gliding over Delaware Avenue. Okay, tell Bleeker to forget it—*if he can!* Here's Williams on the phone, saying he's made his test and can see luminescent spheres. Tell Williams thanks, and to go bury himself fast! Tollerton on the wire, saying test comes out positive and that he's now observing a string of blue globes moving high across the Potomac. Tell him to go underground and take a sleep.

"That you, Tollerton? Thanks for the information. No, sorry, we're not permitted to tell you whether other tests have produced reports confirming your own. Why? For your own sake, of course! Now stop thinking about it and go bye-bye!"

It was a noisy but systematic hurly-burly in which incoming calls squeezed their way between outgoing messages and every long-distance talker yearned for priority over every other. Here, a man clung desperately to a phone during his twentieth attempt to raise station WRTC in Colorado. Giving it up, he made a contact request to the police department in Denver. Over there, in one corner, a radio operator recited into his microphone in a patient monotone, "Calling aircraft-carrier *Arizona*. Calling aircraft-carrier *Arizona*."

In the middle of it all, exactly at the hour of four, two men arrived through the tunnel which for a decade had provided swift means of egress for thousands of still-damp newspapers being rushed to the railroad terminus.

Entering, the first man respectfully held the door open for his companion. The second man was tall, heavily built, with iron-gray hair, light gray eyes that looked calmly, steadily from a muscular confident face.

While this last one stood appraising the scene, his escort said, simply, "Gentlemen, the President!"

There followed a momentary silence while every man came to his feet, looked upon the features they knew so well. Then the chief executive signed them to carry on, permitted himself to be conducted to an enclosed booth. Inside, he adjusted his glasses, arranged some typewritten sheets in his hand, cleared his throat and faced a microphone.

The signal lamp flashed. The president spoke, his delivery assured, convincing, his voice impressive. Two blocks away, hidden in another basement, delicate machinery absorbed his voice, commenced to reproduce it two thousand times.

Long after he had departed, the machinery sped on, pouring forth tiny reels of magnetised wire which were snatched up, packed in airtight containers, and rushed away.

The New York-San Francisco strat-plane left at five o'clock with a dozen canned reproductions of the president's speech hidden in its cargo. It dropped three of them en route before its pilot lost control of his thoughts—whereupon it disappeared forever.

The four-thirty special for London received the first score of copies, bore them safely across the Atlantic, delivered them at their destination. The pilot and co-pilot had been told that the sealed cans contained microfilms. They thought they were microfilms, and thus anything—or any things—which may have been interested in their thoughts were successfully deceived into believing the same.

About three-quarters of the reproductions had been received by the time zero hour arrived. Of the missing quarter, a few had suffered natural and unforeseeable delays, while the remainder represented the first casualties in the new and eerie conflict. The speech could have been made quite easily by the president in person, over a nation-wide hook-up. And just as easily the speech could have been defeated at utterance of the first sentence, by death lurking at one microphone. Now, in effect, there were fifteen hundred presidents ready with fifteen hundred microphones so completely scattered that some waited in American consulates and embassies in Europe, Asia and South America, some were ready on solitary islands in the Pacific, several were aboard warships far out at sea, away from human—and Viton—haunts. Ten were located in Arctic wastes where harmless flickers in the sky were the only Vitonesque phenomena.

At seven o'clock in the morning in the eastern States, at noon in Great Britain, and at equivalent times elsewhere, the news splashed over the front pages of old-fashioned papers, glowed into telenews screens, stood out starkly on stereocine screens, blared from loudspeakers, bawled over public address systems, was shouted from the housetops.

A low, incredulous cry of anguish came from the world of mankind, a wail that grew with growing belief and built itself into a shrill, hysterical scream. The voice of humanity expressed its shock, each race according to its emotional trend, each nation to its creed, each man to his glands. In New York, a frightened mob filled Times Square to suffocation point, surging, shouting, shaking fists at sullen skies, driven bellicose by peril in the manner of cornered rats. In Central

Park, a seemlier crowd prayed, sang hymns, screamed for Jesus, protested, wept.

Piccadilly, London, was messed with the blood of forty suicides that morning. Trafalgar Square permitted no room for traffic, even its famous lions being concealed beneath a veritable flood of half-crazy human figures, some howling for the august presence of George the Eighth, other bellowing orders at the Lord God Almighty. And while the lions crouched even lower than humanity was crouching, and surrounding white faces were staring sweatily at wages-of-sin-is-death orators, Nelson's Column broke at its base, leaned over, propped itself for one tremendous second against another column of shrieks, fell and crushed three hundred. Emotion welled to the heavens, bright, clear, thirst-quenching emotion!

Mohammedans embraced Christianity that morning, and Christians became Mohammedans, Buddhists, boozers . . . anything. The churches swapped inmates with the bordellos and the asylums eventually gained from both. While many of the sinful made haste to bathe themselves in holy water, the pure did some mind-diverting wallowing in iniquity. Each according to his lights, but all a little unbalanced. Every one a Viton-cow satisfactorily stimulated to over-swollen udders!

But the news was out despite every attempt to prevent it, despite various obstacles to its broadcasting. Not all newspapers had acceded to official requests that their front pages be devoted to the authorized script. Many asserted their journalistic independence—or their proprietors' dimwitted obstinacy—by distorting the copy with which they had been provided, lending in humor or horror according to their individual whims, thus maintaining the time-honored freedom of gross misrepresentation which is the freedom of the press. A few flatly refused to print such obvious balderdash. Some mentioned it editorially as a manifest election stunt for which they were not going to fall. Others loyally tried to comply, and failed.

The *New York Times* came out with a belated edition stating that its early morning issue had not appeared because "of suden casualties among our staff." Ten had died in the *Times* office that morning. The *Kansas City Star* came out on time loudly demanding to know what sort of a dollar-snatching gag Washington had cooked up this time. Its staff survived.

In Elmira, the editor of the *Gazette* sat dead at his desk, the television-printed data from Washington still in his cold grasp. His assistant editor had tried to take the sheet, and had slumped on the floor beside him. A third sprawled near the door, a foolhardy reporter who had dropped even as his mind conceived the notion that it was up to him to fulfill the duty for which his superiors had given their lives.

Radio Station WTTZ blew itself to hell at the exact moment that its microphone became energized and its operator opened his mouth to give the news which was to be followed by the presidential speech.

Later in the week, it was estimated that seventeen radio stations in the United States and sixty-four in the entire world had been wrecked mysteriously, by supernormal means, in time to prevent the broadcasting of revelations considered undesirable by others. The press, too, suffered heavily, newspaper offices collapsing at the critical moment, being disrupted by inexplicable explosions, or losing one by one the informed memebrs of their staffs.

Yet the world was told, warned, so well had the propagandists prepared beforehand. Even invisibles could not be everywhere at once. The news was out, and a select few felt safe, but the rest of the world had the jitters.

Bill Graham sat with Lieutenant Wohl and Professor Jurgens in the latter's apartment on Lincoln Parkway. They were looking through the evening editions of every newspaper they'd been able to acquire.

"The reaction is pretty well what one might expect," commented Jurgens. "Some mixture! Look at this!"

He handed over a copy of the *Boston Transcript*. The paper made no mention of powers invisible, but contented itself with a three-column editorial ferociously attacking the government.

"We are not concerned," swore the *Transcript's* leaderwriter, "with the question of whether this morning's morbid scoop is true or untrue, but we are concerned with the means by which it was put across. When the government exercises powers that it has never been given by mandate of the people, and practically confiscates the leading pages of every newspaper in the country, we perceive the first step toward a dictatorial regime. We see a leaning toward methods that will never for one moment be tolerated in this free democracy, and that will meet with our uncompromising opposition so long as we retain a voice with which to speak."

"The problem that arises," said Graham, seriously, "is that of whose views this paper represents. We can assume that the person who wrote it did so with complete honesty and in good faith, but are those opinions really his own, or are they notions which cunningly have been insinuated into his mind, notions which he has accepted as his own, believes to be his own?"

"Ah, there lies the peril!" agreed Jurgens.

"Since all our data points to the fact that the Vitons sway opinions any way they want them, subtly guiding the thoughts that best suit their own purposes, it is well-nigh impossible to determine which views are naturally and logically evolved, which implanted."

"It is difficult," Jurgens conceded. "It gives them a tremendous advantage, for they can maintain their hold over humanity by keeping the world divided in spite of all our own attempts to unite it. From now on, every time a trouble-maker shoots his trap, we've got to ask ourselves a question of immense significance: *who's talking now?*" He put a long, delicate finger on the article under discussion. "Here is the first psychological counterstroke, the first blow at intended unity—the crafty encouragement of suspicion that somewhere lurks a threat of dictatorship. The good old smear-technique. Millions fall for it every time. Millions will always fall so long as they would rather believe a lie than doubt a truth."

"Quite." Graham scowled at the sheet while Wohl watched him thoughtfully.

"The *Cleveland Plain Dealer* takes another stand," Jurgens observed. He held up the sheet, showing a two-inch streamer. "A nice example of how journalism serves the public with the facts. This boy fancies himself on satire. He makes sly references to that vodka party in Washington a fortnight ago, and insists on referring to the Vitons as 'Graham's Ghouls.' As for you, he thinks you're selling something, probably sunglasses."

"Damn!" said Graham, annoyedly. He caught Wohl's chuckle, glared him into silence.

"Don't let it worry you," Jurgens went on. "When you've studied mass psychology as long as I've done you'll cease to be surprised at anything." He tapped the paper. "This was to be expected. From the journalistic viewpoint, truth exists to be raped. The only time facts are respected is when it's expedient to print them. Otherwise, it's smart to feed the public a lot of guff. It makes the journalist feel good; it gives him a sense of superiority over the suckers."

"They won't feel so darned superior when they've got an eye-full."

"No, I guess they won't." Jurgens mused a moment, then said, "I don't wish to seem melodramatic, but would you be good enough to tell me whether any of these Vitons are near us at this moment?"

87

"There are none," Graham assured him. His wide, glistening eye gazed through the window. "I can see several floating over distant roofs, and there are two poised high above the other end of the road, but there are none near here."

"Thank goodness for that." Jurgens' features relaxed. He used his hand as a comb, passing thin fingers through long, white hair, smiled quietly as he noted that Wohl's face also expressed relief. "What I'm curious about is the problem of what is to be done next. The world now knows the worst, but what is it going to do about the matter—what *can* it do?"

"The world must not only know the worst, but also see it in all its grim and indisputable actuality," said Graham, earnestly. "The government has practically co-opted the big chemical companies in its plan of campaign. The first step will be to put on the market large and cheap supplies of the materials cited in Bjornsen's formula, so that the general public may see the Vitons for themselves."

"Where does that get us?"

"It gets us a big step toward the inevitable show-down. We must have a united public opinion to back us in the coming fight, and I'm not talking parochially, either. I mean united the world over. All our numerous squabbling cliques, political, religious, or whatever they may be, will have to drop their differences in the face of this greater peril and unitedly support us in future efforts to get rid of it once and for all."

"I guess so," admitted Jurgens, doubtfully, "but—"

Graham went on, "Moreover, we must gather as much information concerning the Vitons as it may be possible to obtain. That is because what we know about them to date is appallingly little. We need more data, we need it in quantities that can be supplied only by thousands, maybe millions of observers. At the earliest possible moment we must counterbalance the Vitons' enormous advantage in having an ages-old understanding of human beings, and gain an equally good comprehension of them. Know thine enemy! It is futile to scheme, or oppose, until we can make an accurate estimate of what we're up against."

"Perfectly sensible," Jurgens conceded. "I see no hope whatever for humanity until it has rid itself of this burden. But you know what opposition means?"

"What?" Graham encouraged.

"Civil war!" His distinguished features grave, the psychologist wagged a finger to emphasize his words. "You will not get a chance to strike one miserable blow at these Vitons unless first you've managed to conquer and subdue half the world. Humanity will be divided against itself—they'll see to that. The half that remains under Viton influence will have to be overcome by the other half, in fact you may have to exterminate them not only to the last man, but also the last woman and child."

"I can't see them being that dopey," Wohl put in.

"So long as people insist on thinking with their glands, their bellies, their wallets or anything but their brains, they'll be dopey enough for anything," declared Jurgens, fiercely. "They'll fall for a well-organized, persistent and emotional line of propaganda and make suckers of themselves every time. Remember those Japs? Early last century we called them civilized, poetic; we sold them scrap iron and machine tools. A decade later we were calling them dirty yellow bellies. In 1980 we were loving them and kissing them and calling them the only democrats in Asia. By the end of this century, they may be hell's devils again. Same with the Russians, cursed, cheered, cursed, cheered—all according to when the public was ordered to curse or cheer. Any expert liar can stir up the masses and persuade them to love this mob or hate that mob, as suits the convenience of whoever's doing the stirring-up. If ordinary but unscrupulous men can divide and rule, so can Vitons!" He turned from Wohl to Graham. "Mark my words, young man, your first and most formidable obstacle will be provided by millions of emotional dimwits among your fellow beings."

"I fear me you may be right," admitted Graham, uneasily.

Jurgens was right, dead right. Bjornsen's formula* was marketed a mere seven days, in immense quantities, and the first blow fell early in the morning of the eighth day. It fell with thunderous vim which humanity felt like a psychic blast.

An azure sky splashed with pink by the rising sun spewed two thousand thin streamers of flame from the invisibility of its upper reaches. The streamers curved downward, whitening with condensation. Thickening as they lost altitude, they resolved themselves into mighty back-blasts of strange, yellow stratosphere planes.

Below lay Seattle, a few early citizens on its broad streets, a few wispy columns of smoke rising from stoked furnaces. Many amazed eyes turned to the sky, many still-sleeping heads tossed on their pillows as the aerial armada howled across Puget Sound, swooped over Seattle's roofs.

The bulleting rush brought the howl up in pitch to a shrill scream as the yellow horde rocketed over the rooftops, the badge of a flaming sun showing on the underside of each stubby wing. Black, ominous objects excreted in pairs and waggled downward from sleek, streamlined fuselages, fell for a hushed age, buried themselves in the buildings beneath. The buildings promptly disrupted in a mad, swirling mêlée of flame, fumes, bricks and splintered timbers.

For six hellish minutes Seattle shuddered and shook to an uninterrupted series of tremendous explosions. Then, like wraiths from the void, the yellow two thousand vanished into the stratosphere whence they had come.

Four hours later, while Seattle's streets still sparkled with shards of glass and her living still moaned amid the rains, the invaders reappeared. Vancouver suffered this time. A dive, six minutes of inferno, then away. Slowly, lackadaisically, their condensing blast-streaks dissipated in the upper regions, while beneath lay pitted avenues, strewn business-blocks, crushed homes around which wandered silent, thin-lipped men, sobbing women, screaming children, some whole, some not. Here and there a voice shrieked and shrieked and shrieked like one of the damned doing his damnedest in a world of the damned. Here and there a sharp report brought quietness and peace to someone urgently in need of both. A little lead pill was welcome medicine to the partly disemboweled.

It was coincidentally with that evening's similar and equally effective attack on San Francisco that the United States government officially identified the aggressors. The markings on the attackers' machines should have been sufficient indication, but this evidence had seemed too unreasonable to credit. Besides, officialdom had not forgotten the days when it had been considered expedient to strike blows under any flag but one's own.

Nevertheless, it was true. The enemy was the Asian Combine, with whom the United States was supposed to be on friendliest terms.

A despairing radio message from the Philippines confirmed the truth. Manila had fallen, the Combine's war vessels, air machines and troops were swarming through the entire archipelago. The Filipino army no longer existed, and the United States Far East carrier fleet—caught on distant maneuvers— was being attacked even as it raced to the rescue.

America leaped to arms while its leaders met to consider this new problem so violently thrust upon them. Playboy financiers made ready to dodge the draft. End-of-the-world cultists took to the hills and waited for Gabriel to come fit them with halos. Among the rest, the mighty masses making ready for sacrifice, a fearful questioning went whispering around.

"Why didn't they use atom-bombs? Haven't they got any —or are they wary because we've got more?"

With or without atom-bombs, so savage and unprovoked an assault was Viton-inspired, and no doubt about it. But how had the luminosities managed to corrupt and inflame the normally slumbersome Asian Combine?

A fanatical pilot, shot down while attempting a crazy solo raid on Denver, revealed the secret. The time was ripe, he asserted, for his people to enter into their rightful heritage. Powers unseen were on their side, helping them, guiding them toward their divinely appointed destiny. The day of judgment had arrived and the meek were about to inherit the earth.

Have not our sages looked upon these little suns and recognised them as the spirits of our glorious ancestors, he asked with the certitude of one who poses the unanswerable question. Is not the Sun our ancient emblem? Are we not sons of the Sun, fated in death to become little suns ourselves? What is death but a mere transition from the army of abominable flesh to the celestial army of the shining spirit, where much esteem is to be gained in company with one's honorable fathers and one's exalted fathers' fathers?

The path of the Asians is chosen, he yelled insanely, a path sweetened by the heavenly blossoms of the past as well as the unworthy weeds of the present. Kill me, kill me—that I may take my rightful place with ancestors who alone can lend grace to my filthy body!

Thus the mystic rambling of the Asian pilot. His entire continent was afire with this mad dream, cunningly conceived and expertly insinuated within their minds by powers that had mastered the Earth long before the era of Emperor Ming; powers that had the precise measure of the human cow, knew when and where to jerk its dangling udders. The notion of plausibly "explaining" themselves as ancestral spirits did full credit to the infernal ingenuity of the Vitons.

While the Western Hemisphere mobilized as speedily as it could in the face of constant and inexplicable handicaps, and while the Eastern pursued its holy war, the best brains of the Occidental world sought frantically for means by which to refute the insane idea placed in Asian minds, means to bring home to them the perilous truth.

In vain! Had not the Occidentals themselves first discovered the little suns and, therefore, could not dispute their existence? Onward, to victory!

The hordes of the spiritually inflamed poured out of their formally peaceful boundaries, their eyes aglow with ignorance instead of knowledge, their souls dedicated to a divine mission. Los Angeles shrivelled in a sudden holocaust that fell upon it from the clouds. The first lone enemy flier to reach Chicago wrecked a skyscraper, minced a thousand bodies with its concrete and steel before a robot-interceptor blew him apart in mid-air.

By August the twentieth, no atom bombs, no radio-active gases, no bacteria had been used by either side. Each feared the retaliation which was the only effective defence. It was a bloody war and yet a phoney war.

But Asian troops were in complete possession of the whole of California and the southern half of Oregon. On the first of September, the air-borne and submarine transports cut their increasing losses by reducing their flow across the Pacific. Contenting itself with consolidating and holding the immense foothold it had gained on the American continent, the Asian Combine turned its attention in the opposite direction.

Triumphant troops poured westward, adding maddened Viet Nam, Malaysian and Siamese armies to their strength. Two hundred ton tanks with four-feet treads rumbled through mountain passes, were manhandled when bogged by humanity in the mass. Mechanical moles gnawed broad paths through previously impassible jungles, bulldozers shifted and piled their litter, flamethrowers burned the piles. Overhead, stratplanes dotted the sky. In sheer weight of numbers lay the Asians' strength. Theirs was the greatest weapon, the weapon possessed by every man . . . that of his own fertility.

Into India they swept, a monstrous conglomeration of men and machines. The ever-mystical and Viton-infested population received them with open arms and three hundred million Hindus became recruits at one swoop. They added themselves to the swarms of the Orient, thus making one quarter of the human race the poor dupes of an Elder People.

But not all bent the knee and bowed the head. With superb cunning the Vitons boosted the emotional crop by inciting the Moslems of Pakistan to oppose. Eighty millions of them stood with their back to Persia and barred the way. The rest of the Moslem world made ready behind them. Frenziedly, they died for Allah, and impartially Allah fattened the Vitons.

The brief breathing space permitted by pressure being transferred elsewhere enabled America to get its wind and recover from the initial shock. The press, once given exclusively to every aspect of the conflict, now saw fit to devote a little space to other matters, especially to Bjornsen's experiments in the past, and news about Vitons' activities both past and present.

Inspired by the resurrection of Beach's collection of press clippings, several papers searched through their own morgues in an effort to discover cogent items which once had been ignored. There was a general hunt for bygone data, some conducting it in the hope of finding support for pet theories, others with the more serious intention of gaining worthwhile knowledge about the Vitons.

Holding the opinion that not all people could see identically the same range of electro-magnetic frequencies, the *Herald-Tribune* asserted that some were endowed with wider sight than others. Wide-sighted persons, said the *Herald-Tribune,* had often caught vague, unrecognizable glimpses of Vitons many times in the past, and undoubtedly it was such fleeting sights that had given birth to and maintained various legends of banshees, ghosts, djinns and similar superstitions. This implied that spiritualists were Viton-dupes on an organized basis, but for once the *Herald-Tribune* overlooked religious susceptibilities.

Only a year ago, the *Herald-Tribune* itself had reported strangely colored lights seen floating through the sky over Boston, Massachusetts. Reports of similar lights had been made at various times, and with astonishing frequency, as far back as they could trace. A singular feature of all reports was that they'd been received with a total lack of science's much-vaunted curiosity: every expert had dismissed them as odd phenomena devoid of significance and unworthy of investigation.

For example: February, 1938—Colored light seen sailing high over Douglas, Isle of Man. November, 1937—Fall of a tremendous ball of light frightened inhabitants of Donaghadee, Ireland, other, smaller balls of light being seen floating in the air at the same time. May, 1937—Disastrous end of German transatlantic airship *Hindenburg* attributed to "St. Elmo's fire." The scientists tied a tag on this mysterious phenomena —and went back to their slumbers. July, 1937—Chatham, Massachusetts, station of the Radiomarine Corporation reported a message from the British freighter *Togimo,* relayed by the American vessel *Scanmail,* saying that mysterious colored lights had been sighted five hundred miles off Cape Race, Newfoundland.

New York Times, January 8, 1937—Scientists, fed up counting sheep, produced a new theory to explain the blue lights and "similar electric phenomena" frequently seen near Khartoum, Sudan, and Kano, Nigeria.

Reynolds News (Britain), May 29, 1938—Nine men were injured by a mysterious something that dropped from the sky. One of them, a Mr. J. Hurn, described it as "like a ball of fire." *Daily Telegraph*, February 8, 1938—Glowing spheres were reported to have been seen by many readers during an exceptional display of the Aurora Borealis, itself a rare sight in England. *Western Mail* (Wales), May, 1933—Balls of phosphorescence observed gliding over Lake Bala, mid-Wales. *Los Angeles Examiner*, September 7, 1935—Something described as a "freak lightning bolt" fell in bright sunlight at Centerville, Maryland, hurled a man from a chair and set fire to a table.

Liverpool Echo (Britain), July 14, 1938—What witnesses described as "a big blue light" invaded Number Three Pit, Bold Colliery, St. Helens, Lancashire, contacted lurking gases and caused "a mystery explosion." Blue lights that caused no blips on watching radar scopes caused air-raid sirens to be sounded in Northern Ireland, and fighter-interceptors roared upward, January 17, 1942. No bombs dropped, nothing was shot down. The news was suppressed in the papers and the Germans were suspected of some new devilment. Four months earlier Berlin's guns had blasted at "navigation lights" when no planes were over.

Sydney Herald and *Melbourne Leader* had made astonishingly lavish reports on glowing spheres, or fireballs, which for unknown reasons had infested Australia throughout the year 1905, especially in the months of February and November. Eerie conventions had been held in the Antipodes. Veterans of World Slaughter had conferred, sky-high. One such phenomenon, seen by Adelaide Observatory, moved so slowly that it was watched for four minutes before it vanished. *Bulletin of the French Astronomical Society*, October, 1905—Strange, luminous phenomena seen lurking around Calabria, Italy. The same kind of phenomena, in the same area, had been reported in September, 1934, by *Il Popolo d'Italia*.

Someone found an ancient and tattered copy of *The Cruise Of the Bacchante* in which King George the Fifth, then a young prince, described a strange string of floating lights, "as if of a phantom vessel all aglow," seen by twelve members of the *Bacchante's* crew at four o'clock in the morning of June 11, 1881.

Daily Express (Britain), February 15, 1923—Brilliant luminosities were seen in Warwickshire, England. *Literary Digest*, November 17, 1925—Similar luminosities seen in North

Carolina. *Field,* January 11, 1908—Luminous "things" in Norfolk, England. *Dagbladet,* January 17, 1936—Will-o'-the-wisps in southern Denmark, hundreds of them. Scientists sought onion blight at twenty thousand feet, but not one pursued a will-o'-the-wisp. It wasn't their fault; like all saints and sinners, they went where Viton-inspired to go. *Peterborough Advertiser* (Britain), March 27, 1909—Queer lights in the sky over Peterborough. Over following dates, the *Daily Mail* confirmed this report, and added others from places farther away. Something emotional might have been happening in Peterborough in March 1909, but no paper published anything correlative as between human and Viton activities . . . though there are human functions which are not news.

Daily Mail (Britain), December 24, 1912, ran an article by the Earl of Erne describing brilliant luminosities that had appeared "for seven or eight years" near Lough Erne, Ireland. The things that started Belfast's sirens wailing, in 1942, soared from the direction of Lough Erne, Ireland. *Berliner Tageblatt,* March 21, 1880,—"A veritable horde" of floating luminosities were seen at Kattenau, Germany. In the same century, glowing spheres were reported from dozens of places as far apart as French Senegal, the Florida Everglades, Carolina, Malaysia, Australia, Italy and England.

Journalistically enjoying itself, the *Herald-Tribune* went to town by issuing a special edition containing twenty thousand references to luminosities and glowing spheres culled from four hundred issues of *Doubt.* For good measure, it added a parallel-beam photographed copy of Webb's jottings, publishing them with the editorial opinion that this scientist had been working along the right lines prior to his death. In the light of recently acquired knowledge, who could say how many schizophrenics were really unbalanced, how many were the victims of Viton meddling, or how many were normal people fortuitously endowed with abnormal vision?

"Were all those second-sighters as simple as we thought?" demanded the *Herald-Tribune,* paraphrasing Webb. "Or was it that they could scan frequencies just beyond the reach of most of us?"

Then followed more quotations resurrected from the past. The case of a goat that pursued nothingness across a field, then dropped dead. The case of a herd of cattle that suddenly went mad with fear, and raced around a meadow obligingly sweating their emotions into empty air. Hysteria on a turkey ranch when eleven thousand gobblers went nuts in ten minutes . . . thus providing unseen travellers with a snack. Forty-five cases of dogs that howled piteously, put their tails between their legs and belly-crawled away—from nothing! Cases of contagious insanity in dogs and cattle, "too numerous to list," but all of them proof—asserted the *Herald-Tribune*—that animal eyes functioned differently from all but those of a minority of human beings.

The public absorbed every word of this, wondered, feared, trembled in the night hours and by day. White-faced, jittery mobs raided the drugstores, snatched up supplies of Bjornsen's formula as fast as they became available. Thousands, millions treated themselves according to instructions, saw the facts in all their hellish actuality, had their few shreds of doubt torn away.

In Preston, England, nobody perceived anything abnormal —until it was found that the local atomic-defence chemical plant had substituted toluidine blue for methylene blue. In Yugoslavia, a Professor Zingerson, of Belgrade University, dutifully treated himself with iodine, methylene blue and mescal, peered myopically at the sky and saw no more than he'd seen since birth. He said as much in a bitingly sarcastic article published in the Italian *Domenica del Corriere*. Two days later a globe-trotting American scientist persuaded the paper to print his letter suggesting that the good professor either take off his lead-glass spectacles or substitute ones with lenses made of fluorite. Nothing more was heard from the absent-minded Yugoslavian.

Meanwhile, in the west of America, monster tanks made tentative thrusts and occasional forays across the fighting line, clashed, blew each other into metal splinters. High-speed stratplanes, gun-spotting helicopters, highly streamlined helldivers and robot bombs criss-crossed the skies of California, Oregon and militarily important points east. Neither side yet made use of atomic explosives, each hesitant about starting a process beyond human power to end. Basically, the war followed the pattern of earlier and equally or less bloody wars; despite improved techniques, automatic and robotic weapons, despite development of armed conflict to a push-button affair, the ordinary soldier, the common foot-slogger remained supreme. The Asians had ten for the other side's one, and were breeding ahead of their losses.

Distance shrank even more after a further month of battle when supersonic rockets joined the fray. High out of sight and far beyond sound, they streaked both ways across the Rockies, mostly missing their intended targets, yet still striking ferociously at tightly packed haunts of humanity. A ten-mile miss at one, two or three thousand miles range was mighty good shooting. All the way from Bermuda to Llasa, any place became liable to erupt skyward at any time, the noise following afterward.

So the skies flamed and glowed and spewed death with dreadful impartiality while men of all creeds and colors moved through their last minutes and final hours protected mentally by hope of survival and lack of knowledge of what awaited them at the next stroke of the clock. Heaven and earth had combined to create hell. The common people bore it with the animal fatalism of the lower orders, seeing with eyes more understanding than of yore, constantly conscious of a menace more invincible, more revolting than anything born of their own shape and form.

Chapter 9

AMID surrounding wreckage, the Samaritan Hospital still stood untouched. New York had suffered enormously since the Asian invasion had commenced, and great rockets continued to arrive from the enemy's faraway mobile launchers. By sheer good fortune, or by virtue of that occasional haitus in the laws of chance, the hospital remained unharmed.

Scrambling out of his battered gyrocar three hundred yards from the main entrance, Graham gazed at the intervening mound of rubble blocking the street from side to side.

"Vitons!" warned Wohl, leaving the car and casting an anxious eye at the sullen sky.

Nodding silently, Graham nodded that there were a great number of the weird spheres hanging in the air above the tormented city. Every now and then, an underground giant heaved in his earthly blanket, puked a mass of bricks and stones, then roared with pain. Dozens of waiting spheres swooped down, eager to lap his vomit. Born of fire was their food, and well-cooked . . . the feast of human agony.

The fact that the huge majority of human beings were now able to see them made not the slightest difference to these ultrablue vampires. Aware or unaware, no man could prevent a hungry phantom from seating itself on his spine, inserting into his cringing body strange, thrilling threads of energy through which his nervous currents were greedily sucked.

Many had gone insane when suddenly selected for milking by some prowling sphere; many more had flung themselves to welcome death, or had committed suicide by any means conveniently to hand. Others who still clung desperately to the remnants of their sanity walked, crept or slunk through the alleys and the shadows, their minds in constant fear of sensing that queer, spinal shiver caused by the insinuation of thirsty tentacles. The days of God's own image were long forgotten. Now, it was every man a cow.

That cold, eerie shiver running swiftly from the coccyx to the cervical vertebrae was one of the most common of human sensations long before the Vitons were known or suspected; so common that often a man would shiver and his companion jest about it:

"Somebody's walking over your grave!"

There was revulsion in Graham's lean, muscular features as he clambered hastily over the mass of broken granite and powdered glass, slipping and sliding on outcrops of small, loosely assembled lumps, his heavy boots becoming smothered in fine, white dust. His nostrils were distended as he climbed; he was conscious of that sour, all-pervading blitz-odor, a smell of men and matter crushed together and grown stale. Topping the crest, his wary eyes turned upward, he half-ran, half-jumped down the farther side, Wohl following in a tiny avalanche of dirt.

Hurrying across the cracked and pitted sidewalk, they passed through the gap of the missing entrance gates. As they turned up the curved gravel drive leading to the hospital's front doors, Graham heard a sudden, choking gasp from his companion.

"By heavens, Bill, there's couple of them after us!"

Looking behind, he caught a split-second glimpse of two orbs, blue, glowing, ominous, sweeping toward him in a long, shallow dive. They were three hundred yards away, but approaching with regular acceleration, and the grim silence of their oncoming was a horrifying thing.

Wohl passed him with a breathlessly sobbed, "Come on, Bill!" His legs were moving as they'd never moved before. Graham sprang after him, his heart doing a crazy jig within his ribs.

If one of those things got hold of either of them, and read the victim's mind, it would immediately recognize him as a keyman of the opposition. All that had saved them so far had been the Vitons' difficulty in distinguishing one human being from another. Even the vaqueros of the huge King-Kleber Ranch could not be expected to know and recognise every individual beast, and, for the same reason, they had been fortunate enough to escape the attention of these ghastly superherdsmen. But now—!

He ran like hell, knowing full well as he raced along that flight was useless, that the hospital held no hope for the damned, provided no sanctuary, no protection against superior forces such as these—yet feeling impelled to run.

With Wohl one jump in the lead, and the bulleting menaces a bare twelve yards behind, they hit the front door and went through it as if it didn't exist. A startled nurse stared at them wide-eyed as they hammered headlong through the hall, then put a pale hand to her mouth and screamed.

Soundlessly, with terrifying persistence, the pursing spheres swept past the girl, shot round the farther corner and into the passage taken by their intended prey.

Graham caught an eye-corner vision of the luminosities as he skidded frantically around the next bend. They were seven yards behind and coming on fast. He dodged a white-coated interne, vaulted a long, low trestle being wheeled on doughnut tires from a ward, frightened a group of nurses with his mad pace.

The glossy parquet was treacherous. Wohl's military boots hit the polish, he slipped in mid-flight, fought to retain balance, went down with a thud that shook the walls. Unable to stop, Graham leaped over him, slid along the glossy surface, crashed violently into the facing door. The door creaked, groaned, burst open.

His shoulder muscles taut with expectation, he whirled around to face the inevitable. Surprise filled his glittering eyes. Bending down, he hauled Wohl to his feet, gestured toward the end of the passage.

"By God!" he breathed. "By God!"

"What's up?"

"They came around that corner, then stopped dead. They hung there a moment, went deeper in color, and departed as if the devil himself was after them."

Gasping for wind, Wohl said, "Boy, we're damn lucky!"

"But what made them scram?" persisted Graham, looking puzzled. "It has never been known for them to give up like that. I've never heard of them letting up on a victim once they've got his number. Why did they do it?"

"Don't ask me." Grinning in unashamed relief, Wohl dusted himself vigorously. "Maybe we weren't good enough for them. Maybe they decided we'd make a lousy meal and they could do better elsewhere. I don't know—I'm no fount of wisdom."

"They often depart in a hurry," said a cool, even voice behind them. "It has occurred repeatedly."

Swivelling on one heel, Graham saw her standing by the door with which he had collided. The light from the room behind made a golden frame for her crisp black curls. Her serene eyes looked steadily into his.

"Surgery's sugar-babe," he told Wohl, with unnecessary gusto.

Wohl gave her an appraising up-and-down, and said, "I'll say!"

Miffed, she put a slender hand on the door as if to close it. "When you pay a social call, Mr. Graham, please arrive in seemly manner, and not like a ton of bricks." She tried to freeze him with her glance. "Remember that this is a hospital and not a jungle."

"You'd hardly find a ton of bricks dumped in the jungle," he pointed out. "No, no, please don't close that door. We're coming in." He marched through, followed by Wohl, both ignoring her iciness.

They seated themselves by her desk, and Wohl studied a photograph thereon. Pointing to it, he said, "To Harmony from Pop. Harmony, eh? That's a nice name. Was your pappy a musician?"

The ice broke a little. Taking a chair, Doctor Curtis smiled. "Oh, no. I guess he just liked the name."

"So do I," Graham announced. He threw her the I-spy eye. "I hope it'll suit us."

"Us?" Her finely arched brows rose a trifle.

"Yes," he said, impudently. "Someday."

The temperature of the room sank five degrees. She tucked her silk-clad legs under her chair away from his questing eyes. The whole floor quivered, and a distant roar came down from the sky. All three sobered immediately.

They waited until the roar died away, then Graham began, "Look, Harmony—" He paused, added, "You don't mind if I call you Harmony, do you?" and without waiting for her reply, went on, "What's this you were saying about the Vitons beating it frequently?"

"It is very mysterious," Doctor Curtis admitted. "I don't know of any explanation for it, and so far I've had no time to seek one. All I can tell you is that immediately the hospital's staff became equipped to see these Vitons we discovered that they were frequenting the hospital in fair numbers. They were entering the wards and feeding on pain-racked patients from whom, of course, we carefully kept this knowledge."

"I understand."

"For some reason, they did not bother the staff." She looked questioningly at her listeners. "I don't know why they didn't."

"Because," Graham told her, "unemotional people are just so many useless weeds from their viewpoint, especially in a place containing so much fine, ripe, juicy fruit. Your wards are orchards!"

Her smooth, oval face registered the brutality of his explanation with a look of distaste. She continued, "At certain periods, we have noticed that every luminescent sphere in the hospital has hurried away as rapidly as possible, not returning for some time. It happens three or four times a day. It has happened just now."

"And very probably it saved our lives."

101

"Possibly," she admitted with calculated disinterest which deceived neither.

"Now, Doctor . . . er . . . *Harmony*"—he wiped out Wohl's grin with a hard glare—"do you know whether each exodus coincided with some consistent feature in hospital routine, such as the administering of certain medicines to patients, or the operating of the X-ray apparatus, or the opening of particular bottles of chemicals?"

She considered awhile, apparently oblivious of her questioner's intent gaze. Finally, she got up, searched through a file, dialled her telephone, consulted somebody in another part of the building. There was satisfaction in her features as she ended the call.

"Really, it was most stupid of me, but I must admit that I did not think of it until your questions brought it into my mind."

"What is it?" Graham urged.

"The short-wave therapy apparatus."

"Hah!" He slapped his knee, bestowed a look of triumph on the interested Wohl. "The artificial fever machine. Isn't it screened?"

"We've never been able to screen it completely. We've tried to do so, because it interfered with the reception of local television receivers, sending checkered patterns racing across their vision plates. But the apparatus is powerful, its short waves are penetrating, it has defied all our efforts, and I understand that the complainants have had to screen their receivers."

"On what wave-length does it operate?" pursued Graham.

"One and a quarter meters."

"Eureka!" He bounced to his feet, alight with the fire of battle. "A weapon at last!"

"What d'you mean, a weapon?" Wohl was not overly impressed.

"The Vitons don't like it. We've seen that for ourselves, haven't we? Heaven alone knows how its emanations appear to their alien senses. Perhaps they feel it as unbearable heat, or sense it as the Viton equivalent of an abominable smell. Whatever the effect may be, we've the satisfaction of knowing they like to get away from it as fast as they can travel. Anything that makes them want to go someplace else, is *ipso facto*, a weapon."

"I reckon maybe you've got something," Wohl conceded.

"If it is a weapon, or a potential one," remarked Doctor Curtis, seriously, "surely the Vitons would have destroyed it? They never hesitate to destroy where they deem it necessary.

Why should they leave untouched this threat to their existence —if it is a threat?"

"I can imagine nothing better calculated to draw despairing humanity's attention to the properties of therapy cabinets than to go around destroying them."

"I see." Her large, dark eyes were thoughtful. "Their cunning is indeed great. They think way ahead of us all the time."

"All the time so far," he corrected. "What of yesterday when we've still got tomorrow?" He reached for her telephone. "I must pass this information to Leamington without delay. Maybe it's dynamite. Maybe it is what I hope it is—and God help us if it's not! Besides, it may be enough to permit some of his gadgeteers to throw together an apparatus which will give protection to tonight's meeting."

Leamington's tired, worn features grew into the tiny visor. They relaxed somewhat as he listened to Graham's hasty flow of data. Finishing, Bill Graham turned to Doctor Curtis.

"This meeting is a scientific one to be held at nine o'clock this evening in the basement of National Guarantors Building, on Water Street. I'd like to take you along."

"I'll be ready at eight-thirty," she promised.

Professor Chadwick already was in the middle of his speech when Bill Graham, Harmony Curtis and Art Wohl moved quietly down the center aisle, took their seats. The basement was full, the audience silent, attentive.

At one end of the front row, Colonel Leamington twisted around, attracted Graham's attention, jerked an indicative thumb toward a large cabinet standing guard by the only door. Graham nodded his understanding.

With a rolled newspaper in one hand, the other left free for his frequent gestures, Professor Chadwick was saying, "For a couple of months the *Herald-Tribune* has been exhuming masses of data and still hasn't dug out the half of it. The amount of material is so enormous that one cannot help but marvel at the barefaced manner in which the Vitons were able to operate with complete confidence in humanity's lack of suspicion. To them, we must have seemed witless beyond words."

"Which we were," commented a cynical voice from the rear.

Chadwick signed hasty agreement and went on, "Their method of 'explaining' their own errors, omissions, mistakes and oversights by insinuating superstitious notions to 'account' for them, backing up those notions by the performing of so-called miracles when required, and the production of poltergeist and spiritualistic phenomena when asked for, does full credit to the hellish ingenuity of these creatures whom we call

103

Vitons. They have made the confessional-box and the seance-room their centers of psychic camouflage; the priest and the medium have been equally their allies in the devilish work of seeing that the blind masses stay blind." He brushed a sardonic hand from left to right. "Thus the wide-sighted always have been able to take their pick: visions of the holy virgins, or saints, or sinners, or the shades of the late lamented. Step up, boys, they're all yours!"

Someone laughed mirthlessly, a cold, grating laugh that jarred on the hearers' nerves.

"The *Herald-Tribune's* data is, in grim fact, a record of human gullibility, a record of how men in the mass can look facts in the face—and deny them! It is a record of how people can see fish and call them flesh or fowl, according to the conventionalisms of dogmatic tutors as purblind as themselves, according to their personal fears of losing invisible shares in nonexistent heavenly mansions, according to their credulous belief that God may deny them wings if they, in turn, assert that a sight authoritatively declared to be straight from heaven may indeed have come straight from hell." He paused, added in a hearable undertone, "Satan was a liar from the first—they said it!"

"I agree," boomed Leamington, not giving a damn whose personal idiosyncrasies were being kicked around.

"I've discovered a good deal of cogent data, myself," continued Chadwick. "For example, things we now know to be Vitons were frequenting the Fraser River district of British Columbia early in 1938. They got into the papers time and time and time again. A British United Press report dated July 21, 1938, say that the huge forest fires then ravaging the Pacific coast of North America were caused by something described as 'dry lightning,' admitted to be unique phenomena.

"In 1935, in the Madras Presidency of India, was reported an esoteric sect of floating-ball worshippers who, apparently, could see the objects of their devotions which were quite invisible to non-believers. Attempts to photograph what they were worshipping invariably failed, though I know and you know what might have been recorded had the photographers been able to employ Beach's emulsion.

"The *Los Angeles Examiner* of mid-June, 1938, reported a case paralleling that of the late Professor Mayo. Headed: FAMOUS ASTRONOMER LEAPS TO DEATH, it stated that Doctor William Wallace Campbell, president emeritus of the University of California, had met his end by flinging himself from the window of his third-floor flat. His son ascribed his father's act to his fear of going blind. Personally, I feel that while his fear may have had direct connection with his sight, it was not in the manner then believed!"

Disregarding supporting murmurs from his audience, Professor Chadwick said, "Believe it or not, but one man's extrasensory perception, or his wide-sightedness, was so well developed that he was able to paint an excellent picture showing several Vitons floating over a nightmarish landscape and, as if somehow he sensed their predatory character, he included a hawk in the scene. That picture is Mr. Paul Nash's *Landscape of a Dream*, first exhibited in 1938, and now in the Tate Gallery, in England. Nash himself died very suddenly a few years later."

Turning his eyes toward Graham, the speaker declared, "All the evidence we have been able to gather shows beyond doubt that the Vitons are creatures of primal energy held in a form both compact and balanced. They are neither solid, nor liquid nor gas. They are not animal, vegetable or mineral. They represent another, unclassified form of being which they share with fireballs and like phenomena, but they are not matter in the generally accepted sense—they're something else which is strange to us but in no way supernatural. Maybe they're a mess of wavicles complex beyond all possibility of analysis by any instrument we have today; we know they're so peculiar that our spectroscopic tests of them have proved worthless. It seems to me that the one possible weapon we can bring against them is something influencing their own strange matter-state, namely, a form of energy such as a radiation having a heterodyning effect, something that might interfere with the Vitons' natural vibrations. The discovery made only today by Mr. Graham, of the Intelligence Service, amply confirms this theory." Raising his hand and beckoning to Graham, he concluded, "So I now ask Mr. Graham to give you the valuable information he has obtained, and I feel sure that he will be able to assist us still further with some useful suggestions."

In a strong, steady voice, Graham recounted his experience of a few hours before. "It is imperative," he told them, "that at once we should undertake intensive research in short waves projected on the radio-beam system, and determine which particular frequencies—if any—are fatal to Vitons. In my opinion, it is desirable that we set up a suitable laboratory in some faraway, unfrequented spot distant from war areas, for our evidence is that Vitons congregate where humanity swarms most thickly, and very rarely visit uninhabited regions."

"That is an excellent idea." Leamington stood up, his tall form towering above his seated neighbors. "We have ascertained that the Vitons' numerical strength is somewhere between one twentieth and one thirtieth that of the human race, and it is a safe bet that the majority of them hang around fruitful sources of human and animal energy. A laboratory hidden in the desert, a locality sparse in emotional fodder, might remain unobserved and undisturbed for years."

There came a loud buzz of approval from listeners as Leamington sat down. For the first time since the Bjornsen-precipitated crisis, they felt that humanity was getting somewhere, doing something to rid itself once and for all of the burden of the centuries. As if to remind them that optimism should be modified by caution, the ground quivered, a muted rumble sounded outside, then followed the roar from the sky as lagging sound caught up with its cause.

Already Leamington had in mind a suitable site for the establishment of what he hoped would be the first anti-Viton arsenal. Ignoring outside noises, the Secret Service chief bestowed a fatherly smile on his protégé still standing on the platform. Instinctively, he knew that this plan would go through, and that Graham would play the part best calculated to enhance the reputation of the Service. Leamington had never demanded more of his boys than just their bodies and souls. He had never received less than that.

"It is of little avail," Graham reminded, as outside sounds died away, "to battle the Asians without also attempting to subdue their crafty overlords. To wipe out the luminosities is to remove the source of our enemies' delusions, and bring them back to their senses. They're humans, like us, those Asians—take away their mad dreams and you'll take away their fury. Let's strike a blow by giving our solitary clew to the world."

"Why not organise our native scientists and get them on the job?" inquired a voice.

"We shall do that, you may rest assured. But as we know to our cost, a thousand widely separated experimenters are safer than a thousand in a bunch. Let the entire western world set to work, and nothing—visible or invisible—can prevent our ultimate triumph!"

They roared their agreement as he stared absently at the cabinet still standing guard over the only door. The memory of Beach was a dull pain within his mind which held other and equally tragic memories—the rag-doll appearance of Professor Mayo's broken body; the sheer abandon with which Dakin had plunged to his sickening end; the horrid concentration in the eyes of the sufferer with an imaginary dog in his belly; Corbett's dying *crump* as he smacked into stone; the great black banner of tormented atoms which had been unfurled above Silver City.

Not much use damping their spirits in this rare moment of enthusiasm. All the same, it was as clear as daylight that short-wave research could move in only one of two directions—the right one, or the wrong one. Wrongness meant slavery forever; and the first indication of rightness would be the heartless slaughter of every experimenter within reasonable reach of success.

There was murder in prospect, murder of every valuable intellect in the front-line of the eerie campaign. It was a dreadful certainty that Graham had not the heart to mention. As the audience fell silent, he left the platform. The silence was broken by the now familiar feature of sudden death.

The floor jumped six inches northward, settled slowly back. While the occupants of the basement posed in strained attitudes, the tearing rumble of tottering masonry came to them through the thick walls. Then the vile bellow from the sky as if the Creator were enjoying the agonized writhings of his own creations. A pause, followed by the lower, lighter rumble of vehicles dashing along the street, heading for the new area of wreckage, blood and tears.

Sangster was worried and made no attempt to conceal the fact. He sat behind his desk in the office of the department of special finance, in Bank of Manhattan, watched Graham, Wohl and Leamington, but spoke to none of them in particular.

"It's twelve days since that international broadcast giving a line to everybody from hams to radio manufacturers," he argued. "Was there any interference with that general call? There was not! Did one radio station get picked up and tossed around? No, not one! I say that if short-waved research was a menace to the Vitons they'd have played merry hell to prevent it. They'd have listed the radio experts and had a program. There'd have been slaughted all the way from here to there. But the Vitons took no notice. So far as they were concerned, we might have been scheming to wipe them out by muttering a magic word. Ergo, we're on the wrong track. Maybe they avoided therapy sets just to put us on the wrong track. Maybe they're doing the laughs they can't make up the sleeves they haven't got." He tapped his desk nervously. "I don't like it, I don't like it."

"Or maybe they want us to think the same way," Graham put it, easily.

"Eh?" Sangster's jaw dropped with suddenness that brought grins to the others' faces.

"Your views are proof that the Vitons' disinterest ought to be our discouragement." Strolling to the window, Graham regarded the battered vista of New York. "I said 'ought,' mark you! I'm suspicious of their seeming nonchalance. The damned things know more of human psychology than experts of Jurgens' type are likely ever to learn."

"All right, all right!" Mopping his brow, Sangster pawed at some papers on his desk, extracted a sheet, held it up. "Here's a report from the Electra Radio Corporation. Their twenty experts might as well be shooting craps. They say short waves stink. They've thrown at passing luminosities every frequency their plant can concoct, and the spheres merely ducked out as if they'd encountered a bad smell. Bob Treleaven, their leading wiseacre, says he almost believes the cursed things really do sense certain frequencies as their equivalent to odors." He tapped the paper with an accusatory finger. "So where do we go from here?"

" 'They also serve who only stand and wait,' " quoted Graham, philosophically.

"Very well. We'll wait." Tilting back in his chair, the bothered Sangster put his feet on the desk and assumed the expression of one whose patience is everlasting. "I've tremendous faith in you, Bill, but it's my department's money that is being poured into all this research. It would relieve my mind to know what we're waiting for."

"We're waiting for some experimenter to come near frizzling a Viton." Graham's leathery face grew grim. "And although I hate like hell to say it, I think we're waiting for the first of another series of corpses."

"That's what has got me uneasy." Leamington's voice chipped in, his tone low, serious. "These infernal orbs frequently are prying into minds. Some day, Bill, they'll examine yours. They'll realize they've found the ace—and you'll be deader than a slab of granite when *we* find *you*."

"We've all got to take chances," said Graham. "Heck of a one I took when I chose to be born!" He gazed through the window once more. "Look!"

The others joined him, gazed out. A fat, gray cloud was blooming from the base of the Liberty Building. Sound caught up with sight even as they looked, and there came an awful crash that shook the neighborhood. Then the skyward sound arrived, a terrific yelp that changed pitch with Doppler effect as it descended.

Four seconds later, with the cloud at its fattest, the immense bulk of the pitted and glassless Liberty Building leaned over, slowly, ever so slowly, lowering itself with the mighty reluctance of a stricken mammoth. It reached a crazy angle, hesitated in seeming defiance of the law of gravity, its millions of tons a terrible menace to the area it was about to devastate.

Then, as if an unseen hand had reached forth from the void and administered the final, fateful push, the enormous pile fell faster, its once beautiful column splitting in three places from which girders stuck like rotten teeth. The noise of its landing resembled a bellow from the maw of original chaos.

Ground rumbled and rolled in long, trembling waves of plasmic agitation. A vast, swirling cloud of pulverized silicate crept sluggishly upward.

A veritable horde of spheres, blue, tense, eager, hungry, dropped from immense heights, streaked inward from all directions, their paths direct lines concentrated on this latest fount of agony.

Over the Hudson, another string of spheres ghoulishly were following a flying bomb, clinging to it like a tail of great blue beads. The bomb hammered steadily for Jersey City. Shortly, it would tilt downward and start to scream, and the women beneath it would try to outscream it . . . and the Vitons would enjoy them with the silence of dumb vutures.

"One rocket!" breathed Leamington, still staring at the smoke-obscured wreck of the Liberty Building. "I thought at first they'd started with atom-bombs. God, what a size that one must have been."

"Another Viton improvement," opined Graham, bitterly. "Another technical advantage they've given to their Asian dupes."

On Sangster's desk a telephone whirred with suddenness that plucked at their already taut nerves. Sangster answered it, pressed the amplifier button.

"Sangster," rattled the phone, in sharp, metallic accents, "I've just been called by Padilla on the radio-beam from Buenos Aires. He's got something! He says . . . he says . . . Sangster . . . *oh!*"

Alarmed by Sangster's wildly protruding eyes and ghastly complexion, Graham leaped to his side and looked into the hesitant instrument's visor. He was just in time to see a face slide away from the tiny screen. It was a vague face, made indistinct by a weird, glowing haze, but its shadowy features conveyed a message of ineffable terror before it shrank completely from sight.

"Bob Treleaven," whispered Sangster. "It was Bob." He stood like one stunned. "They got him—and I saw them get him!"

Taking no notice, Graham rattled the telephone, raised the operator. He danced with impatience while the exchange tried to get an answer from the other end. No response could be obtained, not on that line, nor on alternative lines.

"Give me Radiobeam Service," he snapped. "Government business—hurry!" He turned to the white-faced Sangster. "Where's Electra's place?"

"Bridgeport, Connecticut."

"Radiobeam Service?" Graham held his lips close to the mouthpiece. "A recent call has been made from Buenos Aires to Bridgeport, Connecticut, probably relayed through Barranquilla. Trace it and connect me with the caller." Still clinging to the phone, he beckoned Wohl.

"Take that other phone, Art. Call Bridgeport's police headquarters, tell them to get out to the Electra plant, and keep for us whatever they may find. Then beat it down and have the car ready. I'll be one jump behind you."

"Right!" With a grunt of eagerness, Wohl snatched up the other instrument, jabbered into it hurriedly. Then he was gone.

Graham's call got through, he talked for some time, his jaw muscles lumping while he listened to the faraway speaker. Finishing, he made a second and shorter call. He looked moodily disappointed as he shoved the phone aside and spoke to the others.

"Padilla is stiffer than an Egyptian mummy. The relay operator at Barranquilla is also dead. He must have listened in and heard something we're forbidden to know. The knowledge he gained has cost him his life. This is a time when I could do with being in four places at once." He massaged his chin, added, "A million to one Treleaven is as dead as the rest."

"Well, you've got your corpses," commented Leamington, with complete lack of emotion.

His remark came too late. Already Graham was outside the door and dashing down the passage toward the levitator shafts. There was something retributory in his fast lope, and a harder gleam lay behind that other gleam filling his wide-sighted eyes. The rods and cones of his pupils had undergone more than spectroscopic readjustment—they now vibrated with hate.

Air sighed in the bowels of the building as Graham's disk dropped at reckless pace, bearing him toward street level and the waiting gyrocar. Reaching bottom, he sprang out, his nostrils distended like those of a wolf which has found the scent and is racing to the kill.

Chapter 10

THE Electra Radio Corporation's small but well equipped laboratory was meticulous in its orderliness, nothing being out of place, nothing to mar its prim tidiness save the body flopped beneath the dangling telephone receiver.

A burly police sergeant said, "It's exactly as we found it. All we've done is make stereoscopic record of the cadaver."

Bill Graham nodded his approval, bent, turned the body over. He was not repelled by the look of horror which vicious, glowing death had stamped upon the corpse's features. At deft speed he frisked the victim, placed the contents of the pockets on an adjacent table, examined them with shrewd attention.

"Useless," he commented, disgustedly. "They don't tell me a thing worth knowing." He shifted his gaze to a small, dapper man fidgeting miserably beside the police sergeant. "So you were Treleaven's assistant? What can *you* tell me?"

"Bob got a call from Padilla," babbled the small man, his frightened eyes flickering from the questioner to the object on the floor. Nervously, his manicured fingers tugged at his neatly trimmed mustache.

"We know that. Who's Padilla?"

"A valuable business connection and a personal friend of Bob's." He buttoned his jacket, unbuttoned it, then returned to the mustache. He seemed to be afflicted with too many hands. "Padilla is the patentee of the thermostatic amplifier, a self-cooling radio tube which we manufacture under his license."

"Go ahead," Graham encouraged.

"Bob got this call and became very excited, said he'd spread the news around so it couldn't be stopped. He didn't mention the nature of this news, but evidently he thought it red-hot."

"And then?"

"He went straight into the lab to ring up somebody. Five minutes later a gang of luminosities whizzed into the plant. They've been hanging around for days, sort of keeping an eye

111

on us. Everybody ran for dear life excepting three clerks on the top floor."

"Why didn't they run?"

"They've not yet had eye-treatment. They couldn't see and didn't know what was happening."

"I understand."

"We came back after the luminosities had left, and we found Bob dead beneath the phone." Another jittery fumble at the mustache, and another frightened shift of gaze from questioner to corpse.

"You say that the Vitons have been hanging around for days," put in Wohl. "During that time have they snatched any employee and pried into his mind?"

"Four." The small man became more nervous than ever. "They have had a poke at four within the last few days. That made it pretty awful for us. There was no way of telling who they'd pick on next. We couldn't work so well daytimes and we couldn't sleep nights." He gave Wohl a pathetic look, and went on, "They got the last one yesterday afternoon, and he went insane. They dropped him outside the gates and left him a gibbering idiot."

"Well, there weren't any about when we arrived," remarked Wohl.

"Probably they're satisfied that this counterstroke has prevented the plant from becoming a possible source of danger to them for the time being." Graham could not restrain a smile as he noted how the jumpiness of the little man contrasted with the elephantine indifference of the police sergeant. "They'll come back!"

He dismissed the witness and other waiting employees of the radio plant. With Wohl's help, he searched the laboratory for notes, memo-pads or any seemingly insignificant piece of paper that might record a clew, his mind recalling the cryptic messages left behind by other and earlier martyrs.

Their efforts were in vain. One fact and one only was at their disposal—the fact that Bob Treleaven was decidedly dead.

"This is hell!" groaned Wohl, despairingly. "Not a lead. Not one miserable little lead. We're sunk!"

"Use your imagination," Graham chided.

"Don't tell me you've picked up a line?" Wohl's honest eyes popped in surprise. He scanned the laboratory, trying to find something he'd overlooked.

"I haven't." Bill Graham grabbed up his hat. "In this crazy business nobody lives long enough to hand us a useful line, and we've no choice but to spin our own. Come on—let's get back."

It was as they flashed through Stamford that Wohl shifted his thoughtful gaze from the road, glanced at his passenger, and said, "All right, all right—is it a family secret or something?"

"What d'you mean?"

"This line you're spinning."

"There are several. To start with, we've not got enough data concerning Padilla. We'll have to get more, and some of it may prove well worth having. Then again, it seems that Treleaven had about five undisturbed minutes at that phone before he was put out of the running. He was on to Sangster for less than a half a minute, and that was his last call in this sinful world. So unless it took him four and a half minutes to reach Sangster—which is not likely—I reckon maybe he phoned somebody else first. We'll find out whether he did and, if so, whom he called."

"You're a marvel—and I'm dumber than I thought," said Wohl.

Grinning sheepishly, Graham continued, "Lastly, there's an unknown number of radio ham stations operating beween Buenos Aircs, Barranquilla and Bridgeport. One or two may have snooped the commercial beams while raking the ether. If any one of them happened to be listening in, and caught Padilla's talk, we want him as badly as do the Vitons. We've got to find that guy before it's too late!"

"Hope," recited Wohl, "springs eternal in the human breast." His eyes roamed up to the rear-view mirror, rising casually, then becoming fixed in fearful fascination. "But not in mine!" he added, in choked tones.

Slewing around in his seat, Graham peered through the car's rear window. "Vitons—after us!"

His sharp eyes switched to the front, the sides, taking in the terrain with photographic accuracy. "Step on it!" His thumb found and jabbed the emergency button just as Wohl shoved the accelerator to the limit. The crisis-bank of extra batteries added their power, and with the dynamo screaming its top note, the gyrocar leaped forward.

"No use—they've as good as got us!" gasped Wohl. He man-handled the machine around an acute bend, corrected three successive side-slips, straightened up. The road was a broad ribbon streaming past their wildly whirling wheels. "We couldn't escape at twice this pace."

"The bridge!" Graham warned. Feeling surprised by his own coolness, he nodded toward the bridge rushing nearer at tremendous pace. "Hop the bank and dive into the river. It's a chance."

"A . . . lousy . . . chance!" breathed Wohl.

Offering no comment, Bill Graham again glanced backward, saw their ominously glowing pursuers about two hundred yards behind and gaining rapidly. There were ten of the things speeding through the atmosphere in single file, moving with that apparently effortless but bulletlike pace characteristic of their kind.

The bridge widened in perspective as it shot nearer; the ghostly horde picked up fifty yards. Anxiously, Graham divided his attention between the scenes in front and at rear. This, he could see, was going to prove touch and go. A split second would be the difference between one chance in a million and no chance at all.

"We'll barely do it," he shouted above the dynamo's howl. "When we hit the water, fight out and swim downstream for as long as you can hold breath. Don't come up for more than a quick gulp. Stay down for as long as they're around even if you have to soak for a week. Better that than—" He left the sentence unfinished.

"But—" commenced Wohl, his face registering strain as the oncoming bridge leaped at their front wheel.

"Now!" roared Graham. He didn't wait for Wohl to make up his mind; his powerful fingers clamped upon the wheel, twisted it with irresistible power.

With a protesting screech from the sorely maltreated gyroscope, the slender car went hell-for-leather up the bank. It vaulted the top a bare foot from the bridge's concrete coping, described a spectacular parabola through the air. Like a monster, twenty-foot missile, it struck the water with force that sent shocked rrops flying high above roadlevel. A tiny rainbow shimmered momentarily in the shower.

Down, down went the machine amid an upsurging fountain of waggling bubbles. It vanished leaving on the troubled surface a thin, multi-colored film of oil over which ten baffled luminosities skimmed in temporary defeat.

It was fortunate that he'd had the foresight to fling open his door the instant before they struck, Graham realized. Inward pressure of water would otherwise have kept him prisoner for several valuable seconds. Sinuously moving his tough, wiry body, and with a mighty kick of his feet, he got free of the car even as it settled lopsidedly upon the river's bed.

Making fast, powerful strokes, he sped downstream at the utmost pace of which he was capable, his chest full of wind, his eyes straining to find a way through the liquid murk. Wohl, he knew, was out—he had felt the thrust upon the car as the police lieutenant got clear. But he couldn't see Wohl; the muddiness of the river prevented that.

Bubbles trickled from his mouth as his lungs reached point of rebellion. He tried to increase the rate of his strokes, felt his heart palpitating, knew that his eyes were starting from their sockets. A lithe swerve shot him upward, his mouth and nostrils broke surface, he exhaled, drew in a great gasp of fresh air. He went down again, swimming strongly.

Four times he came up with the swiftness of a trout snatching at a floating fly, took a deep, lung-expanding gulp, then slid back into the depths. Finally, he stroked to the shallows, his boots scraped pebbly bottom, his eyes rose cautiously above the surface.

The coruscant ten now were soaring from a point on the bank concealed by the bridge. The hidden watcher followed their ascent with calculating eyes, followed them until they were ten shining pinpoints under the edge of the clouds. As the blue specters changed direction, drifting rapidly eastward, Graham staggered out of the water and stood dripping on the bank.

Silently and undisturbed the river flowed along. The lone man regarded its placid surface with perplexity that quickly changed to open anxiety. He ran upstream, his clothes still shedding water, his mind eager yet fearing to see the other side of the bridge.

Wohl's body grew visible through the concrete arch as the runner came nearer. Moisture squelched dismally in Graham's boots while he pounded along the shred of bank beneath the arch and reached the police lieutenant's quiet form.

Hastily combing wet hair from his forehead, Graham stooped over the other's limp legs, wound his arms around them. His hands gripping the back of Wohl's cold thighs, Graham heaved himself upright, his muscles cracking under the other's weight.

He hugged the body, looking downward at its dangling head. Water drooled from Wohl's gaping mouth and over Graham's boots. Graham shook him with a jerky upward motion, watching resultant drops. When no more came, he laid Wohl face downward, squatted astride him, placed wide, muscular hands over breathless ribs, began to press and relax with determined rhythm.

He was still working with an utterly weary but stubborn rocking motion when the body twitched and a watery rattle came from its throat. Half an hour later, he sat in the back

115

of a hastily stopped gyrocar, his arms supporting Wohl's racked form.

"Got a hell of a crack on the noggin, Bill," wheezed Wohl. He coughed, gasped, let his head loll weakly on the other's shoulder. "Stunned me at the start. Maybe it was the door. It faced upstream, and it slapped back on me. I sank, came up, sank again. I was breathing water." His lungs made faint gurgling noises. "I feel like a month-old floater."

"You'll be all right," Graham comforted.

"Goner . . . thought I was a goner. Said to myself this was the end. Hell of an end . . . just rubbish . . . garbage . . . in the river. Up and down, up and down, amid muck and bubbles, for ever and ever and ever." He leaned forward, dribbling. Graham pulled him back again. "I was up . . . fighting like a maniac . . . lungs full. Broke top . . . and a goddam Viton grabbed me."

"What?" shouted Graham.

"Viton got me," Wohl repeated dully. "Felt its ghoulish fingers . . . feeling around . . . inside my brain . . . searching probing." He coughed harshly. "All I remember."

"They must have lugged you in to the bank," declared Graham, excitedly. "If they've read your mind they'll anticipate our next moves."

"Feeling around . . . in my brain," murmured Wohl. He closed his eyes, breathed with vibrant, bronchial sounds.

Pursing his lips, Leamington asked, "Why didn't they kill Wohl as they have done the others?"

"I don't know. Perhaps they decided that he knows nothing really dangerous to them." Bill Graham returned his superior's steady stare. "Neither do I, for that matter—so don't take it for granted that I'm apt to die on you every time I go out."

"You don't fool me," Leamington scoffed. "It's a marvel how your luck's held out so far."

Letting it pass, Graham said, "I'll sure miss Art for the next few days." He sighed gently. "Were you able to get me that data on Padilla?"

"We tried." Leamington emitted a grunt of disgust. "Our man down there can discover sweet nothing. The authorities have their hands full and no time to bother with him."

"Why? Have they got the usual attack of *manana?*"

"No, it's not that. Buenos Aires was badly blitzed by the Asians shortly after we cabled. The city's in a bad state."

"Damn!" swore Graham. He bit his lips in vexation. "There goes one possible lead."

"That leaves us the ham stations to check," observed Leam-

116

ington, dismally. "We're on that job right now. It'll take some time. Those blasted hams have a fondness for hiding themselves on mountain tops and in the depths of jungles. They pick the darnedest places."

"Can't you call them on the air?"

"Oh, yes, we can call them on the air—like I can call the wife when she's someplace else. They listen out when the spirit moves them." Sliding open a drawer, he extracted a sheet of paper, handed it across. "This came in just before you returned. It may mean something, or it may not. Does it convey anything to you?"

"United Press report," read Graham, rapidly scanning the lines of type. "Professor Fergus McAndrew, internationally known atom-splitter, mysteriously disaappeared this morning from his home in Kirkintilloch, Scotland." He threw a sharp glance at the impassive Leamington, returned his attention to the sheet. "Vanished while in the middle of enjoying his breakfast, leaving his meal half eaten, his coffee still warm. Mrs. Martha Leslie, his elderly housekeeper, insists that he has been kidnapped by luminosities."

"Well?" asked Leamington.

"Kidnapped—not killed! That's queer!" The investigator frowned as his mind concentrated on this aspect. "It looks as if he could not have known too much, else he'd have been left dead over his meal rather than snatched. Why snatch him if he was no menace?"

"That's what gets me down." For once in his disciplined life, Leamington permitted his feelings to gain the upper hand. He hammered on his desk, said loudly, "From the very beginning of this wacky affair we've been tangled in a mess of strings all of which lead to people who are corpses, or people who aren't anything any longer. Every time we run after something we trip over a fresh cadaver. Every time we make a grab a vacuum. Now they've started hoisting evidence clean out of existence. Not even a body." He snapped his fingers. "Gone —like that! Where's it going to end? *When* is it going to end— if ever it does end?"

"It'll end when the last Viton ceases to be, or the last human being goes under." Graham flourished the United Press report and changed the subject. "This McAndrew, I reckon, must have a mind fairly representative of the world's best talent at this particular time."

"So what?"

"They won't content themselves with probing his mind, as they've been doing up to now. They'll take his entire intellect to pieces and find what makes the wheels go round.

117

I can't see any other reason for making a snatch rather than the usual killing. My guess is that the Vitons have become uneasy, maybe scared, and they've taken him as a suitable subject for their super-surgery." His eyes flamed with intensity that startled his listener. "They're trying to measure an average in order to estimate probabilities. They're losing confidence and want to know what's coming to them. So they'll weigh this McAndrew's brain power, and from that they'll deduce the likelihood of us being able to discover whatever they're afraid of us finding."

"And then?" Leamington hissed the question.

"We suspect that Padilla found something, maybe by design, or perhaps by accident, but we must also allow for the possibility that he was no more than a wild guesser who got wiped out deliberately to mislead us. A South American red herring." Graham stood up, his tall form towering above his chief's desk. He wagged an emphatic finger. "This kidnaping, if I'm right, means two things."

"Those are what?"

"Firstly, that there *is* a lethal weapon waiting to be discovered by us—if we've the ability to find it. The Vitons are vulnerable!" He paused, then said carefully, "secondly, if their study of McAndrew's mind satisfies them that we have the talent to find and develop this weapon, they'll take every possible action to meet the threat—and damn quick! Hell is going to pop!"

"As if it isn't popping already!" remarked Leamington. He waved an all-embracing hand. "Can you conceive anything more desperate than our present situation?"

"Better the devil you know than the devil you don't," Graham riposted. "We *know* what's popping now. We don't know what they'll start next."

"If they think up any new hellers," said Leamington, "by God, they'll about finish us!"

Graham made no reply. He was buried in thought, deep, worried thought. One, now dead, had credited him with extrasensory perception. Maybe it was that, or perhaps it was second sight—but he knew that a bigger and better hell was on the way.

Darkness, deep, dismal darkness such as can swathe only a city once lurid with light. Apart from firefly flashes of gyrocars hurtling with masked headlamps through New York's glassless and battered canyons, there was nothing but that heavy, depressing, all-pervading gloom.

Here and there circles of wooden posts coated with
118

phosphorescent paint gleamed greenly in the night and warned drivers of immense pits left by blasting rockets. That sour stench of war was stronger than ever, the smell of upheaved earth and fractured mains, broken bricks and torn bodies.

On uptown Sixth a small red torch waved to and fro in the darkness, causing Graham to brake his speedster. It slowed, stopped, and he got out.

"What's the idea?"

A young officer emerged from concealing blackness. "Sorry, mister, your machine's wanted." He remained silent while Graham revealed his identity, then declared, "I can't help it, Mr. Graham. My orders are to commandeer every vehicle attempting to pass this point."

"All right, I will not argue the matter." Reaching inside the glyrocar, Graham hauled out his heavy topcoat, writhed into it. "I'll walk."

"I'm really sorry," the officer assured. "There's serious trouble out west and we need every machine on which we can lay our hands." He turned to two of his olive-drab command, barely visible in the dark. "Rush this one to the depot." Then, as the pair clambered in, he pressed the button of his red-lensed torch, signalled another approaching gyrocar to stop.

Graham paced hurriedly along the road. There were tottering walls at his side, some temporarily shored with timber braces. On the other side gaunt skeletons of what once had been great business blocks stood in awful solitude.

An anti-aircraft battery occupied the square at the end. He passed it in silence, noting the aura of tension emanating from the quiet, steel-helmeted figures surrounding the sleek, uplifted muzzles. A duty of appalling futility was theirs; the guns, the cunning proximity fuses, the more cunning predictors couldn't beat to the draw a rocket travelling far ahead of its own sound. The most they could hope for was an occasional robot-bomb, or a crazy Asian with ambitions of honorable suicide. Nothing else.

Beyond the square, precariously poised on a shattered roof, was a combined listening-post and radar unit. The quadruple trumpets of the former angled uselessly toward the westward horizon; the hemispherical antenna of the latter rotated dutifully but to little effect. Although he could not see them, he knew that somewhere between the roof-post and the guns were more tensed, silent figures waiting by the Sperry predictor— waiting for that banshee wail announcing the approach of something slow enough to detect and, perhaps, bring down.

A bright pink aurora sparkled for one second over the

Palisades, and the bellow of the explosion drifted in eons later. Whatever caused it sent a tidal wave racing up the Hudson. Another sparkle came a moment later, higher up the Jersey side of the river, near Haverstraw. Then silence filled the sky.

But the road was not silent. From the depths immediately beneath came a strange, persistent sound: the sound of a mighty gnawing. That subterranean *scrunch, scrunch, scrunch* was audible all the way along, and accompanied the stealthy walker for a mile.

There, far down below the very foundations of the city, great jaws of beryllium steel were guzzling the bedrock. Mechanical moles were chewing through the substrata, forming the arteries of a new and safer city beyond reach of rockets and bombs.

"When all that's finished," mused Graham, whimsically "the former subway will be the El!"

Turning left, he saw a blotch of solid darkness in the less material dark. The dim form was on the opposite side of the road, hurrying nearer or steel-shod heels that clanked noisily.

They were almost level, and about to pass, when from a swollen cloud hidden in the general blackness there plunged a ball of cold blue light. Its sudden, ferocious onslaught was irresistible. The vaguely seen human figure sensed imminent peril, whirled around, gave vent to a blood-freezing shriek that ended in a gasp.

While Graham clung close to the deeper shadows, his hard eyes registering the incredibly swift attack, the luminosity bobbed around its victim, illuminating him in pale, sickly light. He saw the fine, brilliant streamers of its tentacles insert themselves in the body. The thing burped a couple of rings like immaterial halos that spread outward and faded away. The next moment, the shining devil soared, bearing the body aloft.

Another was similarly snatched from the vacant lot two hundred yards farther along the road. Passing a skeletal rooming house, Graham saw hunter and hunted crossing the open area. Lit by the former's ghostly glow, the latter's fantastically elongated shadow fled ahead of him.

The prey had all the frantic motion of one fleeing from a product of fundamental hell. His feet hit earth in great, clumping strides, while queer, distorted words jerked from his fear-smitten larynx.

Iridescent blue closed upon him and formed a satanic nimbus behind his head. The blue swelled, engulfed both the runner and his final, despairing scream. The Viton spewed two rings before it took the body skyward.

A third and a fourth were picked from Drexler Avenue. They saw the downward swoop of blue. One ran. The other fell on his knees, bent in dreadful obeisance, covered the nape of his neck with his hands. The runner bellowed hoarsely as he ran, his belly heaving, his bladder out of control, his terror-filled tones a veritable paean of the damned. The kneeler remained kneeling, as if before his personal joss. The joss was as impartial as any other god. They were taken simultaneously, sobbed together, soared together, true believer and heretic alike, both the sinner and the saved. The Vitons displayed no preferences, showed no favors. They dished out death as impartially as munitions-makers of meningococci.

Moisture was lavish on Graham's forehead as he stole up the driveway, passed through the doors of the Samaritan Hospital. He wiped it off before seeing Harmony, decided he would say nothing of these tragedies.

She was as cool and collected as ever, and her richly black eyes surveyed him with what he felt to be a sort of soothing serenity. Nevertheless, they saw into him deeply.

"What has happened?" she asked.

"Happened? What d'you mean?"

"You look bothered. And you've just wiped your forehead."

Pulling out a handkerchief, he mopped it again, said, "How did you know that?"

"It was smeary." The eyes showed alarm. "Were they after you again?"

"No, not me."

"Someone else?"

"What's this?" he demanded. "A quiz?"

"Well, you looked off-balance for once," she defended.

"I'm always off-balance when talking to you." He drove other, deadlier matters out of his thoughts and gave her the springtime look. "I'll be normal when I've got used to you, when I've seen more of you."

"Meaning what?"

"You know what I mean."

"I assure you I've not the remotest notion of what you're trying to suggest," she said, coldly.

"A date," he told her.

"A date!" Her eyes supplicated the ceiling. "In the midst of all this, he comes seeking dates." She sat down behind her desk, picked up her pen. "You must be stark, staring mad. Good day, Mr. Graham."

"It's night-time, not day," he reminded. He emitted an exaggerated sigh. "A night for romance."

She sniffed loudly as she commenced writing.

"All right," he gave in. "I know when I'm given the brush-off. I get used to it these days. Let's change the subject. What d'you know?"

She put down the pen. "I was waiting for you to return to your senses. I've been wanting to see you the last few hours."

"Have you, begad!" He stood up delightedly.

"Don't be conceited!" She waved him down. "This is about something serious."

"Oh, lordie, aren't I something serious?" he asked the room.

"I had professor Farmiloe around to tea."

"What's he got that I haven't?"

"Manners!" she snapped.

He winced, subsided.

"He's an old dear. Do you know him?"

"A bit—though I don't want to now." He put on an exaggerated expression of jealousy and contempt. "Aged party with a white goatee, isn't he? I believe he's Fordham's expert on something or other. Probably takes care of their tropical butterflies."

"He was my godfather." She mentioned this fact as if it explained everything. "He's some kind of a physicist."

"Bill," he prompted.

She took no notice.

"I think he's—"

"Bill," he insisted.

"Oh, all right," she said, impatiently. "Bill, if it pleases you." She tried to keep her face straight, but he caught the underlying hint of a smile and gained considerable satisfaction therefrom. "Bill, I think he's got an idea of some sort. It bothers me. Every time somebody gets an idea, he dies."

"Not necessarily. We don't know how many are still living who've been nursing ideas for months. Besides, I'm alive."

"You're alive because you appear to have only one idea," she observed, tartly. Her legs went under her chair.

"How could you say that?" He registered his shock.

"For heavens sake, will you let me keep to the subject on which I wish to talk to you?"

"Okay." He gave her an annoying grin. "What makes you think old Farmiloe is afflicted with a notion?"

"I was talking to him about the luminosities. I wanted him to explain why it's so difficult to find a weapon against them."

"And what did he say?"

"He said that we hadn't yet learned how to handle forces as familiarly as substances, that we'd advanced sufficiently to discover the Vitons but not enough to develop a means of removing them." Her fine eyes appraised him as she went on. "He said that we could throw energy in all sorts of forms at a Viton, and if nothing happened we just had no way of discovering why nothing had happened. We can't even capture and hold a Viton to find out whether it repels energy or absorbs it and re-radiates it. We can't grab one to discover what it's made of."

"We know they absorb *some* energy," Graham pointed out. "They absorb nervous currents, drinking them like thirsty horses. They absorb radar pulses—radar can't get a blip out of a Viton. As for the mystery of their composition, well, old Farmiloe's right. We've no idea and no way of getting an idea. That's the hell of it."

"Professor Farmiloe says it's his personal opinion that these luminosities have some sort of electro-dynamic field, that they can modify it at will, that they can bend most forms of energy around them, absorbing only those that are their natural food." Revulsion suffused her features. "Such as those nervous currents you mentioned."

"And we can't reproduce those with any known apparatus," Graham commented. "If we could, we might be able to stuff them until they burst."

Her smile crept back. "I happened to remark that I'd like to have a magic spoon and stir them up like so many blue puddings." Her slender fingers curled around an imaginary spoon, stirred in vigorous ellipses. "For some weird reason, he seemed fascinated when I made this demonstration. He copied me, waving his finger round and round as if it was some new sort of game. It was only my foolishness—but why should he be equally foolish? He knows a lot more about energy-problems than I can hope to learn."

"Doesn't make sense to me. D'you think he's in his second childhood?"

"Most decidedly not."

"Then I don't get it." Graham made a defeated motion.

"Not giving any indication of what was on his mind, he looked slightly dazed, said he'd better be going," she continued. "Then he wandered out in that preoccupied manner of his. As he went, he remarked that he'd try to find me that spoon. I know that he really meant something by that; he was not reassuring me with idle words—*he meant something!*" Her smoothly curved brows rose in query. "He meant—what?"

"Nutty!" decided Graham. He made a stirring motion with an invisible spoon. "It's nutty—like everything else has been since this crazy affair began. Probably Farmiloe is stupified by learning. He'll go home and try develop a haywire egg-beater, and finish up playing with it while in Fawcett's care. Fawcett's got dozens like that."

"You wouldn't make such remarks if you knew the professor as well as I do," she retorted sharply. "He's the last person who'd become unbalanced. I'd like you to go and see him. He may have something worth getting." She leaned forward. "Or would you rather arrive too late, as usual?"

He winced, said, "Okay, okay, don't hit me when I'm down. I'll go see him right away."

"That's being sensible," she approved. Her eyes changed expression as she watched him stand up and reach for his hat. "Before you go, aren't you going to tell me what has got you worried?"

"Worried?" He turned around slowly. "That's a laugh! Ha-ha! Fancy, me worried!"

"You don't deceive me. All that date-making small-talk of yours didn't fool me, either. I could see you were bothered the moment you came in. You looked ripe for murder." Her hands came together. "Bill, what is it?—something new?—something worse?"

"Oh, darn!" He thought a moment, then said, "You might as well be told, I guess. You'll learn it sooner or later, anyway."

"What is it?"

"They don't seem to be killing them any more. They're snatching them bodily now, and taking them God knows where." He spun his hat round in his hand. "We don't know why they're snatching them, or what for. But we can have our dreams . . . bad dreams!"

She paled.

"It's the latest version of the oldest gag," he added, brutally, "a fate worse than death!" He put the hat on his head. "So for pity's sake, look after yourself and keep out of their way to what extent you can. No ducking out of your dates, even by going skyward, see?"

"I've not made a date."

"Not yet. But someday you will. When all this mess is cleaned up, you're going to be pestered plenty." He grinned. "I'll have nothing else to do, then—and I'm going to spend all my time doing it!"

He closed the door on her faint wisp of a smile. Sneaking through the gates and into the murky road that crawled beneath a sky of jet, he knew that that smile still lingered with the memory of his words. But he couldn't think for long about her smile.

In the distance the hidden clouds dripped great blobs of shining blue; rain from the overhead hell. There was a mutual soaring of ghastly globules a little later. They were too far off for him to see clearly, but he sensed that the phenomena were ascending burdened.

With his mind's eye, he saw stiff, unmoving human figures rising in the tentacled grasp of repulsive captors, while below their helpless bodies ten thousand guns gaped at the lowering sky, a thousand listening trumpets awaited the advent of another enemy which, at least, was flesh. The pond was being scoured for frogs even while the frogs were battling each other, cannibalistically.

"We shall measure our existence by its frogs."

He wondered how this epidemic of kidnapings would appear to an observer not yet treated with Bjornsen's sight-widening formula. Undoubtedly, this awful demonstration of superior powers justified the fearful superstitions of the past. Such things had happened before. History and the oldest legends were full of sudden frenzies, levitations, vanishings, and ascensions into the blue mystery of the everlasting sky.

His thoughts jerked away from the subject, switched to the old scientist who had hurried home with a strange idea, and he said to himself, "Bill Graham, I'll lay you a dollar to a cent that Farmiloe either is demented, departed or dead."

Satisfied with this sportingly morbid offer, he turned down Drexler, sneaked cautiously through the deepest shadows, his rubber-soled shoes padding along with minimum of sound, his agate-like, glistening eyes wary of ambush in the night-time clouds. Down, down below his slinking feet the beryllium-steel jaws gnawed and gnawed and gnawed at the hidden ores and secret rocks.

Chapter 11

PROFESSOR Farmiloe was dead beyond all possible doubt, and Graham knew it the moment he opened the door. Swiftly, he crossed the gloom-filled room, ran his pencil torch over its windows, made certain that its light-bottling drapes permitted no vagrant gleam to pass outside. Satisfied, he found the wall-switch, flicked current through the center bulb.

A two-hundred watts blaze beat down on the still figure of the scientist, making mocking sparkles in his white hair which was framed by arms bent limply on the desk. Sitting in his chair, Farmiloe looked as if he had fallen asleep, couching his weary head within his arms. But his was not the sleep that is broken by the dawn—it was slumber of another kind, dreamless and never-ending.

Gently, Graham lifted the bowed shoulders, shoved a hand through the shirt-front, felt the cold chest. He studied the aged and kindly face, noted that it was quite devoid of that terrorized expression which had distorted the features of other dead.

He had reached a pretty good age, Farmiloe. Maybe his end was natural. Maybe his clock inevitably had reached its fateful time and tick—and the luminosities had not been involved in the tragedy. At first glance, it didn't look as if they'd been involved; that peaceful expression, plus the fact that he'd died and not been snatched. The hell of it was that if an autopsy showed death to be caused by heart failure it would mean nothing, absolutely nothing.

Weirdly vibrant filaments could absorb quasi-electrical nervous currents with sufficient swiftness and greed to paralyse the heart's muscles. People—old people especially—could die of similar trouble having no connection with supernormal manifestations. Had Farmiloe suffered no more than the natural ending of his allotted span? Or had he died because his wise old brain had harbored a thought capable of being developed into a threat?

Looking lugubriously at the body, Graham cursed himself. " 'Or would you rather arrive too late, as usual?' She was damn prophetic there! Johnny-come-too-late, that's me, every time! Why the heck didn't I take after the old geezer the moment she mentioned him?" Ruefully, he rubbed his head. "Sometimes I think I'l never learn to get a move on." He looked around the room. "All right, Fathead, let's see you make a start!"

In mad haste, he searched the room. It wasn't a laboratory, but rather a combined office and personal library. He treated the place with scant respect, well-nigh tearing it apart in his determination to discover whatever it might hold worth finding. He found nothing, not one solitary item to which he could tie a potent line. The mass of books, documents and papers seemed as devoid of meaning as a politician's speech. There was a touch of despair in his lean features when finally he gave up the search, made to go.

Its balance disturbed by his maneuverings, the body slid gradually in its seat, flopped forward, its arms spreading across the glossy surface of the desk. Putting his hands beneath cold armpits, Graham took the pathetic weight, bore it toward a couch. Something fell to the floor, rolling metallically. Laying the body full length, Graham covered its face, composed its worn, veined hands. Then he sought for the thing that had fallen.

It was an automatic pencil—he spotted its silvery sheen close by one leg of the desk. He picked it up. Obviously it must have dropped from Farmiloe's cold fingers, or from his lap.

The find stimulated him afresh. Memory of others' dying ramblings made the pencil seem highly suggestive. Of course, Farmiloe might well have been struck out of this life and into the next—if he had been thus smitten—at the very moment his mind broadcasted the thought that his pencil was about to record. It was a thoroughly un-Vitonic principle to give the sucker an even break: their killings came without warning or hesitation, and they killed for keeps.

At that stage, he amazed himself by perceiving an angle he'd overlooked before, namely, that the Vitons could not read. A point so obvious had not occurred to him until that moment. The Vitons had no optical organs, they employed extra-sensory perception in lieu of same. That meant that they passed sentence of death on whoever nursed dangerous ideas, or conceived the notion of recording such ideas in manner not plain to them. Possibly printed patterns on paper, or written ones, meant nothing to their alien senses; they dealt in thoughts, not in pen, pencil or typeface; they were the masters of intangibles rather than the concrete and substantial.

That meant that if Farmiloe has used this pencil it was likely that his record remained, had not been destroyed, exactly as the other messages had not been destroyed. For the second time Graham went through the drawers of the desk, looking for scratch-pads, notes, any kind of hurried scribble that might convey something significant to an understanding mind. Transferring his attention to the top, he satisfied himself that its writing-block and blotter were quite unmarked, looked through two scientific books, examining them leaf by leaf.

No luck. That left only the *Sun*. The late night final lay spread but unopened in the middle of the desk, positioned as if Farmiloe had been about to peruse it when abruptly he lost interest in the world's news. With his photographic eyes poring over the sheet, the Intelligence man breathed deeply when he found a pencilled mark.

It was a thick, swiftly-scrawled ring; a slashing circle such as a man might make in a moment of frenzy—or in the very last moment of life.

"If they got him," mused Graham, "evidently he did this after they got him. Death isn't coincident with stoppage of the heart; the brain does not lose consciousness until several seconds later. I once saw a dead guy run ten steps before he admitted he was dead."

His tongue licked along dry lips while he tried to decipher this message from the grave. That frantically drawn ring represented Farmiloe's last stand: the fading brain's stubborn effort to leave a clew no matter how crude, hurried or far-fetched. In a way it was pathetic, for it was the professor's dying tribute to the intelligence and deductive qualities of his own kind. It was also wacky, it could not well have been wackier—for the ring encircled the printed drawing of a bear!

In the advertising columns, depicted against an iceberg background, the animal was standing upright, its right forepaw extended in a persuasive gesture, an irritating smirk of commercial pride upon its face. The subject of its appeal was a large and ornate refrigerator beneath which appeared a few cajoling words:

"I stand for the world's best refrigerator—you'll find me on its door."

"That ad-writer doesn't suffer from excess of modesty," grunted Graham. He pored over it defeatedly. "Sleep," he decided. "I'll have to get some sleep, else this'll put me among the knitters of invisible wool!"

Neatly tearing the advertisement from the page, he folded it, placed it in his wallet. Then he switched out the light and departed.

Entering a phone booth in the subway on his route home, he called police headquarters, told them about Farmiloe, gave rapid instructions between repeated yawns. Next, he tried Boro 8-19638, obtained no response, felt sleepily surprised that the intelligence department's office did not answer. He was too far gone in fatigue to query the matter or to develop suspicions and apprehensions. They didn't answer—so to hell with 'em.

Later, he fell into bed, thankfully closed eyes red-rimmed with weariness. One mile away, a high-altitude battery, Sperry predictor, radar early-warning outfit and listening-post stood unattended in the dark, their former operators involuntarily removed from their posts. Knowing nothing of this, he tossed uneasily in fantastic dreams that featured a deserted office surrounded by a sea of living, scintillating blue through which strode the gigantic figure of a bear.

The unease he ought to have felt the night before made up for its absence with the morning. He tried to reach the intelligence department's office on the phone, still got no reply, and this time reacted sharply. Something fishy there, bawled his refreshed and active brain—better watch your step.

He watched his step carefully a little later as he approached the building. The place looked innocent enough; it sat there with all the studied indifference of a recently set mouse-trap. The nearest Vitons were well to the west, dangling from the undersides of fat clouds and apparently contemplating their navels.

He hung around for a quarter of an hour, sharing his attention between the ominous building and the menacing sky. There seemed no way of discovering what was wrong with Leamington's phone except that of going in and finding out. Boldly, he entered the building, made toward a levitator shaft. A man emerged from the attendant's niche at the side of the levitator bank, made toward him.

This fellow had black eyes and blacker hair stuck on a chalk-white face. He had black clothes, shoes, hat. He was a sartorial dirge.

Sliding across the parquet in easy, pantherish strides, he harshed, "You—!" and fired directly at Graham.

If the Intelligence man had been one degree more assured or a fraction less edgy, it would have cost him half his noggin. As it was, he felt the bullet-sections whip wickedly above his scalp as he dived to the floor. Going prone, he rolled madly, hoping to cannon against the other's splayed legs before he could fire again, but knowing that he could not make it in time.

His back muscles quirked in agonized anticipation of a split bullet's quadruple impact. There came the expected blast, sharp and hard. Nervous conditioning forced open his mouth in readiness for the yelp his throat did not utter. In that astounding moment of realization that again he had not been hit, he heard a weird gurgling followed by a thud.

A crimson-streaked face fell into the arc of his floor-level vision, a face in which eyes retained an insane glare even as their luster died away. Graham leaped to his feet with the quick suppleness of an acrobat. He gazed down dumbly at his stricken attacker.

A low groan drew his attention to one side. Jumping the body of the man in black, he sprinted to the stairs winding around the bank of pneumatic levitators, bent over the figure sprawling awkwardly at the bottom of them.

Still clinging to a warm automatic, the figure stirred weakly, moved with little, pitiful motions that exposed four blood-soaked holes in the front of its jacket. The other hand dragged itself up, showed Graham a plain, gold ring.

"Don't worry about me, pal." The figure's speech came in forced, bubbling gasps. "I got down this far . . . couldn't make it any farther." Legs twitched spasmodically. The dying man let go his weapon, dropping it with a clatter. "I got the swine, anyway. I got him . . . saved you!"

Holding the ring in his fingers, Graham's glance flashed between the man at his feet and the somberly dressed shape of his assailant. Outside, hell blew off its top and roared its fury, the building swayed, and nearby masonry poured down, but he ignored these sounds. What was a fatally wounded operative doing at the very entrance to the intelligence department? Why hadn't the office answered his calls of last night and this morning.

"Leave me. I'm done!" Feebly, the operative tried to push away Graham's hands as they tore open the gory jacket. "Take a look upstairs then get out fast!" He choked up a bloody froth. "Town's . . . full of nuts! They've opened the asylums and the crazy are . . . on the loose! Get out, brother!"

"God!" Straightening, Graham knew that the man at his feet had slipped away for ever. Snatching up the dropped automatic, he dashed into the nearest levitator. Masonry was still tumbling outside, but he didn't hear it. What awaited him upstairs?

"Take a look upstairs then get out fast!"

The segmentary automatic ready in his grip, his glistening eyes gazing up the shaft, he danced with impatience as his disk soared with what seemed to be excruciating slowness.

A horrible queasiness permeated his stomach when he looked into Leamington's New York field office. The place was a shambles. He counted them quickly—seven! Three bodies lay near the window, their cold faces indelibly stamped with the mark of diabolical fate. Their guns were in their jacket-holsters, unused. They'd never had a chance!

The other four were scattered haphazardly around. These had drawn their weapons and used them. One of the quartet was Colonel Leamington, his riddled frame retaining dignity even in death.

"The trio by the window were settled by Vitons," decided Graham, forcing aside his dazed horror, compelling himself as calmly as possible to weigh up the situation. "The rest killed each other."

Momentarily oblivious of the warning to get out fast, he moved nearer the chief's desk, studied positions, attitudes. It was not difficult to reconstruct the series of events. Evidently the pair by the door—the last to arrive—had opened up on Leamington and the other, but had not been quick enough. Leamington and his aide had swapped shots simultaneously with the newcomers. The result was a likely one; these modern segmentary missiles were blatantly murderous compared with old-fashioned, one-piece bullets.

All the bodies were those of former intelligence men; that was what had him puzzled. He roved around the room, the gun still in his fist, his brow deeply creased as he tried to find the solution.

"Looks like the luminosities first got those three by the window, leaving Leamington and another unharmed—or, at any rate, alive." His frown grew more pronounced. "They left two alive. Why in hell should they have done that? Something mighty queer there!" He edged his buttocks onto the desk while he surveyed the bodies. "After that, three more came along, perhaps because Leamington had summoned them. They turned up, and must have realized something was wrong—for right away they started the fireworks. All five got theirs. Four flopped for keeps. The fifth crawled out and got down the stairs." He hefted the gun, feeling its weight. "But there's nothing to show *why* the fireworks started!"

Swallowing hard, he collected the plain, iridium-lined rings from the dead men's fingers, dropped them into his pocket. Regardless of what had occurred, all these men had been fellow operatives, trusted workers in Uncle Sam's most trusted service.

A bell chimed softly in one corner. Crossing to the tele-news receiver, he flipped it open, saw the *Times* screen-exhibited first edition. He scanned it carefully.

Asian pressure increasing in the mid-West, yelled the *Times*. Workers' demonstration demands that atom-bomb stocks be released forthwith. European situation extremely serious. Thirty enemy stratplanes brought down in southern Kansas during war's biggest stratosphere dogfight. Four-thousand mile lucky-shot blasts Asian dump, devastating one hundred square miles. Bacteriological warfare shortly, says Cornock. Congress outlaws Viton-worshipping cult.

The page crawled off the screen, was followed by local news. Understanding lightened his face as he read. People were running amok! All over New York, in most of the Occidental world's great cities, people were being kidnaped, spirited into the skies, then returned to earth—and were being returned in mental condition much different from their former state.

Supersurgery in the clouds! The grip tightened upon his gun as the terrible significance burst through the haze created by the slaughter in the office. This was the master-stroke! Ultimate victory was to be made infinitely more certain, and—in the interim—still more emotional honey was to be produced with the aid of helpless recruits conscripted from the very ranks of the anti-Viton armies!

What was it that poor devil downstairs had said? "Town's . . . full of nuts!" That was it! The three by the window had died resisting, or had been killed as unsuitable for supersurgical purposes. Leamington and the other had been snatched, operated upon, and returned. They had returned as mental slaves of their ghastly opponents. The office had become a trap cunningly designed to get the intelligence operatives—the heart of the resistance—singly, in pairs or in groups.

But the last three, arriving together, somehow had realized their peril. With that unflinching devotion to duty typical of their kind they had blasted Leamington and his companion. Sentiment had no place in fast play of this ugly description. Unhesitatingly, the three had wiped out their own chief, blowing him into swift and bloody death because quick-wittedly they knew that he was no longer their chief, he was a mind-warped instrument of the foe.

The field office had been a trap—*possibly was still a trap!* The thought stabbed through Graham's brain, made him jump toward the window. Staring out, he noted that random clouds had drifted away leaving a clear, blue sky in which the morning sun shone brightly.

There might be a hundred, a thousand luminosities swaying around in that azure bowl, some actually drifting nearer, some guarding the trap and now about to swoop. Even Bjornsen's wonderful formula couldn't enable one to pick out glowing ultra-blue from a background of glowing normal-blue. The basic and the hyper shared the same sheen under the early sun, making both confusing.

The knowledge that his anxious stare was accompanied by equally anxious thoughts, and that his broadcast psycho-vibrations might entice adjacent trappers, made him race for the door without further ado. Best to get clear while yet there was time! He hit the levitators, went down with a rush.

Two men were lounging just inside the front door. He spotted them through the transparent tube of his shaft even as his disk made a rubbery bounce and settled at street level.

Without leaving the shaft, he reasoned quickly, "If those guys were normal they'd show some curiosity about those two bodies lying within their sight. They aren't interested, and therefore aren't normal. They are dupes!"

Before his disk quite had ceased its cushioning motion he dropped it farther, his long, athletic form sinking from sight of the waiting pair. They stiffened in surprise, ran toward the shaft. Both had guns.

Five levels below the street, he stopped, was out of the perpendicular tube and across the basement ere hidden compressors ceased their sighing. Ducking beneath the main stairway, he heard feet stamping at the top. Hefting his automatic, he fled through a series of empty corridors, gained an exit at the building's father end. Coming out through a steel trapdoor, he sniffed fresh air appreciatively. It was a welcome change from that underrgound odor of fungus and rats. Wearers of the ring were familiar with six such exits, all unknown to and unsuspected by the general public.

The desk sergeant at the precinct station shoved the phone across the polished mahogany, amputated half a wiener, spoke around it. "That's nothing, feller! Police Commissioner Lewthwaite got his around six o'clock. His own bodyguard done it." Another bite. "What's it coming to when big guys get bumped by their bodyguards?"

"Yes, what?" agreed Graham. He rattled the phone angrily. "Looks like they've wrecked the city phone system as well."

"All through the night," mumbled the sergeant, forcing the words through his gag. He gulped, popped his eyes, yoyoed his Adam's apple. "Dozens of them, hundreds! We've bopped them, beat them, shot their pants off and burned them down—and still they come! Some of the nuts were our own boys, still in uniform." His other hand came up, showing a huge police positive. "When Heggarty reports in, I'll be ready for him—in case he ain't Heggarty! You can't ever tell who's next until he starts something!"

"You can't trust your own mother." Suddenly getting his connection, Graham shouted, "Hi, Hetty!" 'He grinned sourly as he heard the answering, "Hi!" then snapped, "I want Mr. Sangster, pronto!"

A deep rich voice took over. Graham drew a long breath, recounted his experience of half an hour before, pouring out a rapid flow of words as he described the scene in the intelligence department's office.

"I can't get Washington," he concluded. "They say all the lines are down and the beams out of action. For the time being, I'm reporting to you. There's no one else within reach to whom I can report."

"This is terrible news, Graham," came Sangster's grave tones. "From where are you speaking?"

"How the heck do I know?"

"Surely you know where you are at the present moment?" Sangster's voice went two tones higher in surprise.

"Maybe. But you don't—and won't!"

"Meaning that you refuse to tell me? You suspect *me?* You think I may be yet another of the mentally mutilated?" He was silent a while. His listener tried to discern his expression in the phone's tiny television screen, but the thing was out of order, displaying only occasional glimpses between vague whorls of light and shadow. "I suppose I cannot blame you for that," Sangster went on. "Some of their conscripts act like dumb gangsters, but others display extraordinary cunning."

"All I'd like you to do—if you can find a way of doing it—is get my reports to Washington," Graham said. "I'm too much on the hop to seek a way myself. You'll have to help me there."

"I'll try," Sangster promised. "Anything else?"

"Yes. I'd like to secure the names and addresses of any other Intelligence operatives who may be in or near this

134

city. They won't all have fallen into that trap. Sometimes some of them don't report in for weeks. I reckon a few must still be roaming free. Leamington was the only one here who had the information I want, but Washington can supply it."

"I'll see what can be done." Sangster paused, then came through a little louder. "A couple of Leamington's recent queries were handled by this department."

"Discover anything?" Graham asked, eagerly.

"A reply from Britain says that McAndrews' laboratory and notes showed that he'd been conducting an interesting line of research in the variation of particle-velocities under heat treatment. Apparently he was hunting the secret of sub-atomic binding power. He'd had no success up to the time of his disappearance, and the British have given him up for dead."

"That's a safe bet!" Graham asserted. "He's been analysed—and the leftovers have been thrown away. He's in some celestial ash-can—a dismembered rabbit!"

"My own imagination can draw all the pictures without you filling in the colors," reproved Sangster. "Leave me alone with my dreams. It's unnecessary to emphasize their horror."

"Sorry!"

"We've found that no radio amateur eavesdropped on Padilla," Sangster continued. "Whatever he told Treleaven is fated to remain a mystery. Data on Padilla's life reveals nothing except that he was a financially successful radio experimenter. He made a big wad out of simplified frequency modulation. He made his own funeral out of something else—but left no record to indicate what it was."

"I'd given up that lead a couple of days ago."

"You say that as if you've found another and better one." Sangster's voice was pregnant with interest. "Have you?"

"I find one almost every morning," declared Graham, glumly, "and it goes rotten on me by night. As a gallivanting gumshoe, I sure picked myself a heller right at the start!" He pursed his lips and sighed. "What are the governmental experts doing?"

"Nothing, as far as I know. There are two groups assembled in lonely places suggested by Leamington. They've discovered that the very loneliness which is their protection is also their handicap. They plan things, design them, make them—then find that there are no adjacent luminosities on which to test them."

"Gosh, I overlooked that," Graham admitted.

"It's not your fault. None of us thought of it." Sangster was now lugubrious. "If we transfer them to Viton-infested pastures, they'll get wiped out. It's an impasse." He snapped his fingers with impatience.

"Probably you're right, sir," said Graham. "I'll report again directly I've turned up something worth reporting."

"Where are you going now?" The question came sharply.

"I'm deaf in this ear," Graham told him. "Funny—I don't seem able to hear you at all."

"Oh, all right." Disappointment trickled through the wires. "I guess you know best. Take care of yourself!" A loud click signalled that he had rung off.

"When in doubt," offered the desk sergeant, darkly, "see who's making money out of it."

"Who's making it now?" Graham asked.

"Morticians." The sergeant frowned at his listener's grin. "Well, ain't they?"

Chapter 12

THE bronze plate said: *Freezer Fabricators of America, Inc.* Graham walked in, spent five minutes sparring a stubborn executive before that worthy agreed to conduct him to the golden name on the old oak door.

That name was Thurlow, and its owner was a living mummy. Thurlow looked as if he'd sweated himself dry in life-long pursuit of percentages.

"We can't do it," complained Thurlow, after Graham had explained the purpose of his visit. His voice rustled like ages-old papyrus. "We couldn't supply a refrigerator to the Sultan of Zanzibar even if he offered to balance its weight with jewels. Our plant has been engaged wholly on government work since the war began, and we haven't turned out a solitary freezer."

"It doesn't matter." Graham dismissed the point without argument. "I want one for the university to pick to pieces. Give me a list of your local customers."

"Nothing doing!" Thurlow's bony hand massaged his bald, yellow pate. "Things won't always be like this. Some day, my prince will come. Fine fool I'll look with my consumer-list circulating among competitors."

"Are you insinuating—?" began Graham, angrily.

"I'm insinuating nothing." Thurlow waved him down. "How do I know you are what you represent yourself to be? That trick ring of yours doesn't mean a goddam thing to me. I can't read its inscriptions without a microscope. Why don't the authorities provide you with a microscope?" His cackle was funereal. *"Heh-heh-heh!"*

Keeping his temper, Graham said, "Will you give me a list if I bring you written authority?"

"Well," Thurlow ceased his cackling, looked cunning, "if what you bring satisfies me, I'll give you a list. What you bring had better be convincing. No slick competitor is going to gyp me out of a list just because trade's gone haywire."

"You need not fear that." Graham stood up. "I'll get something in clear writing, or else the police will make ap-

137

plication on my behalf." Stopping by the door, he asked one more question. "How long have you been using that bear as a trade-mark?"

"Ever since we started. More than thirty years." Thurlow waxed pompous. "In the public's mind, the standing bear is associated with a product unrivalled in its sphere, a product which—although I say it myself—is universally accepted as—"

"Thanks!' interrupted Graham, cutting short the eulogy. He went out.

The stubborn one with whom he'd first battled conducted him to the front doors, saying, "Did he oblige?"

"No."

"I thought he wouldn't."

"Why not?"

The other looked troubled. "I shouldn't say it but, frankly, Thurlow wouldn't give milk to a blind kitten."

Regarding him shrewdly, Graham punched his arm. "Why let that worry you? Time's on your side. You'll be in his chair when he's stinking."

"If any of us live long enough to see this through," observed the other, gloomily.

"That's *my* worry," said Graham. "Bye!"

There was a phone booth in the corner drugstore. Graham sized up the four customers and three assistants before turning his back to them and entering the booth.

He was leery of everybody. That warning voice within his mind whispered that he was being sought with grim determination, that at long last it had dawned upon the eerie foe that the source of opposition was not so much the world of science as a small group of investigatory aces—in which he was the ace of trumps.

The Vitons had gained compensation for their inherent inability to distinguish one human being from another, humans who seemed as alike as so many sheep. Other humans had been forcibly enrolled and given the duty of segregating intransigent animals from the flock. The Vitons now were aided by a horde of surgically-created quislings, a hapless, helpless, hopeless but dangerous fifth column.

Short of a prowling luminosity picking on him at random, and reading his mind, he had been safe. Now he was threatened by proxies of his own kind. This brother-kill-brother technique was the newest and deadliest menace.

Dialling his number, he thanked heaven that Wohl's dazed mind had not depicted himself and the locality of his home. Wohl's smothered, disorganized brain helplessly had sur-

138

rendered its knowledge of the field office, causing wolfish captors contemptuously to leave him upon the bank in their haste to reach the scene of slaughter.

Graham would never tell the burly police lieutenant that he, and he alone, had put the finger on Leamington and the others.

"This is Graham," he said, detecting the lift of a distant receiver.

"Listen, Graham," Sangster's voice came back urgently. "I connected with Washington shortly after you last phoned. We're linked through amateur transmitters—the hams seem to have the only reliable communications system left. Washington wants you right away. You'd better get there fast!"

"D'you know what it's for, sir?"

"I don't. All I've got is that you must see Keithley without delay. There's a captured Asian strat-plane waiting for you down at Battery Park."

"Fancy me roaming around in an Asian. Our fighters won't give it five minutes in the air."

"I'm afraid you don't appreciate our true position, Graham. Except for occasional and very risky sorties, our fighters are grounded. If they had only the Asians to meet, they'd soon sweep the skies clear of them. But there are the Vitons, too. That makes a lot of difference. When a Viton can swoop on a pilot, compelling him to land his plane in enemy territory as a free gift from us . . . well . . . we just can't afford to give away men and machines like that. The Asians have gained command of the air. It's a fact that may lose us this war. You take that Asian job—you'll be safer in that."

"I'll do it on the run." Watching the shop through the booth's plastiglass panels, he put his lips nearer the mouthpiece, and went on hurriedly, "I called to ask you to get me a list of local customers from Freezer Fabricators. You may have to get tough with a wizened dummy named Thurlow; the tougher you get the better I'll like it. He's long overdue to have his ears pinned back. I'd also like you to make contact with Harriman, at the Smithsonian, ask him to reach any astronomers who're still active, and find out whether they can conceive any possible connection between the luminosities and the Great Bear."

"The Great Bear?" echoed Sangster, surprisedly.

"Yes, there's a bear hanging around that means something or other. God alone knows what it does mean, but somehow I've got to find out. I've a feeling it's mighty important."

"Important—a bear! It can't be any other animal, eh? It has to be a bear?"

139

"Nothing but a smell bruin," Graham agreed. "I'm pretty sure that the astronomical slant is entirely wrong, but we can't afford to overlook even the remotest chance."

"Refrigerators, wizened dummies, stars and bears!" gabbled Sangster. "Jesus!" He was silent a moment, then moaned, "I think maybe they've got at you, too—but I'll do as you request." Then he said, "Jesus!" again and disconnected.

The trip to Washington was fast and uneventful, but his army pilot sighed with relief as the machine touched tarmac at the destination.

He clambered out, saying to Graham, "It's nice to arrive at where you intended instead of where some blue globe compels you to go."

Graham nodded, got into the waiting car, was whirled away at top pace. Ten minutes later, he was savagely pondering the bureaucratic habit of saving two minutes and wasting ten. He paced the waiting room with hard, restless strides. You wouldn't think there was a war on, the way they let you hang around in Washington.

That couple of scientists, for instance. Heaven only knew whom they were waiting to see, but they'd been there when he arrived, and they acted like they hoped still to be there when finally the rock of ages crumbled into dust. Graham gave them an irritated look over. Talk!—they talked and talked as if worldwide destruction and human slaughter were trifling distractions compared with other and weightier matters.

Arguing about Bjornsen's formula, they were. The little one reckoned that modification of eyesight was caused by molecules of methylene blue transported to the visual purple by iodine as a halogen in affinity, functioning as a carrier.

The fat one thought otherwise. It was the iodine that made the difference. Methylene blue was the catalyst causing fixation of an otherwise degeneratable rectifier. He agreed that mescal served only to stimulate the optic nerves, attuning them to the new vision, but the actual cause was iodine. Look at Web's schizophrenics, for example. They had iodine, but not methylene blue. They were mutants with natural fixation, requiring no catalyst.

With blissful disregard for other and more urgent matters, the little one started off again, threatening to bring Graham's temper to the boil. The investigator was just asking himself what it mattered how Bjornsen's formula functioned so long as it did function, when he heard his own name called.

140

Three men occupied the room into which he was ushered. He recognized them all: Tollerton, a local expert; Willetts C. Keithley, supreme head of the Intelligence Service; and finally a square-jawed, gray-eyed figure whose presence brought him stiffly to attention—the president!

"Mr. Graham," said the president, without preamble, "this morning a courier arrived from Europe. He was the fifth they'd despatched to us within forty-eight hours. His four predecessors died on their way here. He brought bad news."

"Yes, sir," said Graham, respectfully.

"A rocket dropped on Louvain, Belgium. It had an atomic warhead. Europe retaliated with ten. The Asians have sent back twelve more. This morning, the first atomic rocket in this hemisphere arrived on our territory. The news has been suppressed, of course, but we are about to hit back strongly. In brief, the much-feared atomic war has begun." He put his hands behind his back, walked up and down the carpet. "Our morale is good despite everything. The people have confidence. They feel sure that victory will be ours in the end."

"I'm sure of that, sir," said Graham.

"I wish I were as sure!" The president stopped his pacing and faced him squarely. "The situation now existing is no longer war in the historical sense of the term. If it were, we should win it. But this is something else—it is the suicide of a species! The man who jumps in the river wins nothing but everlasting peace. Neither side can win this battle—except perhaps the Vitons. Humanity, as a whole must lose. We, as a nation, must also lose, for we are part of humanity. The coolest heads on both sides have realized that from the start, hence the reason why atomic weapons have been held back as long as possible. Now—God forgive us!—the atomic sword has been drawn. Neither side dare take the risk of being the first to sheath it."

"I understand, sir."

"If that were all, it would be bad enough," the president continued, "but it is far from all." He turned to a wall map, pointed to a thick black line broken by a tipsy-vee which speared across most of Nebraska. "The public does not know of this. It represents the area of the enemy's armored penetration within the last two days. It is an Asian salient which we may or may not be able to contain."

"Yes, sir." Graham eyed the map without expression.

"We can make no greater sacrifices. We can hold no stronger foe." The president stepped nearer, his stern eyes looking deep into Graham's. "The courier reported that Europe's situation already is extremely critical, in fact so much so that they can hold out until six o'clock on Monday evening. Until that time, we remain humanity's last hope. After that, Europe's collapse or annihilation. Six o'clock and no later—not one minute later."

"I see, sir." The Intelligence man noted the wide-eyed gaze that Tollerton kept upon him, the fixed, keen stare with which Keithley was watching him.

"Frankly, that means there is no way of escape for any of us except by striking an effective blow at the fundamental cause of all this—the Vitons. Either that, or we cease to survive as sentient beings. Either that, or those left of us revert to the status of domestic animals. We have eighty hours in which to find salvation!" The president was grave, very grave. "I don't expect you to find it for us, Mr. Graham. I don't expect miracles of any man. But, knowing your record, knowing that you personally have been involved in all this from the beginning, I wanted to inform you myself; to tell you that any suggestions you can make will be acted upon immediately and with all the power at our command; to tell you that all the authority you require may be had for the asking."

"The president," interjected Keithley, "thinks that if anything can be done by one man, that man is you. You started all this, you've seen it through so far, and you're the likeliest person to finish it—if it can be finished."

"Where have you hidden the experts?" asked Graham, bluntly.

"There's a group of twenty in Florida, and twenty-eight in the interior of Porto Rico," Keithley replied.

"Give them to me!" Graham's eyes were alight with the fire of battle. "Bring them back and give them to me."

"You shall have them," declared the president. "Anything else, Mr. Graham?"

"Give me absolute authority to commandeer all laboratries, plants and lines of communication that I see fit. Let my requirements for materials be given perference over all else."

"Granted." The president uttered the word with no hesitation.

"One more request." He made it to Keithley, explaining, "His duty will be to watch me. He'll watch me and I'll watch him. Should either of us become a dupe, the other will remove him at once."

"That, too, is granted." Keithley handed over a slip of paper. "Sangster said that you wanted addresses of fellow operatives in New York. There are ten on that list—six locals and four out-of-towners. Two of the local men have not reported for some time, and their fate is unknown."

"I'll try to look them up." Graham pocketed the slip.

"Eighty hours, remember," said the president. "Eighty hours between freedom for the living or slavery for the not-dead." He put a paternal hand on the other's shoulder. "Do the best with the powers we've given you, and may Providence be your guide!"

"Eighty hours," murmured Graham as he raced toward the plane waiting to bear him back to New York.

Down the spine of the New World, a hundred millions were facing three hundred millions. Every hour, every minute thousands were dying, thousands more were being mutilated —while overhead hung the glowing quaffers of the ascending champagne of agony.

The end of the hellish banquet was drawing nigh. The last course was about to be served, an atomic one, in critical masses, served with blood red hands. Then appetites replete with human currents might rest content to wait the further feasts to come, the oldtime, regular guzzlings in humanity's rutting seasons and burying seasons. Eighty hours!

The rush with which he entered his New York apartment took Graham halfway across the floor before he saw the figure dozing in the chair. The center light was cold and dull, but the whole room was aglow with the electric radiator's brilliant flare. Seeing by radiant heat had long lost its novelty to those with the new sight.

"Art!" he shouted, delightedly. "I was about to phone Stamford and ask them to toss you out. I need you badly."

"Well, I'm out," said Wohl, succinctly. "I couldn't stand that hospital any longer. There was an angular ward sister with ambitions. She got me scared. She called me Wohly-Pohly and stole my britches. Ugh!" He shuddered reminiscently. "I bawled for my clothes and they acted like they'd been sold to the junkman. So eventually I beat it without them."

"What—nude?"

"Tut!" Wohl was shocked. His foot nudged a bundle on the floor. "No, in these. The crime wave's awful when even police lieutenants snitch hospital blankets." Standing up, he stretched his arms sidewise, revolved slowly, like a gown model. "How d'you like the suit?"

"Holy smoke, it's one of mine!"

"Sure! I found it in your wardrobe. Bit saggy under the arms, and tight around the fanny, but it'll do."

"Heck of a figure you must have. Too little in front and too much behind," commented Graham. His smile faded as he switched expressions and became serious. He shoved Wohl back into his chair. "Listen, Art. Time's short. I've just got back from Washington, and what I heard there is going to keep me on the jump like a flea on a hot stove. The situation is tougher than I'd imagined." He recounted the march of events since he'd left Wohl in the hospital at Stamford. "So I asked Keithley, and here it is." He handed over a plain, iridium-lined ring. "You've been fired by the police and conscripted by the Intelligence, whether you like it or not. You're now my opposite number."

"So be it." Wohl's studied nonchalance failed to conceal his delight. "How the devil do the authorities manage always to supply rings the correct size?"

"Forget it—we've bigger puzzles to solve." He gave Wohl the clipping he'd taken from Farmiloe's copy of the *Sun*. "We're organizing fast. We've got until Monday evening, by which time it must be conquest or curtains! It doesn't matter whether we starve or die so long as we produce by that deadline." He pointed to the clipping. "That's Farmiloe's dying scrawl. That's our only clew."

"You're certain that it's a clew?"

"Nope! I'm certain of nothing in this precarious existence. But I've a hunch that it is a genuine pointer to something worth knowing—something that cost Farmiloe his life!"

Staring long and hard at the bear posing inanely before an iceberg, Wohl said, "Have you had a refrigerator picked to bits?"

"Sangster dumped one on the university and they took it apart. They went down to the last bolt, screw and piece of wire. There was nothing left for them to do but lick the enamel off the plates."

"It told them nothing?"

"Not a thing. Cold might kill luminosities by slowing down their vibrations, but how're we going to apply it? There's no such thing as a beam of pure cold, nor any likelihood of developing one—it's a theoretical absurdity." Graham glanced anxiously at his watch. "Does that scrawl suggest anything to you?"

"Br-r-r!" replied Wohl, hugging himself.

"Don't act the fool, Art! There's no time for horsing around."

"I always feel the cold," Wohl apologized. He scowled at the taunting advertisement. "I don't like that animal's complacent smirk. It knows we're stuck, and it doesn't care,"

144

He returned the clipping to Graham. "All it tells me is what I knew long ago, namely, that you have an astonishing aptitude for digging up the screwiest leads."

"Don't remind me of it!" Graham's voice was an annoyed growl. He transfixed the clipping with an angry finger. "A bear! We've got something here we think is a clew. Maybe it's the masterkey of our puzzle. Maybe it's salvation in our time if only we can look at it the right way. And it's nothing more than a long, mercenary, self-satisfied looking and probably flea-bitten bear!"

"Yes," Wohl joined in, for lack of anything better to contribute. "A gangling, cockeyed, stinking bear! A lousy polar bear!"

"If only I'd been quicker after Farmiloe, or had met him on his way—" Graham stopped in mid-sentence. A thoroughly startled look sprang into his features. In a voice hushed with sheer surprise, he said, "Hey, you called it a *polar* bear!"

"Sure I did! It's not a giraffe, unless I'm blind."

"A polar bear!" yelled Graham, changing tone with sudden violence that brought Wohl upright. "Polarization! That's it—polarization!" He stirred his finger vigorously in the air. "Circular or elliptical polarization. Hell!—why didn't I see it before? A child ought to have seen it. I'm too dumb to live!"

"Eh?" said Wohl, his mouth agape.

"Polarization, a million dollars to a doughnut!" Graham shouted. His face was deep purple with excitement. It would have looked red to ordinary sight. Grabbing two hats, he slammed one on the startled Wohl's head, where it stuck rakishly. "Out! We're getting out hell-for-leather! We're telling the world before it's too late! Out!"

They fled through the door without bothering to close it behind them. Warily, their eyes watched the heights as they hammered along the sidewalk. Blue dots were glowing in the sky, but none swung low.

"Down here!" puffed Graham. He ducked into a concrete maw whose throat lead to the newer and lower city. Together they went full tilt down the ultra-rapid escalators, hit the levitator banks at first level, descended another four hundred feet.

They were inhaling heavily as they jumped from their disks, found themselves at the junction of six recently made tunnels. Dull rumbles and raucous grinding noises of steadily boring mammoths still spouted from the two newest holes.

Hydrants, telephone booths, public televisors and even a small cigar store already stood in this subterranean area dug

145

only within the last few weeks. Engineers, overseers, surveyors, and laborers were scurrying about laden with tools, materials, instruments and portable lamps. Occasionally, an electric trolley, heavily laden, whirred out of one tunnel and into another. Ominously, workers were fitting radio-active gas detectors to the levitator tubes and the air-conditioning vents.

"Vitons rarely find their way down here," Graham observed. "We ought to be able to phone in comparative safety. Take the booth next to mine, Art. Phone every scientific plant, depot and individual you can find listed in the directory. Tell them the secret may be polarization of some sort, probably elliptical. Don't let them argue with you. Tell them to spread it around where they think it'll do the most good—then ring off."

"Right!" Wohl stepped into his booth.

"How long had you been waiting when I arrived?"

"About fifteen minutes." Snatching the directory, Wohl leafed it to page one. "I'd finished dressing only a couple of minutes when you arrived like a guy shot out of a cannon."

Taking the adjoining booth, Graham dialled, got his number. As usual, the visor was out of order, but he recognized the voice at the other end. "Try polarization, Harriman," he said, quickly. "Maybe it's elliptical. Toss it around as fast as you know how—if you want to live!" He disconnected, giving Harriman no chance to comment.

Seven more calls he made, repeating his suggestion with economy of words. Then he rang Stamford Center Hospital, asked what time Wohl had left. The reply made him sigh with relief. The former police officer could not have been snatched and perverted—his time was fully explained.

He had not really suspected the other of being a dupe, particularly since Wohl had shown himself willing to help spread the very information which the enemy was desperately anxious to suppress. But he could not forget Sangster's glum statement that "others display the very essence of cunning." In addition, there was that persistent and sometimes frightening feeling of being the especial object of widespread search. The enemy, he sensed, knew of him—their problem was to find him.

Shrugging, he dialled again, rattled hurriedly through his information, and heard the other say, "Your buddy Wohl's on our spare line right now. He's giving us the same stuff."

"It doesn't matter so long as you've got it," Graham snapped. "Pass it along to as many as you can."

An hour later, he left his booth, opened Wohl's door. "Chuck it, Art. I reckon we've thrown it too far to be stopped."

"I'd got down to the letter P," sighed Wohl. "A gezeeber named Penny was the next." His sigh was deeper, more regretful. "I wanted to ask him if he could spare a dime."

"Never mind the wit." Graham's features registered anxiety as he noted the hands on the huge turret clock over the booths. "Time's flying quicker than zip, and I've got to meet those—"

A faraway roar interrupted him. Ground trembled and shuddered in quick, tormented pulsations, and a tremendous blast of warm, odorous air swept through the area. Things plunged down the transparent levitator shafts, crashed noisily at bottom. Fine powder trickled from the roof. There was the sound of distant shouting.

The uproar spread, came nearer. Shouting, bawling men raced from the tunnels, made a clamorous, gesticulating crowd that packed the subterranean junction. A gargantuan drummer thumped the ground overhead, and more powder streamed down. The drumming ceased; the crowd milled and cursed.

Somebody drove his way through the mob, entered a phone booth, emerged after a minute. He silenced the others by sheer superiority of lung power, gained a hearing. His stentorian tones bounded and rebounded around the junction, fled in dismal wails along the tunnels.

"The exit's blocked! The phone cable is intact, and those on the surface say there's ten thousand tons choking the shaft. Dupes did it!" The crowd howled, flourished fists, looked around for rope and a few victims. "It's all right, boys," roared the speaker. "The cops got 'em! They were dropped on the run." His authoritative eyes roamed over the mass of weary faces. "Get back to Number Four—we've the shortest dig for a bust-through there."

Muttering among themselves, scowling as they went, the workers poured into a tunnel. Before the last one had been swallowed by its gloomy arch, distant thumps and rumbles burst forth with doubled fury. The beryllium-steel jaws resumed their gnawing.

Catching the speaker as he was about to follow, Graham identified himeslf, asked, "How long?"

"It'll be quickest through Number Four tunnel," replied the other. "There's about ninety feet of solid rock between us and another gang working to meet us. We're joining systems through this hole, and I reckon we can't make it in under three hours."

"Three hours!' Graham had another look at the turret clock and groaned.

Ten of his precious eighty already had drifted away, leaving behind nothing but a shrewd guess yet to be confirmed experimentally. Three more were to be wasted in waiting—waiting for release from earthly depths which, at least, were safer than the perilous surface. Once again a Viton strike had been well-timed . . .or yet again the devil had looked after his own!

It was some small compensation to find that the adjoining system had its exit on West Fourteenth, for it was in the basement of the Martin Building that Graham had arranged to meet the governmental experts along with several others.

Sixty-four of them were fidgeting apprehensively in this deep hideout immediately below the spot where Professor Mayo's crushed body had started the whole series of ghastly events. It was fitting, Graham thought, that the stain of this tragedy should mark the scene of humanity's last boom-or-bust conference.

"You've been tipped about polarization?" he asked. They nodded. One stood up, intending to offer an opinion. Graham waved him down. "No discussions at the moment, gentlemen."

His eagle eyes weighed them individually as he went on, "In spite of their immensely superior powers, we've outwitted our adversaries twice. We've done it with this polarization hint of Farmiloe's, and we did it when first we broadcast news of the enemy's existence. We beat them despite everything they could bring against us. On both those occasions, we succeeded by taking advantage of the Vitons' chief weakness—that they can't be everywhere at once. We're going to use the same tactics again."

"How?" demanded a voice.

"I'm not telling you that in full detail. There may be some among you who are not to be trusted!" His lean, muscular features maintained their grimness as his eyes carefully went over them again. Uneasily, his listeners shifted in their seats, each casting sidelong, wary glances at his neighbors. Their thoughts were readily apparent: what man can I call man—when no man can I call brother? Graham continued, "You're going to be divided into eight groups of eight apiece. You'll be scattered, and no party is going to know the location of any of the other seven. Those who don't know, can't tell!"

More fidgeting, more mutual suspicion. Wohl grinned to himself as he stood at Graham's side. He was enjoying the situation. If among this crowd of reputed bigbrains were a dozen enforced converts of the Vitons, helpless but supremely crafty spies in the human camp, their identity was completely unknown, and there was no readymade means of detecting them. Any man in this audience might well be sitting between a pair of dreadful proxies.

"I'm taking a group of eight, giving them their instructions in private, and sending them on their way before I deal with the next lot," informed Graham. He selected Kennedy Veitch, leading ray expert. "You're in charge of the first group, Mr. Veitch. Please select your seven."

After Veitch had picked his co-workers, Graham led them to another room, told them hurriedly, "You're going to the Acme plant, in Philadelphia. When you get there, you're not merely to carry on with experimentation designed to blot out a few luminosities, for that means—if you happen to be successful—you'll be promptly eliminated by other, nearby globes, and we'll be left wondering why in hell you died. We're sick of wanting to know why guys have died!"

"I don't see how immediate retaliation can be prevented," opined Veitch, his face pale, but his lips firm.

"It cannot—just yet." Graham minced no words, didn't care whether he sounded brutal or not. "You and your men may be blasted to blazes—*but* we're going to know exactly what you've been doing right up to the moment of the blast. You may be blown to hades, and we may be impotent to prevent it—but we'll know *why* you've been blown!"

"Ah!" breathed Veitch. His group crowded around him, wide-eyed, possessed of that curious silence of men facing the zero hour.

"You'll have microphones distributed all over your laboratory and they'll be linked through the city's telephone system. You'll also be connected with the police teletype system, and you'll have a police operator in attendance. The army signals corps will provide you with two boys with walkie-talkie sets. There will be fine-definition scanners tied to far-off television receivers. Adjacent buildings will hold observers who'll watch your laboratory continually."

"I see," said Veitch, slowly and doubtfully.

"Every single thing any of you are about to do you're to describe in full detail before you try it. You'll send it through all available channels, the mikes, the teletype, the radios. The scanners will then watch you do it. Distant observers will watch results. If you suffer, we'll know exactly why you suffered."

Veitch offered no remark, and Graham went on, "If you

succeed in smearing a luminosity, the technical details of how you accomplished the feat will be known fully and accurately to a large number of people spread over a large area. We'll know the sort of equipment required to repeat the blow, we'll rush it out in quantities, and nothing in heaven, earth or hell will stop us." He studied them steadily. "On your way—and best of luck!"

He turned to Wohl. "Ask Laurie to choose his seven, and bring them in here."

"I didn't like the little runt, the one staring over Veitch's shoulder," remarked Wohl, pausing by the door. "His eyes had hoodlum's heebies."

"And what may those be?"

"A fixed, animal glare. Didn't you notice him? Go have a look through the police art gallery—you'll find dozens with the heebies, usually deranged or hopped-up killers." Wohl looked expectantly at the other. "Not all of them have it, but most do. It depends on the state of their minds at the time they were photographed."

"Yes," agreed Graham, thoughtfull. "Come to think of it, I've noticed it in studies of some of those oldtime gangsters: Dillinger, Nelson, the Barrow boys, Louie the Lep, and others. Who knows that they weren't sorry instruments of unseen drinkers, human swizzle-sticks used to stir up more emotion—when there weren't enough honeymooners around."

"By cripes!" said Wohl. "Do you suggest that every bridal room is somebody else's soda-fountain?"

"Not every one. Of course not! But some—some!"

"I'd be in a living hell if I had your mind. Why don't you go hang yourself sometime?"

"We are in a living hell, and you know how many cracked up when they discovered it." He made an impatient gesture. "Veitch won't be out of the building yet. Go catch him, Art, and put him wise." He went toward the door. "I'll call Laurie myself."

His frown was still serious, worried, when he got the next group of experts, conducted them to the room.

Chapter 13

THE Faraday Electrical Equipment Company's laboratory claimed to be the biggest on the American continent; its size suggested the building of airships rather than the evolving of more efficient iconoscopes, tubes, and stereo-screens.

A battery of enormous Diesel-electrics occupied one end of the hangarlike shed. Mighty transformers reared alongside them; the main switchboard was plenty large enough to serve the chief distributing station of a great city.

Tall, complex tubes of every conceivable type were ranged along one wall, some half finished, many completed but not yet tested. Queer frames formed of bars, rods and tubular loops—experimental models of ultra-short wave beam antenna —were propped against the opposite wall.

No production lines ran through this great hangar; it was the company's playground for the most imaginative of its gadgeteers. A veritable litter of scanners, photo-sensitive cells, partly assembled stereo-screens, radio components, wire golliwogs and schematic diagrams marred with doodles lay scattered over tables the size of rooms.

Faraday's thought nothing of pouring a million dollars a year into the wackier channels of research. When the war began, who'd been about to market six-color stereo-scopic television-de-luxe. Faraday!

Duncan Laurie moodily weighed up the technical junkpile at the disposal of his little band, and said to Graham, "Plane polarization ought not to be overlooked. It should be tried in case Farmiloe was slightly off the mark."

"It's being considered," Graham assured him. "We are letting no chances slide, no matter how remote they seem. Why, we've got one crowd out west investigating a report that the Vitons duck around rainbows, like men portaging past rapids."

"Ye gods!" exclaimed Laurie.

"All the work is properly co-ordinated. Your gang is to concentrate on hyperbolic polarization."

"Okay." Laurie pulled meditatively at one ear. "These luminosities seem to reflect over a wave-band running from about three million Angstrom units up to four or five. They're damnably difficult to analyse spectroscopically: we can't line an instrument on one long enough to get anywhere. But it's obvious that they're energy in compact and balanced form, and are inertialess."

"Are fish inertialess?" asked Graham.

"Fish?" Laurie was frankly puzzled.

Graham pointed to an overhead skylight. "We've got to forget our conditioning and try looking at things from a novel angle. Up there is the atmospheric ocean which may be infinitely more tangible to the Vitons than it is to us. It's full of blue, shining fish swimming around in their natural habitat, swimming by some propulsive means not given to us creatures crawling around on the bottom."

"But energy—"

"Ordinary light's a form of energy, and has weight," Graham went on. He heard the rattle of the police teletype as he talked. "Being made of prime forces—wavicles or whatnot —I think these Vitons have a sort of substance, though they're not matter as matter is generally understood. We're faced with a fourth and unfamiliar form of matter, a force-form. They have weight, even though it may be minute from our viewpoint. They have inertia, and have to expend energy to overcome it. That's why they suck us like so many lollipops—to renew their tissues." He smiled at Laurie. "Only my own opinions, mind you."

"Possibly you're right," acknowledged Laurie. He favored the skylight with a look of extreme distaste.

"Now," Graham continued, "reports we've collected since we discovered the shoo-fly effects of short-wave therapy cabinets show that the luminosities are susceptible to a radioband stretching from two centimeters to about one and a half meters. They don't die. They just skedaddle as if stung."

"My guess is that those impulses hamper the whirl of their surface electrons," Laurie opined. "But they don't penetrate."

"Quite! And penetration's what we've got to achieve, not sometime next year, or next month, or next week, but within a few hours! We've chopped at Viton timber and have been smacked in the eye by the splinters. With luck, we're going to bore into their hungry guts by means of polarization. Either that, or we can start mooing, for we revert to what we've always been—just a herd of goddam cows!" He looked squarely at Laurie. "You've got fifty hours. Start at two centimeters and work up."

"We'll do it!" swore Laurie. He gave sharp orders to his band. The tiny group—dwarfed by the hugeness of the place—bustled into activity.

To one side, the teleprinter operator transmitted information as Laurie recited his intentions. Silent but supersensitive microphones also picked up his voice, carried it away in a dozen directions and to varying distances. Scanners fixed to the steel roof trusses recorded the scene from above.

With Wohl at his side, Graham hurried toward the door, and as he reached it the scanners picked up and transmitted a hideous incident that plunged dramatically into the screens of faraway receivers.

All the lights went out simultaneously, the switchboard blew a shower of hot, copper-smelling sparks, and a blaze of vampire blue swelled through an open hopper in the north wall. Elusive gleams of blue reflected the invading Viton from the polished surfaces of jumbled aparatus, shifted and flickered as the apparition arched forward and glided down to floor level.

A human face, fearfully distorted, made leprous by the ghastly ilumination, sweated directly in the luminosity's path—a homoburger waiting the bite! Hysterical gabbling poured from the face's twitching lips, gabbling that ended in a long hoarse sigh.

Helpless feet dragged on the floor immediately below the glowing devil, scuffled loosely around, rapped on table legs. The brilliant orb bobbed up and down, a limp form dangling beneath it. It made a couple of violent jerks, as if forcing energy-milk from reluctant udders. Glass toppled from an adjacent table, hit the floor, and bounced around in horrible imitation of the bobbing globe.

Somebody began noisily to vomit as red flame lanced vividly from the laboratory's west side. Dull, purplish spots appeared momentarily on the invader's scintillating surface. More flame; the sharp, hard crack of the heavy weapon being magnified to deafening proportions.

The luminosity dropped its burden as if discarding an old and empty sack. Vengefully, it shot westward, making a meteoric curve straight into the opposing stream of fire. A voice screamed a terrified obscenity, choked, was silent. The Viton made five savage jerks of guzzlement against the wall.

Swiftness of its departure was breathtaking. Blue whizzed back to the hopper, shone within its open frame, and then was outside. It shrank toward the cloud-wrapped sky. Joe, returning from a bender.

Feet stumbled, voices sounded loudly and querulously in the

153

darkness of a place receiving poor illumination from outside. An unseen hand was quick to close the hopper, making the gloom still deeper. Graham swung wide the door, permitting entry of the afternoon's light.

Away in the farther corner, somebody ran a pencil beam over the switchboard and fuse-boxes, worked at them with fingers that trembled uncontrollably.

Power suddenly poured through a multitude of overhead bulbs. Laurie ran down the center aisle, kneeled beside an eye-rolling, arm-jerking form. Sensing Graham at his side, he glanced up at the investigator, his eyes straining in a face like marble.

"He's batty," observed Graham, in cold, matter of fact tones. The prone man gibbered horribly, clutched Laurie's hand, moped and mowed. "He gave away nothing. He went nuts as it got him."

"God, this is awful!" breathed Laurie.

"We'll get him away." He looked at the thin ring of fearful onlookers. One of them still was clutching a crucifix. "Back on the job, you men. Don't let this get you." They dispersed, slowly, dazedly. He crossed to the hangar's west side where Wohl was bending over another limp shape.

"Dead as the dodo," announced Wohl, unemotionally.

Stooping, Graham extracted a big police positive from the teletype operator's dead fingers. Placing the weapon on a table, he found a small mirror, reflected light into staring optics. It might have been only his imagination, but he thought he saw that subtle something which is life fade gradually from those upturned eyes.

After searching the victim's form, he straightened, said, "Not a mark! His heart was stopped!"

A siren wailed along the road outside, died away dismally at the open door. Four police officers entered accompanied by one man in plain clothes. Quietly, without comment, they took out the uniformed corpse, came back for the fallen scientist. He was mouthing noiselessly as they bore him away.

Three of the officers got into the car, drove off. The fourth took his seat at the teletype. The man in plain clothes went up to Laurie.

"I'm Ferguson, the replacement."

Laurie stood like one stupified, his gaze wandering over his companions. Nervously, he tugged at one ear while his face asked his unspoken question.

"Organization," explained Graham. His gesture was a comprehensive sweep indicating the microphones and scanners. "Already your losses have been made good. Go ahead with

154

your task, and let's have some speed—we've got to move quicker than death!"

Dashing out, Graham clambered into a gyrocar, Wohl taking the wheel. He said, "Bet my own speedster is now a wreck somewhere out west."

"Maybe." Wohl tooled out to the middle of the concrete. "Where to?"

"Yonkers. There's an underground laboratory out there. Steve Koenig's in charge." Noting Wohl's curiosity, he added, "There are only two groups in this neighborhood. I'm not revealing where the others are, even to you."

"Meaning I might be grabbed and tapped for information?" Wohl leered at the sky, and pulled a face. "Where do we stand if the victim is *you?* Or do we then sit down and take it?"

"We will stand. Nobody's under the delusion that I'm invincible. There are plenty of other groups beside the sixty-four boys I claimed. I've had nothing whatever to do with the others, and know nothing about them. People in Washington and other places have placed them where they'll do the most good. Moreover, nobody in this country knows where South America and European experts are located, and they know nothing of ours."

"This," decided Wohl, "certainly is one time when it's folly to be wise."

"I'll say!" Graham's expression was thoughtful. "Things have been arranged in such a way that the same applies to me as to everyone else—what I don't know I can't tell."

They swung right, the dynamo whirling powerfully. In a smooth rush, they swept around a huge crater in the road. Above the enormous hole was a quarter-mile gap in the shattered skyway, a break from the ragged ends of which stubby lengths of twisted, rusting girders stuck.

"Some banger!" Wohl let his streamlined machine plummet along in top gear. He covered two miles in a fraction over a minute, slowed at an intersection, turned left.

At that point the sky flashed into several times its normal brilliance, for a split second cast sharp, clear-cut shadows across the street. Then the phenomenon was gone. Wohl braked the car to a stop, waited expectantly. Seconds later, the ground quivered. The weakened, unsupported shell of a nearby building collapsed into the road with an appalling roar, filling it with rubble from side to side. Several Vitons suspended in the sky began to zoom to the west.

"That was atomic," declared Graham. "Some miles out. Probably a rocket."

"If we'd been half an hour ahead—" Wohl left his sentence unfinished.

"We weren't, and that's that. No use going on now. Turn her round, Art. I'll try the Battery."

They raced downtown, away from the distant and giant mushroom which was crackling with death. Bulleting along, they passed Bank of Manhattan.

Graham remarked, "Seems years since I worked from that office." He was silent a moment, then added sharply, "Pull up on this corner, Art."

The gyrocar swung into the curb, stopped. Graham sat hunched in his seat, his eyes on the rear-view mirror. Opening the door he writhed out.

"What's up? Can you see that mushroom from here?" Wohl fiddled with his wheel, glanced inquiringly at the other.

"The twenty-fourth floor. Yes, it was the twenty-fourth." Graham's eyes glittered. "Something blue and shining flashed out of an open window on that level just after we passed. I caught sight of it out one corner of my eye. The six middle windows in that row belong to Sangster's dump."

"Meaning?"

"Meaning I'm pretty sure that it was a luminosity." The investigator's features showed ire. "Stick around, Art—I'm going to phone."

Without waiting for Wohl's reply, he entered the nearest building, found a telephones in a deserted and half-wrecked ground level office. In strange contrast with its surroundings, the instrument's visor was intact and functioning perfectly, for a girl's face blossomed in its tiny screen as his call got through.

"Hi, Hetty!" he gave her the usual cheer.

"Hi!" she smiled mechanically.

"Mr. Sangster there?"

"No. He's been out all afternoon. I expect him back before five-thirty." Her voice was peculiarly dull and lifeless, but her smile grew more insistent, more inviting. "Won't you come along and wait for him, Mr. Graham?"

"Sorry, I can't. I—"

"We haven't seen you for such a long time," she pleaded. "What with most of the buildings around us lying flat, and this one almost deserted, it's like living on an island, I'm so lonely, so afraid. Can't you come and chat with me until he arrives?"

"Hetty, I can hardly spare the time." He felt moved by her cajolery even as he stared fascinatedly at the screen, noting the tiniest quirk of her lips, the slightest flicker of her eyelids.

"From where are you speaking?" Again that dull, lifeless, phonographic voice.

His temper started to rise, and there was sweat in the palms of his hands. Evading her question, he said slowly, "I'll come around Hetty. Expect me about five o'clock."

"That's fine!" Her smile widened, but her eyes held no collaboratory expression. "Be sure to make it. Don't disappoint me, will you?"

"You can depend on me, Hetty."

Disconnecting, he glared a long time at the screen from which her familiar features had faded. His fury was tremendous. He worked his fingers as if itching to strangle someone. Giving vent to a hearty expletive, he hurried back to the waiting gyrocar.

"They've got Hetty," he told Wohl. "She talked and acted as if animated by clockwork. The place is a trap."

"Like the field office was," remarked Wohl. He swallowed hard, tapped his fingers on the steering wheel while he kept watch on the sky.

"Ten to one my own home is also a trap—both Hetty and Sangster know it well." His mounting fury colored his voice. His fists clenched into hard bunches. "They're creeping nearer and nearer to me every minute. Art, I'm fed up. I can't stand this hunt much longer. I'm going to step up and smack 'em right in the pan—and to hell with 'em!"

"Really?" said Wohl. He propped an elbow on the wheel, and his head on one hand. He studied Graham with academic interest. "Just like that, eh? You pull one down from the heavens and you kick into a pulp whatever it uses for a bottom, eh?" Taking his head off his hand, he shouted, "Don't talk like a blithering idiot!"

"What's eating you?"

"Nothing." Wohl showed his iridium lined ring. "Nothing's going to eat you either, not if I can help it."

"I don't intend to be eaten. That's why I want to smack them with a fast one."

"How're you going to do that?"

"It depends." Climbing into the machine, Graham sat and pondered, keeping wary watch through the transparent roof lest any wandering spheres might drift within telepathic range. "If that trap is toothed with Vitons, then I'm merely talking big, because there's nothing I can do."

"Ah," said Wohl, speaking to the windscreen, "he admits it!"

Graham snorted, gave him a look, and added, "But if, as is likely, they've left the dirty work to a bunch of dupes, I'm going in. I'm going to go in and kick out their teeth and walk away with Hetty. Anything wrong with that?"

The other thought it over. "H'm, I guess it could be done if they're relying on dupes. Yeah, you might do it and get away with it, though it's a hell of a risk. I've one objection, though."

"What's that?"

"All this 'I' stuff you use. Who the heck d'you think you are?" He flashed the ring again. *"We* go in and take Hetty!"

"I didn't contemplate trying it single-handed, nor even with you. I'm not all that daft!" Graham had a last look back at the Bank of Manhattan. "I found a fellow operative when I returned from Washington, and gave him the chore of finding the other nine who're supposed to be functioning hereabouts. If he's managed to trace them, they'll be waiting for me at Center Station. We'll pick them up and see what can be done about this trap. With luck, we may snitch the bait without grabbing the tribulation." He lay back in his seat. "Bank her along Art —we've got less than one hour."

He looked over the eight of them, noting their clean, square-jawed confident features, and knowing that the remaining pair would never be found. There should have been ten all told. Every one of these young huskies was aware of that fact, and every one knew equally well that soon their number might be lessened still further. But no consciousness of this was evident in their expressions or bearing. These were men of the Intelligence Service, men trained to compensate for losses by doing the work of the missing—and more.

"You know what you're to do?" he asked. They nodded. He jerked a thumb upward, reminding them of the observers twenty floors above, peering across two streets and a wrecked block, and into Sangster's office.

"The boys say there are no luminosities in that office, so it's evident that we have to deal only with dupes. I'm going in. You fellows have got to help me get out."

Again they nodded. None could see any reason why Graham should be so keen to risk his life, but it was enough for them that he intended to do just that. They were prepared to play their part.

"All right, fellows—I'm on my way."

"Me, too," announced Wohl, stepping forward.

"For heaven's sake, keep out of this, Art. We don't know what sort of reactions these proxies have. Hetty was a pal of mine, but she doesn't know you from Adam. If you barge in with me you may ball up the works."

"Oh, damn!" said Wohl.

With a grin for his disappointed companion, Graham hastened out, crossed the intervening space under the watching

158

glasses of his observers above, entered Bank of Manhattan. Five men were lounging around the dusty, neglected foyer. Disregarding them, he walked boldly to the pneumatic levitators, ascended to the twenty-fourth floor.

No more loungers were in sight on this level, but he felt that crazy and somewhat corpselike eyes were watching him as he thrust open the door of the department of special finance.

With a casual, "Lo, Hetty!" he closed the door behind him. His keen eyes examined the room, noted the closed door of Sangster's private sanctum, the closed doors of a large cupboard nearby. Sangster himself was not in evidence. Perhaps the girl had told the truth about him.

Outside, a war-worn clock struck twenty in cracked and off-tone chimes. It was precisely five.

Seating himself on a corner of her desk, he swung a nonchalant leg to and fro. "I've been busy, Hetty, as busy as the very devil, else I'd have been in to see you before now. Things are shaping for the showdown—I hope!"

"In what way?" She didn't add, "Bill," as was her habit.

"We're about to produce an anti-Viton weapon at last."

"In short waves?" she asked. Her eyes looked into his, and hair erected on the back of his neck when he saw the emptiness of her formerly lively pupils, a dreadful, soulless emptiness that made her no longer interested in masculine small-talk, feminine fripperies or any of her oldtime conversational subjects. Her interests now were different, appallingly different—anti-Viton weapons, and short waves, plus Graham himself as her masters' fall guy.

"Sure!" He stared fascinatedly at her mechanical features. It was hellish to think that this was no longer the vivacious girl once he had known, that this familiar form had become a fleshly robot. "We're searching way down in the centimeters. We've divided a broad band between many groups of experimenters. An army like that can't fail to strike oil."

"That is heartening," she commented in a voice totally devoid of tone. Her pale, blue-veined hands fumbled in her lap, below the edge of her desk, out of his sight. "Do you know where these groups are, and which lines they're trying?"

Triumph mounted within him as she put this childishly apparent question. It was as he'd expected—this poor, warped brain was working obediently along a single track, mechanically following the course on which it had been set. There was cunning here—but no cleverness. Even a moron would have seen through her query.

A twofold duty had been placed upon her: firstly, to bait the trap; secondly, to obtain essential information before giving the death signal. Obviously, the fearful operation to which her protesting mind had been subjected had not endowed her with telepathic powers—if luminosities could so endow their victims. At any rate, she was quite unaware of his shrewd perception.

Hard put to it to conceal his eagerness, he told her, "Although there are a lot of experimental groups, Hetty, I know the location of them all, every one of them." It was a downright, thumping lie, and he told it with no compunction, making it in boastful tones. "You've only got to suggest a wavelength and I can tell you who's about to try it, and where."

The dummy responded by betraying her manipulators; her poor, distorted brain was too automatic for guile. "Point five centimeters," she responded, speaking the words as if they had been engraved upon her tortured mind. Her hands slid forward, reached under her desk. She was making ready for the information—and his reward.

"That's all I wanted to know," Grham growled. He was on his feet and around her desk before she could move.

Putting out his hands to grab her, he saw the door to Sangster's room whip open, and a menacing figure charge toward him. He flung himself forward and down; his automatic was in his hand as he hit the floor. The maniacal invader paused, took sloppy aim, and the sound of his shot was terrific in the confined space.

Things catapulted over Graham's flat back. The cupboard door swung wide. Momentarily ignoring the first attacker, he blasted at the gap in the cupboard, saw splinters fly from the edges, knew that all four bullet sections had gone inside.

A whooping figure bowed low in the opening, bent farther, spewed a bloody froth. It toppled full length, its gory torso a sudden barrier in the path of his crazy fellow.

Profiting by his peril, Hetty lugged out a drawer, snatched something from it. She leaned over her desk toward Graham, her blank, unemotional eyes lined along the sights of a tiny, old-fashioned revolver. Her knuckles whitened. The desk erupted beneath her when with a desperate thrust Graham heaved it over from his side. The little gun spat upward as Hetty toppled in her chair, and its slug went into the ceiling.

Feet were hammering along the passage outside, and someone was bellowing oaths near the levitator shafts. Graham swayed upward with the lithe grace of a striking cobra, fired simultaneusly with his first attacker. His left arm jumped involuntarily and went red-hot, but his assailant dropped like a slaughtered steer.

Behind him, the door burst inward, revealed two Intelligence operatives, weapons in hand. Hard, explosive noises twanged from the end of the passage. One missile struck metal, whined shrilly as it went on end over end. Two more thudded into the wooden frame of the door; a third clunked softly into flesh. The shorter of the two operatives choked, spat, choked again, leaned weakly against the wall, slid down. He finished in a sitting position, the gun sliding from his fingers, his head lolling forward.

"Full of them!" swore the other. "The place is crammed with them." Peering leftward around the door, he sent two quick shots down the passage. A volley of shots from the right went in the same direction, and in the following few seconds of silence, four more operatives slipped into the room.

"Move fast!" urged Graham. "I want this girl out."

Whirling around with the intention of grabbing Hetty and bearing her away bodily, he caught a glimpse of distant blue through the open window. "Vitons!" There were about twenty of the shining spheres, shooting along one behind the other like a string of immense beads, aiming directly for the room, and nearing swiftly. The shepherds were coming to the aid of their dogs.

More feet thundered recklessly along the passage. His companions opened fire as he sprang toward the door. The sitting operative pawed blindly for his gun, fell on his side, closed his eyes and dribbled blood.

Thumps, groans and mad, aphetic mouthings sounded in the corridor. The next instant, a swarm of staring dupes were in the room. They made their assault with complete disregard for personal safety and with the energetic lack of organization of automatons on the loose. They were robots conditioned only to kill, somehow, anyhow.

A colorless face in which blank eyes goggled ghoulishly came close to Graham's own. Its lopsided mouth was oozing saliva. He hit it with every ounce he possessed. The face vanished as if snatched into the cosmos. Another replaced it and he promptly smacked it to the floor.

Somebody lifted a crazy, face-twitching body, hurled it half-way across the room. A stricken dupe writhed snakishly on the floor, snatched at Graham's left leg. He used his right to kick the other's schnozzle into something resembling a squashed strawberry. An operative's gun roared close to his ear, deafening him, and filling his nostrils with the stink of cordite.

The mad mêlée swept him out of the uproarous office, along the passage to the levitator shafts. A weight descended crushingly on his shoulder, a thousand hands seemed to be reaching for him at once.

He saw Sheehan, an operative, shove the muzzle of his gun straight into a slobbering mouth and let her blow. Gobs of noggin, slop and goo flew in all directions as the part-headless victim toppled under his stamping feet. Far behind him, or in front, or in some direction—he didn't know where—a voice was hollering something about Vitons. He bulled into the horde of dupes, his struggles more maniacal than their own. Then the whole of existence became an inferno of raging fire through which he sank and sank and sank until every sound had ceased.

Chapter 14

EASING the bandage around his head, Graham gazed at the distant pile of Bank of Manhattan, then turned to the others.

"How the devil did we manage to get out of that mess? What happened?"

"Me and my pair had five on our hands in the foyer," explained Wohl. He fondled a damaged knee, winced. "We heard the shenanigans upstairs come echoing down the levitator shafts as the other six went to your aid. A short time later, two of them came down like bats out of hell, bringing you with them. You'd been conked, and I'll say you looked lousy!" He favored the knee again, muttered an oath. "Your stretcher-bearers said they'd got out one jump ahead of visiting luminosities."

"And Hetty?"

"There!" Wohl handed him a pair of field glasses. "She went Mayo's way."

"What, flung herself out?" Wohl's answering nod plunged him into thought.

So the duty imposed upon that poor, warped mind had been a threefold one—she was to end herself with her usefulness.

He was moody as he looked at the tragic bundle on that far sidewalk. In a little while, they'd pick her up and send her to decent repose. Meanwhile, it was fortunate that they'd got out fast and in the nick of time, for once again they were unidentifiable among New York's slinking, wary millions.

Short of sheer chance, or the aid of a dupe, they were as difficult to pick out as individual bees in a mighty swarm. There was good parallelism in an imaginary revolt of the bees. The same elusiveness would protect from superior mankind the few intellectual insects who were seeking a means of replacing formic acid with Black Widow venom. If it came to that, they were bees—bees whose nervous honey was not for others.

He said to Wohl, "Two brought me down? Only *two?*" His inquiring eyes moved to the four dishevelled operatives standing near, and two of them fidgeted uneasily, "What of the other four—were they killed?"

"A couple of them were." One of the restless pair waved his hand toward Bank of Manhattan. "Bathurst and Craig stayed behind."

"Why?"

"Most of the dupes were scattered, wounded or dead, but the Vitons were entering. They were coming in at the top while we were trying to get you out at the bottom. So Bathurst and Craig hung back, and—" His voice trailed off.

"Decoyed them, knowing there could be no escape?" Graham suggested. The other nodded assent.

Two had remained to attract the still invincible but over-eager foe; to run and shriek and shriek and die—or become dupes in their turn. They had raced higher in the building, knowing that they would never reach the top, but knowing that by the time their recoiling minds were seized and analysed, the others would be safely merged in the concealing mass of humanity.

It was a sacrifice made for him. There was no comment Graham could make that would not sound fatuous, and he knew that none was asked or expected. In the tradition of the service, two Intelligence operatives had done their duty as they deemed it—and that was that!

Rubbing his throbbing left arm, he lifted the thin bandage beneath the sleeve. A mere flesh wound.

Wohl said, "Let that be a lesson to you: don't rush in where angels fear to tread. It buys you nothing but grief."

"I'm hoping it's bought us salvation," Graham retorted. Taking no notice of Wohl's mystification, he turned to the four operatives.

"You two," he said, selecting a pair, "beat it out to Yonkers. You won't be able to get there direct—there's hard radiation across the route. It may be necessary to take a round-about road. But you must get there at all costs."

"We'll make it, never worry," assured one.

"Okay. Tell Steve Koenig he's to try point five centimeters sooner than immediately, and that's a hot tip. You'd better split and go different ways if you can: it will double your chances of getting through. Remember—point five centimeters. That's all that Koenig will want to know." He addressed the other couple. "Marconi's have established their underground plant at Queens end of the low-level city. They're fiddling around on their own, without orders from Washington, but they could use the information I've got. So rush along and tell

Deacon we've reason to believe that point five-centimeters is the critical wavelength."

"Yes, Mr. Graham," answered one.

He spoke to all four. "You'd better say, too that if either of them gain success they'll have to move fast if they want to stay in business. They'll have to protect their own plant with the first installation they produce, and then the stations from which they draw power. Then—and not until then!—they can supply official demands. Tell them it's absolutely essential that they refuse to be moved by any bureaucratic panic until they've protected their own plants and power-stations. D'you understand?"

"Sure, Mr. Graham." They went out, cautiously, yet fast.

Grimness was in the set of his jaws when he remarked to Wohl, "If we discover a way to turn out suitable weapons, we're not going to have them destroyed at the source."

"That's logical," agreed Wohl. He cocked a questioning eye. "You've found something, Bill?"

"Yes, I got the specific detail for which Hetty's mind had been directed to seek. Undoubtedly, the luminosities intended to suck her knowledge as she acquired it and take action accordingly." He ripped a dangling pocketflap from his tattered jacket, scowled at it, flung it away. "If possible, she was to ascertain the location of any experimental group working on or near point five centimeters. Had she been able to identify them, they'd have been smeared around. Probably they'd have smeared other groups simultaneously, just to keep us confused. We'd have had no clew to a potent wavelength—but they'd have put finish to the one they fear."

"Gosh!" Wohl registered a mixture of glee and admiration. "And that's what you dived in to get? The Vitons might just as well have told you themselves!"

"They did," was Graham's succinct reply. "They informed us by proxy. Very kind of them—damn their guts!" He had a look at his watch. "We've to carry on from this point, getting results in a few precious hours. Polarization's the trouble—we're dealing with short radio waves, not ordinary light."

"Never mind," Wohl comforted. "So far you've done fine."

"Me? You mean *we!*"

"I mean you," Wohl persisted. "You've done fine. Every cloud has a silver lining."

"We'll have to see that silver darned quick, else it'll come too—" He stopped, rubbed his pulsing arm, stared at the other. "I seem to remember something about photons changing their double-eights to true spirals when rebounding from polished silver."

"What of it? I spiral off glass—when it holds beer."

"Silver might do it," Graham went on, ignoring him. "The problem's largely one of refraction versus reflection, but silver might do it. There's a good chance that so short a wave might spiral if the beam could be bounced off a silver plate—especially if we use a Bergstrom magnetic-field impeller to make the stuff hard and fast by cutting down absorption."

"You bet!" Wohl's grin was apologetic. "It ought to work just like you say. I get the whole idea so clearly I could see it with muffled ears in a dungeon next month."

"The odd chance in a thousand," murmured Graham. "It will be worth trying if Laurie hasn't thought up something better." Ceasing to nurse his injuries, he became suddenly dynamic. "Jump to it, Art—we're going back to Laurie."

A hundred highly skilled craftsmen now toiled and sweated inside the great Faraday shed. They had been commandeered from various local radio and scientific instrument works, and every man knew his stuff so well that Laurie and his little band could concentrate unhampered on their own special jobs.

Valuable hours of non-stop work were represented by the compact but complicated apparatus which glistened and shone in the center of the littered floor. Long, slender tubes sparkled in the assembly's heart: cylindrical screens projected from its turntable framework beneath which were a dozen rubber-tired wheels. From its seat mounted before a small control-board the entire set-up could be moved and rotated electrically like a crane, drawing power from cables which snaked out of its end couplings and ran across the floor toward the generators.

Here, a worker bent over a true-surfaced peralumin disk and silver-plated it by wire-process metallization. While his electric arc sputtered its rain of minute drops, another worker close by plated another disk with granulated silver by-passed into an exoacetylene flame and thus blast-driven into the pre-heated surface. Any method would do so long as there was someone capable of doing it with optical accuracy.

Another worker was burnishing a heavily plated disk on a confiscated buffing machine, frequently checking results with a micrometer gauge. Behind him, one of Laurie's experts was completing the assembly of a hemispherical trellis antenna. Two more scientists fussed around a big, cylindrical funnel; one fitting front and rear skeleton-sights to its upper surface, the other making minute adjustments to its complex impeller.

Two hours to go!

Graham came in with an old-fashioned printed paper, rested one foot on the assembly's turntable while he scanned the front page. Iowa threatened by battle for Omaha. Asian armor enters Luxembourg. Madrid obliterated in atom-blast. Scandinavia's last stand today. More atomic rockets flay Britain. It was gloom, gloom, gloom all the way. His eyes found the side column just as Laurie came up. French collapse imminent. He shoved the paper into his pocket.

"Bad news?" inquired Laurie.

"Not so good. There's something else, too. It came from Philly by ham radio. Veitch's nearly completed apparatus was blown to pieces early this morning."

"Ah!" Laurie's bushy brows drew together in a frown. "That suggests he was on the right track. If he was on the right track, then we're on the wrong one."

"Not necessarily. Veitch had a dupe in his crowd. We warned him, and he said he'd kid the fellow along. He didn't want to remove him in case he was replaced by another. Better the devil you know than the devil you don't."

"The dupe did it?"

"Yes—killing himself in the blast. Honorable harakiri, sort of. A couple of others are wounded." He looked meditative. "I'd have phoned Vietch before now if it hadn't been that all his lines are reserved strictly for outgoing traffic. He ought to have been ready long before anyone else, since he had tons of stuff transported from Florida and it needed only reassembling."

"H'm-m-m! Any other news?"

"Only that Sangster's been located, I was worried about him. They found him in an underground hospital. He was in William Street when that big section of skyway collapsed. He'll recover."

Leaving Laurie, he visited the open space fronting the shed. Here, in the middle of the cleared area, was a ring of giant copper earths, all ready to connect with the multiple condensers of the transmitter's intricate grounding system.

A parade of blue dots, made tiny by distance, wended its way far to the east, somewhere over Long Island. His eyes gleamed as he watched them. Nice fix they were in, he thought, with chronic disregard for his own greater fix. Like hundreds of worried bee-keepers trying to search thousands of hives containing tens of millions of bees. They could go here, and there, and to dozens of other places, but they couldn't be everywhere at one and the same time. That was their weak spot.

His gaze returned to the copper earths, and he wondered whether even this efficient system would absorb the terrific shock imposed upon it by a vengeful enemy. He doubted it.

A system ten times the size would not be sufficient to cope with the hell's fury such as had fallen upon Silver City.

The most they could hope for was to destroy one Viton— and let the rest of the world know why Faraday's had been thrown all over the landscape, let it thus know that there still was hope if the struggle could be maintained a little longer. Yes, the end of only one Viton would be enough.

Behind the transmitter's intended site was a wide pit, its six-inch wall of sprayed-on, quick-drying cement diving into the depths like a gigantic pipe. There was a slidepole down its center.

One man was going to operate the transmitter. If he could do it, that man was going to try to save himself from the certain holocaust that success would bring by plunging down the shaft deep, deep into the ebon depths. It was a primitive sanctuary—but the fastest out that could be contrived in the circumstances.

Returning, he asked Laurie, "How long?"

"Fifteen minutes." Laurie mopped his damp and anxious brow. "We'll be all set in fifteen minutes. If it works, we'll have plant ready for ten more assemblies." He waved a hand to indicate the bustling crowd. "And providing we don't get slaughtered, we'll fling them together in a couple of hours."

"No you won't." Graham's contradiction was flat and authorative. "You're going to rush those spares away to a safe distance right now. The whole area is liable to be tossed moonward when those Vitons get the rats, and the spares had better be someplace else during the showdown." Finding a microphone, he chattered into it rapidly.

Three minutes later, a line of trucks swung before the doors, each picking up its load and lumbering heavily away. Workers departed in silent, ruminative groups, leaving behind a shop cleared of all but the polarized-wave projector shining in the middle of the floor. A quartet of scientists hurried to complete various connections, make a few last-minute adjustments.

He leaned on the turntable, watching them with a cold patience that surprised himself considering that the testing time was so near. After days of nervous strain, he was suddenly as impassive as a stone Buddha—like a man who finally finds himself in the dental chair after a jumpy hour in the waiting-room. His gaze settled on one of the working four, a half-pint individual with a tonsure around his balding head.

As this expert completed his task, Graham spoke to him

in harsh, deliberate tones. "I don't fancy handling a trick circuit jumping the power line to the impeller switch." The concentrated venom in his voice appalled his hearers.

The runt he had addressed turned on him a wizened, monkeyish face in which pale blue eyes regarded him blankly. Dropping a piece of thin cable, he felt casually in his pocket as if seeking a pair of pliers.

Graham shot him where he poised, the powerful, point-blank blast fairly flinging the fellow backward. While Laurie and the rest looked on white-faced, Art Wohl stepped unconcernedly to the body, felt in its pocket, extracted a small, egg-shaped object.

"Holy smoke, a bomb! He'd have shredded us along with the dingbat!"

"Never mind. Take it away, Art, and dump it in that reservoir out back." He transferred his attention to Laurie. "Unhook that power by-pass and check the circuit, Duncan. See if the output is all right. If so, we'll run the thing out and tie it to those earths."

A minute later, Laurie pronounced, "It's ready for action. It'll never function more perfectly even if it achieves nothing."

"Good!" They drove it out, earthed it. Laurie departed with his three men, leaving only Wohl.

Graham sat high up in the assembly, the power, impeller, elevator and turntable controls within easy reach. A dull, cloudy sky was heavy overhead. He had an argument with Wohl as the smoke and spume of a rocket-shot sprang high in the south.

"Beat it, Art," he ordered. "There are Vitons over there." He indicated a horde of glowing balls roaming in from the north-east. "This is no time to squat here and debate with you. Chase after Duncan and the others—I'll give you half a minute to get clear."

"But—" began Wohl, protestingly.

"Scram!" roared Graham in a frantic voice.

He watched Wohl slouch miserably away, waited until he was out of sight beyond the hangar. Before him as he sat, the cylindrical funnel projected like the barrel of a monster gun. The approaching luminosities were now only a mile distant.

Wide-sighted eyes raked the sky as he gave Wohl time to gain safe distance. The origin of the Vitons would never be known, he decided. Their existence would remain as much a mystery as that of pneumococci, poodles, or any other form of life. But it was his pet theory that they were true natives of

Earth, and it was also his hunch that they were about to be wiped off Earth forever—if not by one battling human group, then by some other.

Zero hour had come, the fateful moment had arrived. He swung the great funnel, lined it upon the advancing orbs. The funnel moved lightly on its gimbals, and the entire assembly spun smoothly on its turntable frame. He heard power being made by the whining generators in the hangar, and noted that the time was ninety minutes from Europe's deadline. Snapping a switch, he let the power pour through.

There followed a few seconds' pause while the tubes warmed up. Over there, in strategic posts ten or twelve floors high, distant observers watched through field glasses that trembled in their hands.

The half-centimeter beam fountained into the shaft, polarized, directable. It spiked from the funnel's maw, the axis of its whirling impulses parallel with the skeleton-sights lined upon the Vitons.

This frequency lay beyond even the Bjornsen vision-range, and the beam could not be seen. But its effect was startlingly visible. The leading luminosity of a prowling string of ten stopped in mid-air as if barred by an unseeable obstruction. It turned deeper in color, from bright blue to dark purple, almost instantaneously switched to orange of extreme brilliance, then popped into nothingness. It was gone so utterly and completely that its going shocked the army of hidden observers.

The remaining nine Vitons bobbed around undecidedly, and another stopped, went through the blue-purple-orange-obliteration cycle before the rest scattered at top speed. They bulleted straight upward, into the clouds.

Somebody was bellowing like a mad bull as Graham elevated the funnel and caught a third in full flight. Somebody howled an idiotic remark about it being more sporting to get 'em on the wing.

With the tail of his eye, he saw an enormous gout of yellow-white flame vomit from the general area of Broadway. The noise followed, then the air-blast. It rocked him in his seat. His lips closed firmly, the strange bellowing ceased, and he realized that he had been bawling himself hoarse.

Some sixth sense—probably his extra-sensory perception —made him whirl his assembly around. He spun dizzily behind the impeller casing, caught a line of spheres rushing him from the south.

He started yelling again as the leader went deep purple. The following luminosities slowed so suddenly that he fancied they had feet, braced forward, and still skidding. Their velocity was too great for that. They crashed headlong into their stricken fellow at the moment it flared into an eye-searing orange.

"One for Mayo!" he hollered, jigging on his seat. "One for Webb! One for Beach, you dirty, stinking gobs of parasitic lousery! Another for Farmiloe, and the whole damn lot of you for Bjornsen!"

Ceasing his insane howls, he watched the results of the aerial collision. For the space of a single heart-beat, the wildly whirling conglomeration of energy maintained enlarged but spherical form in the astounded heavens. Then it exploded with a terrible roar.

Graham's ear-drums bounced against each other. Displaced air almost tore him from his precarious saddle. The entire apparatus wrenched at its fastenings and groaned. While the high-up mess of wavicles went haywire, fierce rays struck him like vicious sunburn, forcing him to close his eyelids to protect his pupils.

But he couldn't keep quiet, he wouldn't keep quiet. This was the end of the trail, this was his lone half hour if never he enjoyed another, and, above all, this was retribution. He whooped like a charging Sioux as deftly he swung the funnel through a ninety degree arc and blasted two scintillating menaces dropping upon him from above.

Now it was clear how they'd set off those tanks in Silver City. A dozen of them, or twenty, or perhaps fifty had committed suicide, plunging into the tanks, merging as they struck. That merging had destroyed their natural balance, collectively converting them into a super-detonator. They had in their ancient lore a secret only recently discovered by their human slaves: the secret of violent disruption when energy-forms—radio-active or Vitonic—exceed critical mass.

That silver nitrate had received the world's worst wallop, a sock in the neck that made the atom-bomb look piddling. And that great black finger pointing to where Silver City's souls had gone had been a monstrous column of maddened atoms seeking new unions as they splashed upward.

Whirling his turntable again, he threw a free sample of hell at an oncoming sextet, saw them dispel their energy in visible frequencies and cease to be. These Vitons could afford to be nonchalant about stuff coming at them along Lissajous' complicated path, for nature had conditioned them to the solar output. They could stand it. Maybe they liked it. But hyperbolic: *that* corkscrewed into their very guts!

There was a tremendous array of luminosities collecting on the extreme limit of the northern horizon. He tried to reach them with his beam, found he was unable to discern any result, concluded that they must be beyond effective range. More man-made volcanos belched in the east. The air held smells of ozone, burning rubber and wet cement. Voices made indistinct by distance were shouting all around.

He thought of America's grounded air fleet, ten thousand fast, efficient machines that dared not ascend so long as there were luminosities to take control of the pilots' minds and set one against another. That was going to be altered pretty soon. Winged warriors were going to darken the sky, while below them people spoke the sweetest word of any man's war—"Ours!"

So far, he'd wiped out only the reckless, lazy or unwary, but now they knew their danger. A mass attack was about to be made, an onslaught in which the Vitons would demonstrate once and for all the fullness of their united power. They would bullet toward him in companies, battalions, brigades, in numbers far greater than he could slaughter. They were going to blot him off the face of the disputed Earth, and the projector along with him. The end was near, but it had been a great run.

Searching the sky, he saw a squadron of Asian stratplanes zooming eastward with the calm confidence of things in cahoots with God. Puff-balls and sparks sprang into being behind and beneath them. He wondered whether their fanatical pilots had witnessed the fate of some of their supposed ancestral spirits, concluded that they had not.

The news ought to have got around by now. It would be all over the New World, and probably Europe had full details. Europe would hold on, knowing that victory was now a matter of time rather than doubt. Maybe one of the other groups also had succeeded. Anyway, it didn't matter— this success at Faraday's was humanity's triumph.

He ceased his pondering when the faraway cohorts soared upward. They made so huge and fantastic an aurora that it became hard to conceive their complete invisibility to ordinary, untreated eyesight. They were a bright blue myriad, a veritable army whose numbers filled the northern sky with a panorama of glowing horror, a heavenly host not born of heaven and long rejected by hell. The speed of their advance was almost incredible.

Even as Graham braced himself for what was coming, a small patch in the enemy's center darkened to purple, went orange, puffed out of existence. It had him puzzled for a moment, then he remembered—Yonkers.

172

"Good old Steve!" he roared. "He's done it. Give them hell, Steve!"

Shooting power along, he sprayed the rapidly swelling horde. Blue switched to purple and orange, became nixed. An untouched section detached itself from the main body, fell headlong on Yonkers, some changing color as they fell.

The rest shot vengefully toward Graham. He knew what was going to happen, sensed it from the way in which they gradually concentrated themselves as they sped along. Up to the last moment he let them have it hot and strong, cancelling them wholesale with furious words and lethal impulses. Then, as they merged suicidally, he reached the pit in four frantic leaps, embraced the pole, let the force of gravity snatch him down.

Ghastly, glowing blue momentarily wavered and undulated over the mouth of the shaft as he dropped at breathtaking speed. The whole sky had become a bowl of glossy azure. Then, abruptly, it flamed unbearably. A brain-searing roar as of the cosmos being ripped to tatters smashed into his already maltreated eardrums. The slide-pole danced like a juggler's wand.

Helplessly, he was flicked off the pole, fell into shaking depths. The shaft quivered from base to mouth, its walls crumbled, earth, stones, lumps of concrete poured after him in a deadly rain. Something bigger and blacker than the rest came unstuck, fell ponderously through general blackness, landed dully on yielding flesh.

Graham emitted a queer sigh. His mind wandered off, a barge of funereal ebony floating in sooty seas.

It was comfortable in bed, so comfortable that the illusion was well worth preserving. Shifting his head contentedly, Graham felt a sharp pain lance through it, opened his eyes.

Yes, he was in bed. He waggled his fingers, felt around. Definitely a bed. Amazedly, he surveyed a white sheet, studied a picture on the opposite wall. It was *A Stag At Bay*. He extended his tongue at it.

A chair creaked at his side, he winced as he turned his head to look, discovered Wohl's broad-shouldered figure.

"Good evening, Rip van Winkle," greeted Wohl, with unctuous politeness. He indicated a clock and a calendar. "It's ten in the evening of Thursday. For three days you've been deaf, dumb, dopey and doubled up. In other words, you've been your natural self."

"Is that so?" Graham's snort was a little less fiery than

173

of yore. He glared toward the stag. "Did you hang that blasted thing? If so, it isn't funny."

Wohl looked at it, endured the pain of thought, then said, "Haw-haw!"

Struggling upward, Graham propped himself on one elbow, ignored his throbbing cranium. "Get me my rags, you ignorant flattie—I'm going places."

"Nothing doing." Wohl's broad hand pressed him gently down. "This is one time when I give orders and you take 'em." He made the declaration with unashamed relish, and went on, "Those luminosities devastated an area a couple of miles in diameter, killed many observers. It took us twelve hours to locate your funk-hole and dig out the lump of cat-meat that was you. So lie down and be at peace while Uncle Art tells you some bedtime stories."

Producing a printed newspaper, he opened it, gave a brief sketch of the day's events, reading in a voice that fairly gloated.

"Mayor Sullivan says city now adequately protected. Electra's hundred scores new high for one day's projector output. Two more Asian strat-plane squadrons land at Battery Park and surrender." Glancing at his listener, he remarked, "That's merely local stuff. An awful lot has happened while you snored on like a fat hog."

"Humph!" Graham felt peeved. "What about Koenig?"

"He lost two operators when Yonkers took it on the chin. A lot of surrounding observers went west, too. But the rest are all right." Wohl reversed his paper. "Listen to this," he invited. "Nebraska line straightened. Our armor pushes on against weakening opposition. Rebellion spreads through Asian ranks as first transmitters reach front and destroy overhead luminosities. Pacifist Asians seize Chung-king and start manufacture of anti-Viton beams. Europe pressing eastward at fast pace. Washington expects Asian offer of armistice and aid in wiping out luminosities." He rolled up the paper, shoved it under Graham's pillow. "The war's as good as over, thanks to you."

"Nuts!" said Graham, sourly. He lifted himself again. "Get me my cover-ups. I'm not a thieving louse like you—I don't snitch blankets."

Wohl came to his feet, stared in mock horror. "By God, Bill, you look awful. You look real bad. I guess you need a doctor." He moved toward the door.

"Don't play the fool," shouted Graham. Hurriedly he sat up, held his head together until it decided not to fall apart.

"Fetch me my pants before I get out and paste you one. I'm beating it out of this dump."

"You don't know what's good for you," Wohl reproved from the doorway. "You're in a new underground hospital —it's now the Samaritan."

"Eh?"

"The Samaritan," Wohl repeated. He leered at the stag. "Ah!" Graham promptly lay flat, produced a hollow groan. "I feel terrible, Art. Maybe I'm dying. Go fetch me a doctor."

"Well!" said Wohl. He struck an attitude, protruding his buttocks, and holding an imaginary bow. "Look—Cupid, me!" Then he went out.

She came in presently, sat down, put on her best bedside manner, and inquired, "How're you feeling now?"

"As usual—with my hands." Putting out a hand, he took hold of hers.

She dumped it back firmly. "This is no place for that sort of thing."

"You've never given me the chance any place else," he pointed out.

Saying nothing, she stared at the stag without seeing it.

"Hell of a thing," he said.

"I beg your pardon?"

"That." He nodded toward the picture. "Somebody's sarcasm, I guess. Yours?"

"Mine?" She was patently surprised. "Nonsense. If you don't like it, I'll have it moved."

"Please do. It reminds me too much of me. Too much of everybody, if it comes to that."

"Indeed? Why?"

"At bay. We've been at bay back to the dawn of history. First without knowing it, then with full knowledge. It's nice to know that's over. Maybe we'll now have time for fun. You helped with the one, you can help with the other."

"I am not aware of having given any valuable assistance," she said, primly.

"You tipped us about Beach, and therapy cabinets, and Farmiloe. We'd still have been chasing shadows but for you." He sat up, gazing at her. "I'm not chasing any more shadows. I've had enough."

Making no reply, she turned her head sidewise, looked upward meditatively. He drank in the curve of her cheekbone, the sweep of her lashes, and knew she was conscious of his gaze.

"Up there, Harmony, are the stars," he continued. "There may be people out that way, people of flesh and blood like us, friendly people who'd have visited us long ago but for a Viton ban. Hans Luther believed they'd been warned to keep off the grass. Forbidden, forbidden, forbidden—that was Earth." He studied her again. "Every worthwhile thing forbidden, to those folk who'd like to come here, and to us who were imprisoned here. Nothing permitted except that which our masters considered profitable to themselves."

"But not now," she murmured.

"No, not now. We can emote for ourselves now, and not for others. At last our excitements are our own. Two are company, three are none—especially when the third's a Viton. Has it stuck you that in the truest sense we're now alone?"

"We—?"

Her face turned toward him, her eyebrows arched.

"Maybe this isn't the place," he observed, "but at least it's the opportunity!" He bent her across his lap, pressed his lips on hers.

She pushed at him, but not too hard. After a while, she changed her mind. Her arm slid around his neck.